JUST A LITTLE MISCHIEF

MERRY FARMER

JUST A LITTLE MISCHIEF

Copyright ©2021 by Merry Farmer

This book is licensed for your personal enjoyment only. This book may not be re-sold or given away to other people. If you would like to share this book with another person, please purchase an additional copy for each recipient. If you're reading this book and did not purchase it, or it was not purchased for your use only, then please return to your digital retailer and purchase your own copy. Thank you for respecting the hard work of this author.

This book is a work of fiction. Names, characters, places, and incidents are products of the author's imagination or are used fictitiously. Any resemblance to actual events or locales or persons, living or dead, is entirely coincidental.

Cover design by Erin Dameron-Hill (the miracle-worker)

ASIN: B08YGTR1D7

Paperback ISBN: 9798745335013

Click here for a complete list of other works by Merry Farmer.

If you'd like to be the first to learn about when the next books in the series come out and more, please sign up for my newsletter here: http://eepurl.com/RQ-KX

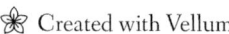 Created with Vellum

CHAPTER 1

LONDON, ST. JAMES'S PARK – NOVEMBER 1890

It was a bad idea. Every bit of it. Xavier Lawrence turned up the collar of his wool coat and tucked his hands under his arms as he walked with his friends along the perimeter of St. James's Park. There was a nip in the air, but it wasn't so much the cold that made him shiver and shrink in on himself, it was the dare his friends had proposed.

"Come on, Xavier," Adam nudged him, swaying close enough for Xavier to smell the alcohol on his breath. "You're new to London, but that doesn't mean you have to stay a virgin forever."

Adam and Nick snorted with laughter, practically falling all over themselves as they stumbled along the path.

"I'm not a—oh, never mind," Xavier said, letting out an irritated breath. He could barely see the cloud of frost it made in the scattered lamplight of the park. St. James's Park was dark after dusk, which suited the men who roamed in the shadows on a night like this one perfectly.

"How long has it been, then?" Nick tittered—yes, tittered like one of the misses in the house where he served as a footman. "Surely not since you came down from West Riding, eh?"

"There's hardly been time," Xavier started to argue. "We've barely been here a fortnight. Lord Selby has been deeply occupied with family matters since we arrived and—"

He gave up explaining when Adam and Nick proved they hadn't been listening to anything since the words "deeply occupied" by guffawing and sniggering until they sagged against each other. Xavier rolled his eyes, but didn't truly blame them for having too much to drink at The Cock and Bear earlier. All three of them were in service, and it was a rare occasion when their nights off coincided. It was even rarer that the three of them would be in London at the same time at all. Adam's and Nick's families traveled down frequently and spent more than just the season in their comfortable Mayfair townhomes, but Xavier hadn't been to London at all since becoming Blake's—that is, Lord Blake Williamson, the Duke of Selby's—valet years ago. Blake despised travel, and up until recently, he despised London. And Xavier still hadn't entirely resolved himself to referring to his august employer by his given name, but Blake insisted that was the way of The Brotherhood. Still….

Xavier was letting his mind wander too much to keep his thoughts away from the dare at hand.

"I remain unconvinced that this is a good idea," he hissed to Adam and Nick after a man in a dark coat with his hat pulled low wandered past them, glancing a little longer than he should have.

Adam made a sound of sloppy derision and pushed away from Nick to drape his arm over Xavier's shoulder. "St. James's is the best cruising location in London," he slurred, wafting fumes of alcohol in Xavier's direction. "Anyone can catch a bit of a bauble or a fit of a fumble or a tad of a tumble—oh dear, what was I saying?" He laughed, stumbling a bit as they walked, and dragging Xavier's shoulder down.

"What our esteemed friend is trying to say," Nick went on, sniffing and attempting to sound like his titled employer, "is that out there in the dark is a likely lad just waiting to thrust his pretty little hand down your trousers to get you off."

"And if you're lucky, not to mention in the proximity of an obliging shrub, he'll drop to his knees and suck you so hard you'll be like a wolf howling at the moon," Adam finished. He followed his statement with a howl of his own.

"Shush!" Xavier hissed, glancing around. "Are you trying to draw the coppers? They're probably everywhere in here, blackmailers too, just waiting to bring us all up on charges. You've seen the newspapers recently. They can't get enough stories of our sort being nabbed with our trousers down."

Indeed, there had been more than a few sensational arrests of "inverts and perverts" in St. James's Park reported in papers of late. Ever since the Cleveland Street Scandal a few years ago, newspapers were constantly printing reports filled with salacious gossip about men caught trysting where they'd thought they wouldn't be caught. After years, decades, of relative obscurity, between the evils of the Labouchere Amendment and the public's thirst for titillation, what had once been the sort of thing one simply didn't talk about while carrying on regardless, had turned into fuel for the fire of outrage that made newspapermen wealthy.

"We're just trying to initiate you into the joys and wonders of London," Nick said, dragging Xavier to a stop near one of the paths that crossed through the center of the park. "Don't you get tired of playing with your own willy all the time?"

"Yeah, let some other likely bloke play with it for a change," Adam added, far too loud for Xavier's comfort.

"Keep your voices down," Xavier scolded them again. He shook his head. There was only one way to shut the two nutters up. "Alright, I'm going in," he said, turning to start along the path.

"Are those the words of endearment your last bit of fun said?" Nick called after him.

Xavier turned to make a rude gesture at his friends—

and they truly were his friends, but perhaps more so when they weren't drunk out of their minds—and hurried into the beckoning shadows of the park.

"I must be mad," he murmured to himself, tucking his hands into his coat pockets and trying not to look as conspicuous as he felt.

He reminded himself that he didn't actually have to find a man who would exchange a quick fumble for a few coins. He could cross the park and circle back, then tell Adam and Nick that he'd gone through with it. Paying for something like that felt dirty, even if that was what men like him, Adam, and Nick generally did in London. He'd never had any trouble finding a friend for a bit of fun at home, near Selby Manor. He'd always been rather popular with that set, though he wouldn't ever think of describing himself as fast. He was valet to a duke, after all. There were standards to maintain.

Standards which he felt even more keenly, now that Blake was in such a horrible, tragic spot. They'd just come to London less than a fortnight before—both as a way to hide Blake's daughters, Lady Margaret and Lady Jessica, from Lady Selby, and so that they could track down Lady Selby and Blake's heir, Lord Stanley—and Xavier had been extra vigilant about not drawing notice to the family in any way, good or bad. He felt a great deal of personal responsibility toward Blake and his children. Not only had Blake hired him as valet knowing his proclivities, doing so had restored Xavier's flagging reputation with his family after his previous employer had sacked him. Sacked him for *refusing* an inappropriate advance, of all things. Even though Xavier had sworn to the man he would never tell a soul. The last thing Xavier wanted to do now that he was in London was bring more shame down on Blake's shoulders. He admired his employer and friend above anyone else, and wanted to make the man proud.

"Got a match?"

The friendly voice that issued from the shadows as Xavier walked past a spreading oak came as such a surprise that Xavier gasped and jerked to see who had spoken. He twisted, searching, and found a handsome young man with some of the most striking features he'd ever seen leaning against the oak's trunk, his hands in his pockets.

"I...er...are you addressing me, sir?" Xavier's heart sped up and his hands instantly went clammy.

The handsome man shrugged and pushed away from the tree. "I don't see anyone else."

Xavier swallowed. "Oh. Right." He craned his neck, looking this way and that, searching the darkness for his friends, policemen, his mother, anyone who might rain holy terror down on him for even thinking of talking to a gorgeous stranger. He returned his focus to the handsome man, who had strolled to stand so close to him that Xavier caught the scent of his shaving soap. The man didn't have a cigarette or a pipe or anything that would require a match. "Um, no," he said, bristling with anxiety. How was one supposed to do this at any rate? His plan was specifically *not* to do it. "I'm afraid I left my matches at home."

The handsome man shrugged and hooked his arm suddenly through Xavier's. "I guess we'll just have to go home and fetch them, then."

They started forward. Xavier thought he might fall over his own feet. Everything around them suddenly seemed threatening and full of eyes. He might as well have been walking through the park naked, he felt so conspicuous.

"Not a man of many words I see," the handsome man said.

"It's not that," Xavier mumbled, glancing this way and that. "It's just that I've only arrived in London recently, and my friends put me up to this, and I honestly have no idea what in God's name is going on."

The handsome man laughed. "If it makes you feel better, I don't generally do this myself." He slowed his pace, his arm losing some of its tension. In fact, Xavier hadn't realized how tense the man was until he relaxed a bit. "Stop glancing around," he whispered. "It looks suspicious. Pretend that we're old school chums or something like that."

Xavier nodded tightly, then stopped and stared at the man. "Hang on, you're American." He felt like a fool for not noticing the man's accent before. Then again, he'd been too stunned by the man's strong cheekbones, expressive mouth, and intoxicating scent to notice much of anything.

"Does that excite you?" the man asked.

Xavier's brow shot up to his hairline. In fact, it did, but the question was so blatant and titillating that he hardly knew what to do with himself.

The handsome man must have seen that he had Xavier completely off-guard. He glanced around quickly, then pulled him off the path and down to the shadows near the base of one of the bridges spanning the lake. Judging by a muffled sound coming from the other end of the bridge, someone was already plying their trade in the shadows.

The handsome man spun Xavier so that his back was against the foot of the bridge and started in on the buttons of his coat. "What do you like?" he murmured, leaning in to whisper against Xavier's ear as he worked. "I can't say I know what the going rate for anything is these days, but I'm certain we could negotiate."

"I—oh!" Xavier let out a shaky cry as the man sucked on his earlobe. He had the horrible feeling that his boots were sinking into the mud of the lakeshore, but his cock was going in a different direction entirely.

Even more so when the handsome man finished with his coat and cupped his stiffening erection. He hummed as if impressed, "I see I have your attention."

"You have more than that," Xavier croaked. Flirting? Was he *flirting* with the man? What was he thinking? It was near midnight in the middle of a royal park. He must have gone mad.

But the handsome man smelled divine, and he was

gorgeous, and as he leaned in, Xavier could feel the heat of his well-formed body, even through their clothes. It was everything Xavier could do to maintain his dignity of bearing when the man unfastened Xavier's trousers and slipped his hand against his cock.

"What do you say?" the man murmured, kissing Xavier's neck. "A pound for a pound?"

Xavier's eyes popped open and he tensed. "That's an exorbitant sum for a fumble in the dark." He would have felt far more confident saying as much if his voice didn't crack and if he wasn't already leaking pre-come all over the man's hand.

"I told you I didn't know the going rate for these things," the man said, then shocked Xavier by slanting his mouth over his and devouring him with the single most sinful kiss Xavier had ever experienced.

Perhaps this wasn't such a bad idea after all. Desperation had pushed Alexander Plushenko into St. James's Park that night, but something entirely different might come out of it. Zander had tried everything he could think of to raise the money he needed to pay the rent on his third-rate rooms in the West End after his rotten flatmate had absconded with an entire year's worth of his savings. The ballet didn't pay as much as it should have to anyone who wasn't a principle, and there wasn't time between rehearsals and performances for him to earn what he needed honestly. He'd balked at the idea when one of his fellow dancers took him aside and told him how he could earn a quick coin or two, but hunger and the threat of homelessness were powerful motivation to do the unthinkable.

But there he was now, pressed up against the muddy base of a bridge in St. James's Park, fondling the rather impressive cock of a sweet-looking young man with a proper accent, kissing him into oblivion. The lad had the most intriguing mouth as well, and surprisingly good breath for a man randomly cruising the park at night. Zander didn't mind kissing him at all. In fact, he forgot about stroking him off entirely and just held him as he made love to the man's mouth. He wanted to pluck the hat right off the gent's head and run his free hand through his hair as well.

"I think I'm doing this wrong," he panted, breaking the kiss and leaning back a bit, though he couldn't bring himself to remove his hand from the gent's prick.

"No, you're doing it very right," the gent sighed roughly. He grabbed the back of Zander's head and yanked him in for another kiss.

Zander threw caution to the wind, sliding his tongue along the gent's and making a sound of surprise when the young man slipped his hand under the hem of Zander's jacket to tug his shirt free from his trousers. The moment the gent's long, slender fingers spread against the bare flesh of his belly, Zander knew he'd made a horrible miscalculation in targeting the man. He was young and lovely and eager as fuck, and in an instant, Zander couldn't remember what he was supposed to be asking for, other than for the man to move his hand down a couple of inches.

"Slow down, slow down," the gent panted breaking away from Zander's mouth and tilting his head back against the bridge. "I'm too close." He'd knocked his hat askew.

"Isn't that the point?" Zander asked with a teasing grin, doing what he wanted to do and tossing the gent's hat aside entirely so he could thread his fingers through his hair. It felt like strands of silk.

The gent laughed. It was a low, vibrating sound that went straight to Zander's prick. "When am I ever going to have the privilege of a handsome American getting me off again?" he asked. "I'd like to make it last, thank you. And, my God, you're built like Adonis."

He'd managed to untuck Zander's shirt entirely and had both hands spread across his abdomen. Having the man's elegant hands on him in itself was heavenly—which was utterly mad, considering he was supposed to be engaged in the highly distasteful task of prostituting himself to pay the rent—but when the gent unfastened his trousers, he thought his knees might give out.

"Let's see if you're built like a god everywhere," the gent said, biting his lip as he glanced into Zander's eyes.

Zander thanked the stars above that there was enough light for him to see that impish look on the gent's face. He had a certain gamine charm to him that never failed to fire Zander's blood. If they'd met in a different place, under different circumstances....

Hell, why was he worried about meeting the man under different circumstances? Different circumstances wouldn't have enabled them to fondle each other's cocks five minutes after meeting or thrust their tongues against each other's while making ridiculous sounds of abandon, and he most certainly wouldn't have wanted to miss out on that. He'd never wanted a man so instantly or so thoroughly in his life. He couldn't explain why, but that hardly seemed to matter.

"This is madness," he laughed against the gent's ear, kissing his neck, and jerking into his touch. "I'm supposed to be asking money for this."

"And I was just going to walk through the park so I could lie to my friends about going through with the dare," the gent said.

For some reason, that sent even more arousal flaring through Zander. "So I'm a dare, then?"

"A dare I'm glad I took," the gent panted, then grabbed Zander's hips and yanked him close so they could grind together.

Zander had gone into the park knowing there would be a fair chance he'd change his mind about what he was doing. Change his mind he did, but not in the way he'd anticipated. "Do you want to come home with me?" he whispered, heart racing. "Forget this tumble in the park nonsense. Do you want to spend the night with me?"

"Oh, God, yes," the gent said. "How far do you—"

His question was cut off by the shrill cry of a policeman's whistle. More than one. Scuffling and curses came from the shadows on the other side of the bridge. The crackling tension in the air shifted from sensual to dangerous.

"Shit." Zander pulled away from the gent, tucking himself awkwardly back into his trousers.

"Oh, God," the gent said in an entirely different tone than he'd used just moments before.

In the scant lamplight, Zander caught the terror in the young man's eyes. He seemed frozen as well, as though his worst nightmare had come to fruition. Zander wasn't about to see someone so lovely suffer the cruelty men like them were subject to at the hands of the police.

"Come on," he said, working fast to tuck the gent back into his trousers and to yank the front of his coat together. "You have to get out of here. Run as fast as you can and don't look back."

"But what about you?" the gent said, still dazed, even though he pulled his boots up from the mud where they'd been standing and hurried up the riverbank to snatch his hat from the grass.

The police whistles sounded again, nearer, and Zander caught sight of several shadows darting for safety.

"Don't worry about me," he said, pushing the gent to run after them. "I'm more than capable of taking care of myself."

"Are you—"

"Go!" Zander shouted, no longer worried about staying quiet.

He pushed the gent as hard as he could, then watched as he dashed away with the others.

Zander's relief only lasted for a moment, though. Just as he was breathing a sigh of relief that the sweet young gent had made it to safety, an officer raced toward him from the darkness and grabbed his arm.

"Hold it right there, Nancy," the man growled.

"What is the meaning of this? I haven't done anything." Zander's protest would have meant more if his trousers weren't hanging open with his still hard cock straining for freedom.

"You're under arrest, sweetheart," the policemen sneered.

Zander cursed under his breath. He must have had the worst luck in the world. He didn't try to fight as the officer jerked his arms behind his back to throw shackles on his wrists. He did, however, glance off in the direction his fine young gent had gone. To his horror, he saw the man's pale, terrified face peeking out from the shadows, his delicious mouth dropped open in a silent shout of protest. There was nothing either of them could do about it, though. Zander had been caught like the idiot he was.

All he could do was smile weakly at his gent and jerk his head, ordering him to go and save himself. The gent nodded, then disappeared into the night. Zander bitterly regretted the fact that he'd never see the lovely thing again or get a chance to finish what they'd started.

CHAPTER 2

LIVERPOOL – MARCH 1891

The *RMS Umbria* towered above every other ship along the Liverpool waterfront—or dock or marina or slip, or whatever the place where ships connected to the shore was called. Xavier knew as little about naval terminology as he did about the ocean itself, or about the vast country of America that he was about to see for the very first time. After a lifetime spent toiling away in the north of England, then in London for a matter of months, Xavier's entire world was about to explode with experience and color. He could hardly wait.

"Careful there, Xavier. You'll strain your neck if you keep your head tilted back like that," John Dandie—a friend of Blake's who was traveling with them on the mission to retrieve young Lord Stanley from his erstwhile mother in New York—teased him. "And if you don't stop gaping, a sea bird will fly straight into your mouth."

Xavier shut his mouth quickly and straightened from where he'd been gaping up at the goliath ship, one hand on his hat to keep it from tumbling off, well aware that John was teasing him. He'd nearly lost that hat once before, and he wasn't keen to lose it now, but the *Umbria* was a modern marvel that he couldn't stop staring at. It was a steam-powered ship with two massive smokestacks, but it was also fitted with three tall masts and auxiliary sails. Even from the gangplank, as Xavier walked aboard behind Blake and Niall, he could see that the ship was outfitted with the utmost luxury. He spotted a wide promenade that already had finely dressed ladies and gentlemen walking along it, as well as an upper deck toward the back of the ship where the second-class passengers roamed, waving goodbye to their friends on the shore. Smartly-dressed porters dashed this way and that along the decks, helping arriving passengers with their things or fetching refreshments for the first-class passengers.

"You're back to gaping again," John chuckled. He walked behind where Xavier pushed a small trolley containing Blake's and Niall's trunks and his own suitcase for the journey. John seemed as excited about the voyage as Xavier was, but perhaps for a different set of reasons.

Xavier glanced behind John to where Detective Arthur Gleason made up the fifth in their party. Xavier wasn't entirely certain why the mysterious detective was coming to America to help them search for Lord Stanley, considering he had been their adversary during the first part of the search. But everyone who had been within ten yards of John Dandie and Arthur Gleason recently could feel the sexual tension enveloping the two men. It was as likely as not that they both saw the trip to New York as one long courtship dance. Xavier only hoped that the two of them could contain themselves long enough not to draw the attention of whatever police force was responsible for the ship.

He'd had enough of police raids to last a lifetime after his incident in St. James's Park months before. Not a day went by when he didn't think about everything that had happened that night and blush. The mad dash to get away from the police had been a baptism by fire when it came to understanding the danger that men like him faced from carrying on in public. But what he truly couldn't forget from that night was his handsome, American stranger, the man whose kiss he would carry with him for the rest of his life, whose taste would linger forever on his lips, and who's shape seemed to be imprinted on his hands now. He didn't even know the man's name, but forgetting him would be as impossible as forgetting the sunrise.

"There we are," Niall said once they'd stepped over the threshold and onto the ship proper. "It finally feels as though we're getting somewhere."

"It will feel more like we're getting somewhere once

the ship departs," Blake said with a sigh, removing his hat briefly so he could rub his forehead.

"We will succeed, my lord," Xavier told Blake with what he hoped was an encouraging smile.

Blake smiled gratefully at Xavier, but from behind, Gleason asked, "Shouldn't you be calling him 'your grace', since he's a duke?" with a cheeky grin.

Blake's smile warmed. "I've been trying to convince Xavier to call me 'Blake' for the past two years, since he's been one of the most faithful friends I've had in that time, but the man is a stickler for protocol. For him, 'my lord' is as informal as calling me 'old chum'."

Xavier blushed, unable to decide whether he was offended by Blake's teasing or flattered by it. John and Gleason laughed—although when they exchanged a look, John's laughter turned brittle, and he snapped away with a frown, as though laughing with Gleason were a sign of weakness. He walked ahead to flag down one of the porters.

"Every once in a while," Blake went on, gesturing for them all to move out of the way so another party could board the ship behind them, "when Xavier is feeling particularly sentimental, he drops all pretense of formality and addresses me by the friendly endearment, 'sir'."

Niall hid his chuckle behind his hand, but Gleason wasn't so circumspect. "You old devil, you," he ribbed Xavier.

"Lord Selby may be a duke," Xavier defended

himself, "and as such, he may be entitled to be called whatever he chooses, but propriety must be observed in some way. I am only a valet."

"Come now, Xavier. You are much more than that to our family," Blake said. "It's all I can do to stop the girls from calling you 'Uncle Xavier'."

Xavier blushed even harder at that. Lady Margaret and Lady Jessica were all sweetness and light. Blake and Niall weren't the only ones who felt anxiety over leaving them in the care of Stephen and Max Siddel at the Darlington Gardens Orphanage—which stood nearly adjacent to their townhouse in Earl's Court—for the duration of the journey to America. The girls had been thrilled to spend more than a month with their friends, but the adults were all desperately and sentimentally worried about them.

John returned with the porter he'd snagged a moment later. "This fine lad says he can lead us straight to our cabins if we would just follow him."

"It would be my pleasure, sirs," the porter said with a short bow.

Xavier's brow shot up. He'd never been bowed to in his life. He supposed how one was treated was all about who one was with.

The porter led them along the deck to one of the entrances to the first class section of the ship at the front of the *Umbria*. Xavier could hardly drink in enough of everything he saw around him. The interior of the ship felt like a fine, if somewhat tight, hotel, complete with wood-paneled walls, velvet furnishings, and fine art hanging on the walls. To one side, he caught sight of an open door with a placard declaring it the Music Room above it and the stylish furnishings of the room beyond.

They went the other way, though, traveling down a short flight of stairs—the porter helped transport their baggage down the stairs—to an equally well-appointed lower deck. Xavier caught sight of the promenade out one door, and a vast and sumptuous dining hall off to the other side. The hallway that the porter led them down, however, took them through a series of halls with identical doors marked with numbers.

"Eighteen and nineteen are down that way," the porter gestured in one direction, "and twenty and twenty-one are on the other side." He signaled the opposite way.

"Thank you," Blake told the man with a smile, offering him a generous tip.

The porter's face lit up. "Anything you need for this voyage, your grace, just let me know. My name is Edward."

"Thank you, Edward." Blake nodded to the young man.

They waited for a moment as Edward scurried off. John and Gleason both veered off to cabins twenty and twenty-one, but Blake, Niall, and Xavier waited until the hall was deserted before moving to the other two.

"Right," Niall said. "Perhaps it is an abundance of

caution, but let's get my and Blake's things set up in eighteen before anyone suspects we're bunking together."

Xavier hid his smile as he wheeled the trolley with their trunks down the side corridor to the two doors facing each other near the end of the hall. Niall held the keys to both rooms and opened eighteen, stepping in and holding the door for Blake. Xavier grinned at that as well. Outsiders would turn up their nose or balk in disgust at the unique kind of love Blake and Niall had for one another, but the two were as in love and devoted to each other as any couple Xavier had ever seen. They were affectionate when they thought they could get away with it—and sometimes when they couldn't—and the care and sweetness they showed each other always left Xavier sighing with longing. Who said there was no such thing as romance for men like them?

He unloaded the trunks with Niall's help, then insisted on unpacking them and hanging both Blake's and Niall's suits in the tiny wardrobe on one side of the room. The cabin itself was astoundingly luxurious. Xavier hadn't known what to expect, but the furnishings were as fine as anything he'd seen in the estates he'd visited, the bed seemed comfortable and spacious, and the series of large portholes along one side of the room let in a decent amount of light. There were gaslights as well, but they wouldn't be needed until later.

"You don't have to fuss over all that now," Blake said when Xavier was only halfway through putting away his things and noting to himself what needed to be pressed.

"Why don't you settle in to your own cabin, unpack your things, then take a stroll around the ship to gauge the lay of the land, as it were."

"Gauge the lay of the sea?" Niall offered.

Blake laughed.

Xavier stood straight after putting away one of Blake's suits and tried not to look awkward. "My cabin, my lord?" he asked. They hadn't discussed the details of where, exactly, on the ship Xavier would be staying. He assumed Blake had booked second-class passage for him and that he'd spend a good part of his journey rushing back and forth along the length of the ship.

Instead, Blake handed him the key to cabin nineteen. "It's all yours. First-class passage for a first-class friend."

Xavier's mouth hung open as he accepted the key from Blake. "Are you certain, my lord?" he asked, a bit hoarse.

Blake grinned. "When else is a boy from West Riding going to get the chance to cross the Atlantic in the most luxurious accommodations money can buy?"

"I—I shouldn't, my lord," Xavier said, turning the key over in his hands as though it would lead to a treasure trove. "It's above my station."

"Your station is whatever I say it is," Blake told him, clapping a hand on his shoulder. "Consider this a gift for everything you've been forced to put up with because of me these last few months." He was solemn, so Xavier merely nodded in answer. "Now go." Blake thumped his arm. "Take your bag and get settled in your opulent surroundings. And I am serious about taking a turn about the ship to let us know where all of the hiding places and rendezvous nooks are located." He winked sportingly.

Xavier flushed and reached for the mostly empty trolley. "Thank you so much, sir," he said, swelling with pride and affection. "I'll just return this while I'm at it, and if there is anything else you need from me at any point in the journey—"

"I'll track you down, crack the whip, and put you to work," Blake said.

Xavier sent his employer a final, grateful grin before taking the trolley and his things and wheeling them out into the hall. He was glad that Blake was in one of his rare, cheery moods, and he hoped that after Niall shut the door behind him, the two of them would spend a few cozy minutes before letting the cares of their mission and the world weigh on them. They deserved all the happiness they could get after what they'd gone through.

Once he returned from handing the trolley off to a crewman in the hall, Xavier let himself into cabin nineteen. He drew in a breath of excitement as he carried his suitcase into the room and deposited it on the wide bed. The room was a mirror image of the one Blake and Niall were sharing, which humbled Xavier. He truly didn't deserve to share the same sort of accommodations as a duke, but now that the key was in his hand, he raced through putting his things away so that he could feel like the room was home. Even if it would only be home for a week or less. The voyage could take anywhere from five to seven days, depending on weather, which was a modern marvel itself. The part of him that was inexperienced with travel couldn't wait to discover more about how a goliath of a ship could speed across a vast ocean in no time at all.

Once unpacking was done, the real excitement began. Xavier left his cabin and explored his way through the first-class hallway, seeing what there was to see. The rooms themselves didn't hold much interest, except in terms of how many of them there were. He'd read somewhere that the *Umbria* could carry well over three hundred passengers. The public rooms at the far end of the first-class hall were far more captivating than the rooms. The dining hall was vast and pretty, with an open balcony above that led to the music room. Whatever orchestra had been engaged to entertain passengers would be heard by diners as they ate. First-class also contained a smoking room for the gentlemen, a few parlors, and special sitting rooms for ladies.

The deck and promenade were far more intriguing to Xavier, though. The promenade was covered and ran the length of the ship on the same deck where his and his friends' cabins were located. The upper deck was open to the sun and the sky directly above the promenade. That was where Xavier found he wanted to be so that he could watch the last passengers climb aboard and marvel at all the things he'd marveled at earlier. The ship wasn't scheduled to depart for another hour, but the deck was teeming with people who had come up to wave the shore goodbye.

He started around the deck, making his way from the section that was primarily first class to the back of the ship, where second class began. He was curious to see what the difference in accommodation for the classes were, but almost immediately, something else caught his eye and froze his steps. It pushed the air from his lungs and sent his heart racing.

There he was, leaning against the ship's railing and staring out at the shore with a pensive look, his gorgeous American. He was even more handsome in the daylight than he'd been in the shadows of St. James's Park. His broad shoulders were hunched slightly, he was thinner and paler than Xavier had imagined him to be, and his expressive face seemed filled with troubles, but he was undoubtedly the man Xavier hadn't been able to stop thinking or dreaming about since that embarrassing, wonderful night in November.

As if he could feel him looking, the handsome man of his dreams turned and stared right at him. Xavier felt even more glued to the ground, heat rising up his neck to his face, particularly when the man burst into an amazed smile and straightened. His frame was even more powerful and graceful than Xavier remembered it to be, and as he pushed away from the railing and strode toward him, Xavier's heart ran riot in his chest.

"If you only knew how wide your eyes are right now, you'd be as afraid as I am that they're about to pop right out of your head," the man said, smiling broadly enough to reveal his astoundingly perfect teeth.

"I...I didn't...I couldn't...." Xavier blinked and cursed himself for sounding like a complete idiot in the face of the man who had given him the best kiss of his life. And who had had his hand down his trousers. That was a terrible thing to remember on a crowded deck in the middle of the afternoon. His cock didn't seem to care about etiquette and propriety, though.

The handsome man thrust out the same hand, nearly making Xavier whimper with delight. "Alexander Plushenko," he said. "My friends call me Zander."

"Am I a friend?" Xavier croaked.

Zander's smile widened. "As soon as you take my hand and tell me your name you will be."

Xavier pinched his eyes shut for a half second, calling himself every name imaginable, and grasped Zander's hand. It was large and warm and immediately reminded him of all the things it could do. "Xavier Lawrence," he managed to squeak out.

"It's a pleasure to meet you again, Xavier." Zander smiled, his eyes dancing with excitement. He didn't seem to want to return Xavier's hand.

"Oh, God," Xavier gulped, his smile turning into a look of horror. "I'm sorry. I'm so, so sorry." He pulled his hand out of Zander's grip, suddenly feeling like the worst sort of cad imaginable.

"For what?" Zander asked, losing his smile as well.

"I ran." Xavier winced painfully. "I fled like a coward

and abandoned you to the police. I...I should have stayed, I should have tried to do something to help you."

Zander clapped a hand on his arm. "You did the right thing. I set myself up for that mess. If you'd stayed, you would have been arrested too."

"Arrested?" Xavier felt worse than ever. "You were arrested?"

Zander nodded. "Caught with my willy out and everything. Fortunately," he went on with more cheer than Xavier thought the situation called for, "I argued that I'd just been relieving myself."

Xavier flinched. "They didn't believe that, did they?"

"They couldn't prove otherwise." Zander shrugged. "They didn't catch me with anyone. Which meant I only spent three months in jail on charges of sodomy before the case went to court and the charges were dropped instead of being sentenced to two years of hard labor."

Xavier's stomach twisted so tightly he thought he might be sick. "I'm so sorry," he repeated. "That must have been a nightmare."

"It wasn't the best Christmas I've ever spent, no," Zander replied.

Xavier felt even worse. He'd spent a jolly Christmas in Darlington Gardens, watching Blake's girls and Stephen and Max's orphans get up to mischief and defend them all from a police raid. Zander had likely spent it alone in a cold cell, being mistreated in the worst of ways. He owed the man so much to make up for everything.

"I don't know what I can do to make amends for it all," he began.

Before he could finish, they were hailed with a call of, "You two! You look like fine, strapping men. Come over here and help."

Both Xavier and Zander turned to find a steely, grey-haired, old woman dressed to the nines being followed up the gangplank by an exhausted and sweating porter pushing a trolley stacked high with trunks and traveling bags. The woman must have been eighty if she were a day, and she snapped her fingers at Xavier and Zander.

"Well?" she huffed in her sharp, American accent. "Don't just stand there like signposts. Do as you're told and help me with my things."

Zander turned to Xavier with a bright and mischievous smile. Rather than telling the old lady that they weren't ship's crew, Zander murmured, "This should be fun," and tugged on Xavier's cuff to pull him closer to the old woman.

CHAPTER 3

A hundred different emotions, each more powerful than the next, slammed into Zander at once when he glanced across the *Umbria*'s deck and spotted his gentleman from St. James's Park—joy that squeezed his heart, shame over the way they'd parted, regret over the way they'd met, and deep, pulsing hope that this time he could do things right. After the indignities and humiliations he'd suffered for the last five months, all he wanted was to do one thing right.

Xavier—that was his gent's name, and how funny that their names had a natural rhythm to them that fit together—was even more handsome in daylight than he'd been in the shadows of St. James's Park. He had a sort of brightness and glow about him as Zander grinned and tugged him over to the trolley of trunks belonging to the old woman that the sweating ship's porter was struggling with. Xavier was surprisingly agile as he leapt to steady one of the suitcases piled on top of the trunks, his graceful hands stopping the whole pile from spilling over.

But it was Xavier's intelligent, brown eyes, so full of soul, that Zander couldn't look away from as he took the trolley's handle from the porter and steered it toward the doorway to first class. Zander hadn't had an adequate look at those eyes in the dark, but now he wanted to do nothing more than stare into their depths to see what sort of secrets they might reveal.

Which was utterly ridiculous and far too sentimental for even his sometimes-maudlin tastes. He shook his head and laughed at himself, poking his head around the edge of the laden trolley to ask the old woman, "Where would you like these to be taken, my lady?"

"It's not my lady anything," the old woman snapped, dropping her shoulders in exasperation. "I am through with this damn fool country and it's silly titles and rules of deference. I don't care if a man was born in a palace with a title so long it takes half an hour to recite it—if he's an idiot, he's an idiot."

Zander exchanged a look with Xavier—who looked as though he might swallow his tongue—and burst into laughter. "Yes, ma'am," he said, laughing even more at the deep, pink flush that spread across Xavier's cheeks, as though someone had spilled fine wine there.

"That's Mrs. Pennypacker to you," the old woman informed him. She tapped the end of the closed parasol she carried impatiently against the deck, then said, "Well, what are you waiting for? My things won't unpack themselves."

She turned and marched forward, her shoes clicking against the deck under her long skirt as she walked.

Zander turned to a still-stunned Xavier. "Well, come along, then," he said in imitation of Mrs. Pennypacker, then pushed the trolley forward.

"We can't just follow an old woman into her cabin," Xavier whispered, grabbing the trolley's handle to help Zander push anyhow. "We're not ship's staff."

"I think it's crew when you're on a ship," Zander replied with a mischievous glint in his eyes, "and I don't think Mrs. Pennypacker cares who we are as long as we help."

"But what if we're found out?" Xavier went on as they rolled the trolley through the doorway to first class, then paused as Mrs. Pennypacker checked her key, looked at the signs indicating where the various cabins were located, then marched on.

Zander shrugged. "If we're found out, we apologize for the misunderstanding and graciously find someone else to help her. But at this point, I think the old bat just wants to get settled in."

Xavier tilted his head to the side in consideration, then pushed the trolley on without another word. They were lucky that Mrs. Pennypacker's room was on that deck and that they didn't have to carry the trolley and its contents down the stairs. Her room was about halfway along the narrow corridor that ran the length of the ship and down a short side corridor. Zander's eyes went wide as he glanced around the spacious cabin once Mrs. Pennypacker opened the door. He'd thought his accommodations in second class were fine, but the first-class cabins were as beautiful as any hotel he'd ever been in. Not that he'd been in many, but the ballet company had hosted a party or two at the Savoy that he'd attended. Until he'd been ignominiously fired.

That thought threatened to derail the first bit of joy Zander had felt in months, so he shoved it aside and asked Mrs. Pennypacker, "Where would you like us to put your trunks, ma'am?"

Mrs. Pennypacker stared at him as if he'd asked where he should store the bucket of frogs she'd ordered. "How should I know?" the old woman shrugged. "Put everything away in the wardrobe and the bureaus."

"Ma'am, do you have a maid to assist you on this voyage?" Xavier asked with all the deference and charm of a proper English gentleman.

Mrs. Pennypacker clicked her tongue and rolled her eyes. "If I had a maid, I wouldn't need two strapping young men like you to do the job for me, now would I?"

Zander grinned at Xavier again, trying hard not to break down into laughter. He couldn't have planned a jollier reunion with his gent if he'd tried. It was the perfect way to get around whatever awkwardness they might be tempted to feel after the way they'd parted. "Yes, ma'am," he said. "Right away, ma'am." He nodded to Xavier, gesturing for him to take the suitcases from the top of the trunks and move them to the bed.

"Surely, you won't need all of your things during the voyage," Xavier said as though it were his business to know and care. "Do you have a few, preferred gowns that you would like to wear while keeping the rest in their trunks?"

"How am I supposed to know in advance which things I'll want to wear on any given day?" Mrs. Pennypacker sighed. "Unpack the whole thing."

"Very well, ma'am." Xavier bowed so perfectly to her that Zander had to hide his grin behind one hand.

More than that, as they took the trunks off of the trolley and opened them to remove and hang their contents, Xavier seemed to know exactly what he was doing. He handled each item of clothing as though it were a treasure, even brushing them with his hands and making sure the flounces and lace were straight before hanging them in the wardrobe. Zander took it upon himself to wheel the trolley back out into the hall and to find places to store the suitcases and trunks once Xavier emptied them, but he was far more interested in watching the way Xavier's hands caressed the expensive fabric and straightened buttons and fastenings.

"You're very good at that," Zander commented quietly when Mrs. Pennypacker went to stare out one of the portholes along one side of her room.

"I should be," Xavier said with a sly grin. "I'm valet to

the Duke of Selby, and before that, I trained as a tailor in one of the finest establishments in Leeds."

Zander's brow shot up. "And here I thought you were some sort of young lordling yourself."

Xavier's eyes went wide with surprise. "Me? A lord? I should think not."

"You've certainly got the mannerisms for one," Zander said with a wink.

Xavier blushed and stammered in a way that made Zander want to throw caution to the wind—and Xavier up against the cabin wall—and kiss him until he forgot his name. He inched closer to Xavier, close enough to touch him, and fixed him with a wicked look.

He opened his mouth to say something else designed to make Xavier blush, but Mrs. Pennypacker turned away from the porthole, shook her head, and sighed, "Why my granddaughter adores this Godforsaken country so much is anyone's guess."

Zander and Xavier jumped apart, and Xavier fussed with a stack of sensible underthings. Zander faced Mrs. Pennypacker with a polite smile, then asked, "Were you in England to visit your granddaughter, then?"

"I was," Mrs. Pennypacker said. "For my sins. That's the third great-grandchild those two miscreants have given me in the last five years. Why can't you young people keep your hands off each other?" she asked, shaking her head.

Zander sent a heated look Xavier's way, though Xavier was paying very close attention to packing away

Mrs. Pennypacker's things in the bureau. His entire neck had gone red, though. A neck Zander would very much have liked to leave a mark or two on.

"Don't just stand there ogling that one's bum," Mrs. Pennypacker went on, shocking Zander out of his impish thoughts. He wasn't being that obvious, was he? Except, he knew he was. "I have a few delicate items in that case there which need to be stored in a secure location." She pointed to the smallest case, which rested on the bed.

Without thinking, Zander crossed to the bed and threw open the case, expecting it to contain gloves or underthings, or something else Xavier would know how to store. Instead, he gasped as he dropped the case's lid. It was filled with enough jewelry to fund a small country for a year. With one glance, Zander caught sight of rubies, emeralds, sapphires, and diamonds. There were enough pearls to fill the ocean as well. Zander hadn't seen so many glittering, sparkling things outside of the window of one of the jewelry stores in Hatton Gardens.

"I didn't say you should open that." Mrs. Pennypacker stomped across the room with surprising speed and slammed the lid of her jewelry case shut.

"I'm terribly sorry, ma'am," Zander said with all the genuineness he could manage. "I didn't think."

"No, I suspect you're too pretty to think."

Mrs. Pennypacker's comment had Zander's jaw dropping for a moment. He didn't know whether to be offended or to laugh. Instead, he shook his head and said,

"Perhaps you should ask if the ship has a safe or some other secure place to store these instead of in your cabin."

"Doesn't the room have a safe?" she asked.

Zander exchanged a look with Xavier. Xavier shrugged. They spent the next minute or so opening cabinets and drawers to see if there were any sort of thing.

"There should be," Xavier said at last, "but there doesn't seem to be one. I agree with Zander that you should ask if the ship has a secure place to put them for the duration of the voyage."

Mrs. Pennypacker snorted. "Not on your life. I'm not letting these things out of my sight. You'll have to find someplace to put them in here where no one will find them."

Zander and Xavier engaged in another search until Xavier suggested they tuck the case of jewels under the sink in the lavatory. "No one will look for them there," he insisted.

"If you say so," Mrs. Pennypacker said, narrowing her eyes for a moment before giving that up with a sigh. "And now, you will accompany me out to the deck and find me a nice chair in the sunshine where I can lounge like your queen and wave goodbye to this horrible country."

Zander's sense of the fun of the situation returned. "Yes, ma'am," he said, straightening to his full height and puffing out his chest before offering Mrs. Pennypacker his arm.

The old woman looked as pleased as punch to take it, but pivoted to gesture impatiently to Xavier as well.

"Come along, you," she said, holding out her hand until Xavier stepped forward to offer his arm as well. "I didn't single out the two of you for your brains. I want to be escorted around this ship by the two handsomest young bucks on it."

Zander laughed out loud before he could stop himself as they stepped out into the hall. "I would say that you have excellent taste, ma'am, at least, regarding my friend Xavier here, but that would make me sound conceited."

"Nonsense," Mrs. Pennypacker said as they walked slowly along the hall, heading back out to the deck. "It's not conceit if it's true. You're both young, handsome, and virile. Just the way I like my men."

Xavier made a strangled sound that turned into a cough, drawing the attention of a pair of ladies just outside the first-class doorway as they stepped back into the fresh air. The two ladies giggled and smiled at Mrs. Pennypacker as though she were quaint, though Zander thought Mrs. Pennypacker might very well be the smartest woman on the ship, in more ways than one.

"How old are you, Mrs. Pennypacker?" he asked cheekily.

Mrs. Pennypacker feigned shock and indignation. "How dare you ask a woman her age?" Zander knew her indignation wasn't genuine when she went on to add proudly, "I'm eight-three years young and still spry enough to travel across the ocean on my own and to promenade the deck of a fancy ship like this with two men less than a third of my age."

"You have my extreme admiration, ma'am," Zander laughed. "Do you know where you'd like to sit to watch this Godforsaken country slip away into the horizon?"

"Oh, anywhere," Mrs. Pennypacker said.

They walked around to the front of the ship and a small deck that was slightly elevated. Several folding chairs had been set up for what looked like the expressed purpose of lounging and lording it over everyone else on the ship, which meant Mrs. Pennypacker would be in heaven. Zander helped her up the stairs to that deck—the first time she demonstrated her age and a touch of fragility—and he and Xavier helped her get settled.

"Is there anything else we can fetch for you, ma'am?" Xavier asked, hands clasped behind his back. "A blanket, perhaps? Refreshments?"

"No, no." Mrs. Pennypacker waved them away. "I just want to sit here and contemplate the joy of the fact that I never have to see England again."

Zander laughed, but the sound turned wistful as he glanced across the ship to the shore. He might have been born and raised in New York, but he'd spent some of the happiest times of his life in England. He'd been there for nearly ten years, and if he were honest with himself, London felt more like home than New York. But after the events of the last few months and the way the life he'd built for himself had crumbled so completely, he didn't know if he'd ever see London again. It hurt more than he wanted to think about.

A tap on his hand shook him out of his thoughts, and

he turned to smile down at Mrs. Pennypacker. She held a handful of bills, which she pushed into his hand. "Thank you for all your help, young man," she said with a wink.

Zander gaped at the tip she'd given him, not sure what to make of it. "You're welcome," he said at last. He wasn't sure it would be right to accept the generous sum of money, but honestly, he needed it, and Mrs. Pennypacker was clearly wealthy.

"Now run along and enjoy the excitement of a ship putting out to sea," Mrs. Pennypacker said to him and Xavier. "I'm just going to take a little nap."

"Very well, ma'am," Xavier said with a perfect bow, then walked around her chair to Zander's side.

The two of them made their way down to the main deck and continued toward the front of the ship. Zander stared at the bills in his hand for a moment before dividing the whole in two and handing half to Xavier. "Here," he said. "You deserve this as much as I do."

"I couldn't possibly," Xavier said. "You take the whole thing."

Zander writhed with guilt, but said nothing and slipped the money into his pocket. Suddenly, every bit of awkwardness that could have existed between them was there. They weren't two friends being mischievous and helping out an old woman, they were two men who had experienced something heady together and who had parted under cringe-worthy circumstances. Not only that, the deck was far too crowded for Zander's liking.

"Would you like to go for a walk around the ship?" he

asked, suddenly anxious that Xavier would say no. "Maybe find someplace quieter where we could talk?"

Thankfully, Xavier broke into a smile. "I'd like that."

The two of them started across the front of the ship, intending to walk along the deck that didn't face the shore, and Zander felt as though for the first time in a long time, things were looking up.

CHAPTER 4

Xavier's heart raced, and the ground beneath him—or rather, the deck beneath him—suddenly felt unsteady. And it wasn't because the ship was finally being tugged out of its dock and pushed out into the open waters of the Irish Sea. As land slipped away behind him, he felt as though his life might just be slipping into an entirely different place as well. Helping out Mrs. Pennypacker had been a lark—and he'd been astounded by the amount of jewelry the woman was traveling with—but as he and Zander found a quiet spot against the railing, facing out at the empty sea and all the possibilities of the voyage before them, Xavier's nerves took over.

"So, you're a valet for a duke," Zander said, finding a spot against the railing that was well away from any other travelers. He leaned his forearms against the top of the railing and rested his foot on the lowest rung, looking utterly casual. Xavier was distracted by the way the sea breeze ruffled Zander's blond hair and the pink flush on his cheeks after their brisk walk and the fun of jumping to do Mrs. Pennypacker's bidding. And Zander had the most beautiful blue eyes Xavier had ever seen—eyes that were full of mischief and sorrow, fun and strength.

He shook his head as he remembered he'd been asked a question and attempted to lean casually against the railing as well. He was certain the result was stiff and clumsy and made him look like a right git. "Er, yes," he said. "I've been valet to Lord Selby for several years now."

"Do you like chasing around after a nob?" Zander asked, a teasing sparkle in his eyes.

Xavier's face went hot as his mind went straight to the alternative meaning of the question that did *not* imply being a valet to a duke. "Oh...well...um...nobs pay well?" he tried.

Zander laughed humorlessly and straightened. "No, they don't."

Xavier prayed for a bolt of lightning to strike him dead on the spot. "I'm so sorry about what happened—"

"How does one get a position as a valet for a duke?" Zander overrode his bumbling embarrassment with enough force to leave Xavier wincing. He shifted to rest his hip against the railing. Xavier was momentarily distracted with the thought that every pose Zander struck showed off some part of him to his credit. Now his muscular arms seemed to be highlighted for some reason.

"I applied for the position, I was interviewed, and I got it," he said, blinking his way back to paying full attention. God, what was wrong with him? He was perfectly capable of having a normal conversation with a man, whether he was the most beautiful man to ever roam the earth or not. "That is to say," he squeezed his eyes shut for a moment, then went on, "Lord Selby was in need of a new valet after his previous one found a new situation. He is a man in need of great discretion, as he told me during our initial interview, and chose me because he believed me to be trustworthy and capable of keeping his secrets."

Zander sent Xavier a wry smirk. "I've heard the name before. Lord Selby, the Disgusting Duke."

Xavier winced. He wasn't aware that the vicious nickname had gone beyond a few hoity-toity members of the aristocracy who thought their own, numerous affairs were somehow forgivable because they were with women, whereas Blake's passionate devotion to Niall was unforgivable, simply because Niall was another man.

"Lord Selby is one of the finest men I have ever known," Xavier defended him, standing straighter and assuming an imperious air. "He has endured more than most men are asked to face in a lifetime, all within the last year. He has had his reputation shattered because of whom he chooses to love, and his family torn from him by the fickle whims of a wife who was never true to him to begin with and whom he had no wish to marry in the first place."

"All right, all right," Zander laughed, standing straighter himself. "No need to defend the man to me. Everyone who is anyone in Covent Garden knows the brave story of Niall Cristofori and Blake Williamson and everything the two of them have endured to be together."

Xavier blinked in surprise, though he felt like a bit of a fool for learning that Zander already knew more of the story than he'd let on. "Are you part of the theatrical set, then?" he asked.

"I was, until recently, employed with the Markova Ballet Company," Zander said, his expression turning shadowy. "We performed across the street from the Concord Theater, where Mr. Cristofori mounts all of his plays. So we were all very well informed about the unfolding drama."

"So you're a dancer, then?" Xavier's interest was piqued. That would have explained the man's perfect physical condition. The thought had him sweeping Zander's form with a look of interest that he quickly forced himself to conceal.

He knew he concealed it badly when Zander grinned saucily and said, "We're not talking about me yet. I'm still interested in how one becomes a valet after being, what did you say earlier? A tailor in Leeds?"

Xavier was far more pleased than he should have been that Zander remembered that detail about him. He forced himself to relax and lean against the deck's railing again. He even glanced out over the water as the ship turned slightly to steady his nerves.

"There isn't much to it," he said with a shrug. "I enjoyed being a tailor very much, but it was a choice between starting at the bottom, working my fingers to the bones for a pittance for however long it might take to establish my own business, or accepting employment which included living arrangements in a grand estate and extraordinarily generous compensation."

"So you gave up your dreams for money," Zander said with a teasing grin.

"I did not," Xavier insisted. "I still do what I love, only now for one man instead of dozens."

"Oh, so that's what it's like?" Zander's eyes filled with mischief.

Xavier flushed hot and stammered for a moment before saying, "*That* is absolutely *not* what it is like. You Americans read far too much into every little thing."

"I'm only teasing," Zander laughed. "You're far too much fun to rile up. Something about breaking through all that stiff, British propriety."

"My behavior is a reflection on my employer," Xander defended himself, chin tilted up. "And Lord Selby deserves far more respect than he gets."

"I believe you," Zander said, genuine, but still seeming to have a laugh at Xavier's expense.

Xavier wasn't sure he minded, though. There was something intimate about the man wanting to tease him and get under his skin. It didn't feel crass or demeaning, like Adam's and Nick's teasing often did. Zander seemed to be ribbing him for the expressed purpose of pulling his guard down, and who knew what the intriguing man would do once that guard was down?

"I am a dancer," Zander went on with a nod, turning to stare out at the sea once more. His expression and tone signaled that he was finally willing to shift the conversation to himself. "At least, I was until about five months ago." He sent Xavier a tense, sidelong look.

It took Xavier a moment to put the pieces together, and when he did, his heart sank. "Oh my God, I'm so sorry."

Zander shook his head. "I've always wanted to be a dancer. Ever since I was a boy and saw a troupe of dancers at Coney Island one summer. They were captivating, and I knew right then and there I wanted to be one too."

Xavier was tempted to reassure Zander that he was utterly captivating in every way, but instead, he asked, "You're from New York, then?"

Zander nodded. "Born a mere month after my parents arrived there from Russia. My father was involved in an assassination attempt on Czar Alexander II, and when it failed, he packed everything he could that night, including his pregnant wife and two children, and fled for America." He laughed and shook his head. "It's still a source of frustration to my father that someone actually succeeded in assassinating the bastard fifteen years after his friends' attempt."

"So you're from a family of revolutionaries, are you?" Xavier found the whole thing fascinating.

But Zander huffed an ironic laugh and shook his head. "Not anymore. Now I'm from a family of bitter, frustrated laborers who believe that soul-crushing, unskilled work is the only way to atone for attempting to rise above one's station, and who believe that anything beautiful or artistic should be treated with suspicion."

Xavier's brow shot up. "That must be...uncomfortable."

Zander sent him an ironic grin. "It was, but at least we all cared for each other. In our own ways. It's also the reason I begged, borrowed, and stole—well, not stole, I'm no thief—in order to secure a position with a ballet company abroad. And let me tell you, that took some doing."

"What did you have to do?" Xavier asked, astounded that anyone would work so hard and go to such lengths—in a foreign country, even—to achieve their dream.

"Don't go making impertinent assumptions about what I might or might not have been willing to do to convince Liev Markova to take me on," Zander said with mock indignation, pointing a finger at Xavier.

Xavier gasped as he realized what his words could have meant, then stammered and blubbered until he managed to squeeze out, "That isn't what I meant at all." His face had heated with embarrassment so much that he was certain he could stand in as one of the lighthouses they passed as the *Umbria* was tugged farther out into the sea.

Zander smiled and laughed at him, "God, but you're fun to tease."

Xavier had absolutely nothing to say to that, and could only stand there and blush for an entirely different reason.

"Markova's sister was a friend of my mother's in Russia," Zander went on to explain. "Mama wrote a letter to her friend, her friend wrote to Markova, and Markova sent an invitation to me to train with him, and the whole thing only took about ten months."

"*Only* ten months," Xavier laughed.

"That felt like an eternity to a sixteen-year-old boy."

Xavier's brow went up. "You were only sixteen when you left your family to train with a ballet company in London?"

Zander nodded. "I was all wide eyes and awkwardness, desperate to get away from the dreariness of the Lower East Side tenements and my father's temper. I'm amazed that he let me go at all, but for all his faults, Papa cares for me. Or else he thought I'd make enough money on the stage to send home an improve his life."

Xavier snapped his mouth shut, suddenly anxious about what sort of life Zander might have lived. Worse than that, it set him to wondering what sort of a life Zander had been pushed out of and why. "You lost your position with the ballet company because of me," he said, his voice hoarse and his heart beating so hard he thought he might be sick.

"No," Zander laughed, though there was more than a

little wistfulness in his voice. "I lost my position in the ballet company because I made one piss-poor decision out of a desperate need to pay my rent after having every cent I had stolen by a faithless flatmate."

Xavier gaped at him. That could very well have been the worst luck he'd ever heard of. "But it's still my fault," he insisted, his gut churning with guilt—although that could also have had something to do with the way the ship pitched slightly as it slipped away from the tugboats and began to make its way into deeper waters on its own. Xavier glanced around as more passengers headed onto the deck where he and Zander stood so that they could get a better look at the view and lowered his voice, "If I hadn't gone off with you that night...." There were too many people nearby who might overhear for him to go on.

Zander slipped closer to him, leaning his elbows on the top of the railing again and nodding for Xavier to do the same so they could continue talking in relative privacy. When Xavier hunched down, his arm touching Zander's, Zander said, "As I recall, you did not get to the point of *going off* with me that night, though I could tell you were close." He winked.

Xavier nearly choked. "That's not the point at all," he whispered, caught between giddy arousal and throbbing guilt. "The point is, you were arrested because of me, weren't you?"

Zander lost his impish grin and sighed. "I was arrested because I was stupid enough to think a quick fumble in a public park—one that I fully intended to block out of my mind for the rest of my life once it was over—was an easy way to pay my rent."

"But still," Xavier whispered, wanting to sink in on himself with embarrassment.

"In fact," Zander went on, his smile returning, "I owe you a huge debt of gratitude."

Xavier flinched. "Me?"

"Yes, you." Zander leaned closer. "I haven't been able to shake this uneasy feeling that if I'd singled out someone other than you, and if I'd been able to go through with it, I might have considered it easy money. In which case, I might have done it again. And again and again. And if I hadn't been caught that first time and managed to convince the judge that I only had my cock out because I'd been taking a piss—and as a stupid American, of course I had no idea what went on in St. James's Park at night—I would have spent more than a few months in jail."

Xavier was stunned by the entire story. "So you weren't brought up on charges of Gross Indecency?"

"Those were the charges I was brought up on," Zander laughed humorously, "but I was only charged with being a public nuisance, and only then because I think Markova intervened somehow."

"Hold on." Xavier straightened. "Mr. Markova intervened with the courts for you, but then he fired you?"

"He wasn't concerned about me, only about the reputation of his company," Zander said, straightening as well.

"He didn't want the scandal to hit the papers—and you know they would have brought the name of the ballet company into the story, because everyone knows the West End theaters are full of perverts and inverts." He rolled his eyes and shifted to lean his hip against the railing again. "So I was let off with time served, charged a fine I had to sell everything of value I had left to pay, evicted from my flat, fired from my job, and forced to telegraph my father for help. His version of help was an order to come home to New York at once and passage on this ship to get there." He sighed. "At least he didn't disown me."

Xavier was so stunned by the story that he couldn't think of a thing to say once Zander was done telling it. "So that's it, then?" he asked. "You're on your way home to New York at your father's insistence."

"That is the final chapter of Alexander Plushenko's Grand Adventure in England, yes," Zander said. "Returning to the bosom of his family with his tail between his legs." He crossed his arms and glanced out over the sea, shaking his head.

"What about the ballet?" Xavier asked. "What about your dreams?"

"New York has ballet companies too, you do realize," he said with a teasing smile that didn't quite reach his eyes. "I'll apply for a position with one of them." As soon as he spoke the words, he looked away, unable to contain the wistfulness in his eyes as they took on the same sort of stormy feeling of the sea.

It was clear to Xavier that Zander didn't believe he would be able to find a position dancing again. The invisible weight on the man's shoulders was that of a dream that had died and the specter of a life that he'd be forced to live, knowing he'd once had everything, then lost it.

"I'm sorry," Xavier said, yet again. He wanted to rest a reassuring hand on Zander's arm—or even be so bold as to hug him—but he didn't dare to. Not with so many fellow passengers wandering around them now, and not when he knew, in spite of what Zander had said, that a good portion of the blame for everything that had happened to Zander was his fault.

The two of them stood there in silence for several more minutes, watching England grow farther and farther behind them. What had started out as a sense of excitement for the unprecedented journey in front of him turned to anxiety over what might happen to Zander once they reached New York. Xavier tried to tell himself he barely knew the man and that a few, fumbling moments of intimacy in the dark didn't amount to a lasting connection, but it was pointless. He did feel connected to Zander in a very real way, and he cared about what might happen to the man.

As if he could somehow sense Xavier's anxiety, Zander stood with sudden tension, glancing down the deck. "Don't look now, but we're being watched," he said in a low voice.

Of course, Xavier looked. He straightened and followed Zander's line of sight, spotting Det. Gleason watching them from the edge of the deck near the front of the ship. "Oh, that's just Det. Gleason," he said, letting out a breath of relief.

"*Just* a detective?" Zander asked incredulously. "It generally isn't a good thing when a detective is watching our sort."

"You don't have to worry about him," Xavier reassured him. "For several reasons. He's come along on the voyage to help locate and recover Lord Selby's son once we reach New York," he explained. "And he came along at Mr. John Dandie's very special insistence." He hoped stating it that way would be enough for Zander to guess which way the wind was blowing, just as he hoped John would forgive him for hinting at some of his personal business. Particularly since John continually denied there was any personal business involved with Det. Gleason at all—which was absolute rubbish, and everyone knew it.

"I see," Zander said with a slow nod, his grin returning. "Interesting."

"Det. Gleason is one of the most interesting men I've ever encountered," Xavier went on. "He's traveled the world, apparently. He was in the navy for a time, stationed in Japan. And he stayed there for a time once his commission ran out."

"That is interesting." Zander grinned at Gleason.

Xavier waved to let Gleason know they'd seen him, and Gleason nodded back before moving on, likely to stare unnervingly at other people. "I envy the man his travels," he said. "I should like to see the whole world someday. I've never been anywhere outside of England. I've hardly been anywhere *inside* of England."

Zander's face suddenly lit up. "Would you like to see the world?"

A thrill of excitement zipped through Xavier. "I most certainly would."

Zander grabbed his hand. "Then come with me," he said, tugging Xavier away from the railing.

CHAPTER 5

Xavier was a hundred times better than Zander remembered him to be. It was like having a taste of chocolate, then being denied for months, dreaming about it, recalling the memory of that nibble, wanting more, and then discovering that not only was chocolate every bit as good as the memory, it was even better, with sticky toffee bits and everything. And Zander couldn't wait to get to the sticky toffee bits of Xavier.

They dodged the *Umbria*'s passengers as everyone spread out around the ship. The ship had moved far enough out to sea that there weren't as many interesting things to wave to on the shore, so first and second-class passengers alike were looking for other ways to entertain themselves until supper was served in a few hours.

"Are you certain we should be—" Xavier started when Zander dragged him through the doorway to second class, veering around a pair of chatty women still wrapped in their traveling coats and down the tightly-curving stairway to the deck below.

"Certain we should be what?" Zander asked as they waited on the landing for an elderly couple chattering in Italian to meander all the way down to the next floor. He, at least, was certain they should be better friends, certain they should spend as much of their journey together as possible, and certain they should pick up where they'd left things in St. James's Park. He wasn't so proud or so stodgy as to think a little bit of fun during the transition between dreams and nightmares would be a bad thing.

"Certain we should be here," Xavier finished after a slight hesitation.

Zander blinked at him. "What's that supposed to mean?"

The Italian couple made it to the deck, and as soon as he could do so politely, Zander grabbed Xavier's hand and dashed past him, heading toward the second-class dining room.

"Are we allowed to just wander around in second class like this?" Xavier asked.

Zander stopped just outside of the dining room door, his brow shooting up at Xavier's question. "Where else would be wander?"

Some sort of realization dawned in Xavier's eyes. "Oh, God. I should have realized. You're traveling second class."

Zander blinked. "Aren't you too, mister valet to a duke?"

Xavier blushed the most delicious rose-wine color. The man was an entire palate of reds and pinks, and Zander found it to be the easiest thing in the world to get him to blush. "I'm in first class," Xavier admitted. "That's the 'to a duke' part of 'valet to a duke'. Lord Selby arranged for me to have the cabin across the hall from his." He looked a bit sketchy for a moment, darting an anxious look around, then said, "So that I can be ready to attend to him quickly when he needs me."

Zander doubted that. If he had to guess, based on the rumors, he'd be willing to bet the room Xavier had been given was formally assigned to Niall Cristofori. That was a minor detail compared to the fact that Xavier would be making the Atlantic crossing in style.

"Well then, I'll just have to rechristen you Mr. Fancy, then," he said with a grin. He tugged on Xavier's sleeve again and drew him back toward the door to the dining-room. "I said I'd show you the world, though, and here it is."

They stepped into the dining-room and were immediately met with a cacophony of sounds of all kinds. As massive as the *Umbria* was, there wasn't a great deal of room for second-class passengers to spread out and move around. Xavier and his toffs probably had all the room they needed and then some toward the front of the ship. And while the second-class accommodations of the *Umbria* had been advertised as some of the most luxurious available on any passenger ship—and they were nice—it was hardly enough to contain the explosion of color and sound, sights and scents from those for whom reaching England was the halfway point of their journey instead of the starting point.

"I've never seen anything like this," Xavier said, walking by Zander's side as they made their way around the spacious room.

"Which part?" Zander asked as they passed an Irish mother with bright red hair trying to keep six little red-headed girls occupied with paper dolls. Next to their table were four men shouting animatedly at each other over a game of cards in a language that was close to Zander's parents' Russian, but not close enough that he understood a word of it. "Is it the ship's facilities or the people making use of them?" he asked with a grin, already knowing what Xavier's answer would be.

"It's like Piccadilly Circus on a Friday night, only captured in a bottle," Xavier said, swiping his hat off his head.

Zander took his hat off as well. He'd forgotten he was even wearing it in his excitement to show Xavier all of the magnificent people he'd already met after boarding the ship. He and several of the other second-class passengers had been aboard since that morning, carefully tucked out of the way so that they wouldn't be a nuisance for first-class passengers, like Xavier and his duke. The extra time had allowed Zander to nominally befriend some of the others already. As soon as he spotted one new acquaintance in particular, he changed direction, weaving through the tables, to draw Xavier along to the far corner of the room.

"Satish-ji," he called out to an older, brown-skinned man in a loose-fitting suit that looked like pajamas, wearing a turban. Satish sat on top of the table in the farthest corner, his legs crossed, eyes closed, smiling placidly to himself. "Satish-ji, meet my friend, Xavier."

"We can't just disturb him like this," Xavier whispered to Zander, trying to hold him back. "He's in a trance or something."

"Meditation is not a trance," Satish said in perfect, beautifully accented English, opening his eyes. He still managed to look as tranquil as a river on a sunny day, in spite of the increasing noise of the dining room as more and more people entered looking for something to do. "It is a practice meant to settle the mind in times of transition."

"That is certainly what this voyage is," Zander said with a laugh that came out a bit more bitter than he intended it to.

Satish glanced sideways at him, the same way he had when they'd first spoken as Zander helped the older man carry his traveling bags aboard that morning. Zander had the feeling Satish could sense every one of his troubles and set-backs, even though they hadn't spoken a word about them.

"Satish, I was wondering if you would be willing to show my friend Xavier some of the interesting exercises you taught me this morning," Zander went on. "They really are amazing," he added for Xavier. "I thought they were just simple stretches, but they left me feeling as though I'd danced for hours."

Satish glanced from Zander to Xavier and back with a knowing smile. "In other words," he said, "your friend wishes to show off the strange and exotic yogi that fate crossed his path with in order to impress you."

"Oh, I'm certain that's not what it is at all," Xavier said, once again, blushing up a storm. Zander could hardly contain himself at the sight of Xavier's adorable modesty. "Zander promised to show me the world, and I think this is what he meant is all."

Satish hummed, sending them a mysterious grin, then slowly shifted out of his crossed-leg stance. His body flowed like water as he moved into a kneeling pose on the table, then folded forward into a new pose that gradually transitioned into him standing on the tabletop. Zander sent an expectant look to Xavier, eager to see what he thought, as several people at the surrounding tables stopped what they were doing to watch Satish move through his exercises.

Xavier watched, clearly impressed, as Satish lifted with perfect balance onto one foot, shifting through a series of movements that were as graceful and athletic as any dance Zander had ever performed. When he'd joined Satish that morning, learning the movements, he'd seen at once how useful they might be for a dancer. So much that he wondered why more ballet companies didn't seek out the services of yogis.

Of course, as soon as Satish finished his exercises, and once the smattering of applause he received caused him to frown, Zander got his answer.

"I shouldn't have done that," Satish said, stepping down from the table to stand with Zander and Xavier. "You westerners have no understanding whatsoever of true spiritual practice and oneness with the divine."

"But you have to admit, your yoga—as Satish calls it," Zander added for Xavier before turning back to Satish, "is fabulous exercise."

Satish sighed impatiently. "As I tried to explain to you this morning, yoga is not a series of pretty stretches to strengthen your body. It is a way to join mind, body, and soul and to turn inward, to ignore the distractions of the world, to reach a point of inner peace." He glanced to Xavier. "It is more than that by far, but those are the simplest terms I can find to explain it to this impatient rapscallion."

"Oh?" Xavier asked, clearly impressed by Satish.

"Why did you show me the movements if you didn't think I would understand, then?" Zander asked, teasing Satish the way Satish had been teasing him from the start. He could tell that as put out as Satish appeared now, he was merely trying to have a go at him.

"Because your mind needs training far more than your body does, young man," Satish scolded him. "You are too anxious and in too much of a hurry for a man your age."

"But aren't all young men in a hurry?" Zander argued. "I thought that's what made us young."

Satish laughed and thumped Zander's arm. "You have me there. I was in a hurry at your age too."

Zander grinned at Xavier, eager to hear what Xavier thought of the whole thing. Xavier mostly looked stunned and overawed by Satish, and everything else around them.

That look of discovery from Xavier deepened when a large, buxom woman who was dressed in clothes that were just a little too colorful and a hair too revealing called out from two tables away, "You! *Cosa bastante joven*! Come over here."

Zander and Xavier exchanged a look, as though they didn't know which of them the woman was talking to, then nodded their goodbyes to Satish to head over to her table.

Zander opened his mouth to greet the woman, but before he could, she nodded to the chairs across the table from her and said, "*Siéntense*! Sit."

As soon as they did, exchanging an amused look in the process, the woman began shuffling through a deck of cards she'd been playing with. Zander looked a little more closely and noted that they were tarot cards, not regular playing cards. "Are you a fortune-teller?" he asked, sitting straighter and sending Xavier an excited look.

"I am Doña Ana," she said. "And I am more than you could possibly imagine."

Zander suddenly placed her accent as Spanish. He

grinned at Xavier, tickled that he'd been able to take his new friend from England to India to Spain in a matter of minutes.

"I'm not entirely certain I'd like to have my fortune told," Xavier said, trying to be polite, but fumbling a bit, as though he were out of his depth.

"Nonsense," Doña Ana said. "Every young man wishes to know what the cards have in store for him."

"I don't know if—"

"Ah!" Doña Ana cut him off, pulling a card out of her deck and holding it up for a moment before slapping it on the table.

Zander didn't know the first thing about tarot or fortune-telling, only that the women who dressed up in shawls and tinkling jewelry on Coney Island during the summer made a fortune off of gullible tourists. Most of them were just girls from the tenements who knew how to put on a show and not Romani at all. The card that Doña Ana uncovered when she moved her hand meant nothing to him. It was a young man who seemed to be juggling several coins.

Doña Ana glanced up at Xavier with a smile all the same. "You are a man of means, I see," she said, eyeing him flirtatiously. "A fine man from a good family with a bright future ahead of him."

"I, er—"

Xavier was cut off a second time as Doña Ana drew another card, held it up just as dramatically as the first one, then slapped it on the table beside the first. Xavier jumped in his seat, his eyes going wide. Zander had to cover his mouth with one hand to keep from laughing.

Doña Ana moved her hand to reveal some sort of card with a sad-looking maiden in a flowing gown. "Ah, you have a young lady, I see," she said.

It was all Zander could do not to dissolve into laughter then and there.

"She is very beautiful, very fine, but your parents, they do not approve of her," Doña Ana said in a breathless, sympathetic voice. "But she is the love of your life."

"I, well, that is—"

A third time, Doña Ana cut Xavier off with a dramatic flourish, taking a third card from her deck. Her eyes blazed with intensity and she smiled triumphantly as she slapped the third card on the table beside the others, then uncovered it.

"Ah," she sighed with sudden melancholy. "You will be parted from your love. She will be as unreachable as if a sea separated you. *Mi querido*, I am sorry, but a curse has been placed on you."

"A curse?" Xavier swallowed. "How could I have been so foolish?"

Zander snorted with laughter, then attempted to hide it by faking a cough.

"You are in luck," Doña Ana went on, her eyes shining. "It just so happens that I am adept at breaking curses. All I would need from you is two American dollars, and you and your fine lady will live many happy years together." She held out her hand, palm up.

"Don't listen to her," another lady with a Spanish accent—one dressed in an equally questionable style to Doña Ana said, striding up to the table. "She's a swindler, on her way to cheat as many Americans out of their dollars as she can."

"How dare you?" Doña Ana sprung up from the table and rounded on the second woman. "You are nothing but a cheap whore."

"And you aren't?" The other woman planted her hands on her hips as she snapped back. "Nine years you worked at Rosa's place across the square from me. Don't pretend I don't know who you are."

Doña Ana looked mortally offended and rattled off something in quick, sharp Spanish that Zander couldn't even begin to understand. The other woman gasped at whatever was said and replied in Spanish as well. The two of them descended into an argument that rose in volume and intensity—not to mention rude gestures—as more of the passengers around them turned to watch.

Zander could hardly contain his laughter. He nudged Xavier to stand. Xavier seemed more than eager to do just that. As a few other passengers attempted to intervene, they backed away from the argument, heading across the dining room toward the doors.

"Maybe that's enough of a tour around the world for now," Zander laughed. "I think the one woman was right about Doña Ana trying to cheat people out of their money anyhow."

"You do?" Xavier asked, picking up his pace as they

reached the dining room door and moving on to a quieter section of the ship.

Zander had an idea, and started toward the part of the ship that would take them to the engine room. "She was dressed perfectly reasonably when I saw her board the ship this morning," he went on. "Honestly, I thought she was a governess of some sort, she looked so laced up. I think women like Doña Ana are as clever as paint. She knows exactly what she's doing, we just weren't going to fall for it."

"We weren't?" Xavier asked, a hint of teasing in his grin.

"Well, I wasn't," Zander replied. "I'm not so sure how your fine lady would take the news of your impending separation, though."

That had Xavier laughing out loud, which was a sight to see, as far as Zander was concerned. He had mischievous plans to show Xavier another sight worth seeing, though, and he was reasonably certain he couldn't keep the roguish look off his face as they reached the door to the section of the ship nearest the engine room. He paused to glance around, making certain no one was near enough to catch them, then slipped through.

The world of that part of the ship was entirely different from either first or second class. There was something rougher, noisier, and more energetic about it than either of the passenger areas.

"Are you certain we should be here?" Xavier asked as Zander drew him down toward the boiler room. "Impersonating members of the ship's crew for Mrs. Pennypacker is one thing. If we're caught down here, I feel like we're as likely as not to be tossed overboard."

"They wouldn't dare," Zander said as they neared the heat and noise of the engines. "You're far too fine and important for that."

Xavier laughed and rolled his eyes a bit, but that stopped when they reached the entrance to the boiler room. The door already stood open so that heat could pour out, but that wasn't why Zander had brought Xavier down there. As soon as Xavier saw the reason, his eyes went wide and he uttered a giddy, "Good Lord."

It wasn't the boiler itself or the piles of coal that were being shoveled into it that had snagged Zander's attention earlier when he'd stumbled across the room on his first perusal of the ship, it was the large, sweaty, muscular forms of the crewmen who worked shoveling the coal into the boiler. They were even more of a sight to look at now that the ship was underway and operating under steam power. Now the burly men were all stripped to the waist and straining to feed the ship the fuel it needed to make a show as it traveled out to the Atlantic.

Zander bit his lip and raised his eyebrows to Xavier, indicating that he'd found the most interesting sight on the entire ship.

"We can't stand here watching them," Xavier whispered—or rather, tried to whisper but had to nearly shout to be heard over the sound of the engine.

"Why not?" Zander asked, crossing his arms and

leaning against the door frame. "Every great work of art deserves to be studied with appreciation. And I'd say there are several in there."

Xavier's mouth twitched as though he were trying desperately not to laugh. Zander was suddenly struck by the memory of how that mouth had tasted and how eager it had been before. He almost didn't hear when Xavier said, "We can't just stand here ogling—"

"Oy! You two! No passengers allowed in the boiler room!" one of the crewmen shouted.

Zander jerked straight and burst into a laugh. He saluted the glaring crewman before grabbing Zander's hand and dashing away before anyone came after them.

He pulled Xavier along, looking for a quiet corner more than a way back up to the deck. Fortunately, that part of the ship was filled with corridors that led to what must have been storage rooms and other places no one had any reason to be just then. He found just the sort of shady, out of the way spot he was looking for and dragged Xavier into it.

"Impersonating a porter in order to assist an old woman," Xavier began to laugh, "making friends with an Indian gentleman, spying on the boiler room. I'm beginning to think you're half mad, Zander. Either that or—"

Zander didn't give him a chance to finish. He pushed Xavier against the wall, grabbing Xavier's hands and planting them against the wall under his, then leaned in to kiss him. Every bit of passion and anticipation he'd stored up for months came pouring out of him as he threw everything he had into the kiss. He was too eager at first, potentially bruising Xavier's lips as their mouths crushed together. Xavier's sound of surprise quickly turned into a moan of longing as Zander thrust his tongue against Xavier's.

He eased up, exploring rather than taking, tasting and remembering and memorizing every sensual detail he could about this man that he hardly knew, but couldn't live without. Every minute they'd spent together was like a lifetime, and every hour they'd been apart since before was like a century. He angled his hips against Xavier's without shame, wanting him to know just how hard and ready he was already. His breath caught and his cock jumped in response when he felt how eager Xavier was for him as well.

"Let's go somewhere," he panted between kisses to Xavier's lips, jaw, and neck. "I don't care where. Let's go and finish what we started. I haven't been able to think of anything else for months."

Xavier groaned, head tilted back as Zander pressed his lips to the pulse in Xavier's neck. The tension coursing through Xavier was intoxicating, and Zander felt like he'd lose his mind if he didn't have all of him soon. He kissed his way back to Xavier's lips and slid his hands down to his sides as their tongues danced, but when he reached for the fastenings of Xavier's trousers, Xavier tensed a little too much.

"We can't," he panted, struggling just enough to get Zander to stop. "God, I want to," he added in a voice so thick with arousal that it sent Zander dangerously close to the edge, "but we can't. Not here. And I...I have to attend to Lord Selby, in case he needs help dressing for supper."

Zander could feel Xavier's arousal shifting quickly to anxiety, and perhaps even terror, with every new second that ticked past. He shouldn't have stopped kissing him. He'd made the inexcusable error of giving Xavier time to think.

"I should be going," Xavier went on, stammering a bit and pushing away from the wall and Zander. He tugged fitfully at the front of his jacket, then touched a hand to his head. "Blast. I've left my hat in that dining room."

"Come get it with me," Zander said, his voice hoarse and full of regret for how things were unfolding. "I left mine there too."

"No, I can't," Xavier said, backing away farther. "I need...I have to go," he said, then turned abruptly and raced away.

For a moment, as Zander watched him dash off, it looked as though Xavier would trip over his own feet in his haste to get away. Once he turned the corner, Zander leaned against the wall and hissed a curse. He'd gotten carried away, been far too eager. Randy was more like it. His delight at discovering Xavier was everything he'd imagined him to be during the last five, painful months had made him sloppy. He should have known his gent would need to be wooed a little before they could tumble into a happy little pile of wickedness.

Zander scrubbed a hand over his face and pushed away from the wall. He took a few deep breaths to steady himself before heading out to the deck. They had time. Depending on the weather and the speed they were able to achieve, they might have as much as a week to get to know each other better. And once Xavier let his guard down, who knew what might happen?

CHAPTER 6

It didn't matter how many times Xavier had attempted to tell himself he'd done nothing wrong by exercising discretion and separating himself from Zander so that neither of them would be caught in a compromising position, the guilt of running out on what had actually been a lovely and exciting situation wouldn't leave Xavier alone. Guilt had turned his food to ash in his mouth as he'd dined with Blake and Niall, John and Gleason—in the first-class dining room, no less, as though he were entitled to it—and it made for a restless night as he tossed and turned in the magnificent bed of his luxury cabin.

By morning, he was far less at ease than a country boy traveling in style across the Atlantic should have been. His head throbbed, and his knees felt wobbly in a way that had nothing to do with the deep ocean that the *Umbria* had reached.

"Are you certain you don't need to find some sort of cure for seasickness?" Blake asked in the morning, as Xavier helped him to dress.

Not that Blake needed much help dressing. He insisted on doing most of the job himself, and on top of that Niall was there to do up buttons and straighten ties in a way that made Xavier think he'd rather be undoing them. In fact, Xavier had felt like he'd walked in on far too intimate a moment that morning, before Blake and Niall had even gotten out of bed—they shouldn't have told him to come in when he knocked—and that his services weren't actually required during the liminal state of the ocean crossing.

Of course, the reminder of two men in love who enjoyed each other's company only served to highlight the stirring feelings Xavier had for Zander, even though there was a world of difference between two men who had known and loved each other for ten years and two who had shared ten minutes of intense intimacy in a public park.

"Xavier?" Blake's question jerked Xavier out of his thoughts.

He flinched and turned toward Blake from the wardrobe, where he'd been mindlessly fiddling about with the suits Blake wasn't planning to wear anytime soon. "Sorry," he said, squeezing his eyes shut for a moment as he cursed himself. "I am not seasick, my lord. But thank you for your concern."

"He's not seasick," Niall repeated with a sly grin,

straightening the lay of Blake's smart suit jacket. He kissed Blake's lips lightly, then said, "He's an entirely different kind of sick."

"Oh?" Blake caught Niall's mischievous look, raised his eyebrows, then turned a teasing look of his own to Xavier. "What sort of sick is he, then?"

"I am quite well, my lord," Xavier said with a formal nod, clasping his hands behind his back and praying that the two would let the matter drop.

Niall stepped away from Blake to fetch his pocket watch from the bureau. "Our Xavier seems to have made a friend," he said, a flash in his eyes.

Xavier let out a breath, his shoulders sagging. If he denied it, Blake and Niall would only pry the truth out of him. They were going to tease him no matter what he did, so rather than drawing the process out, he sighed and said, "His name is Alexander Plushenko, and he is, or was, a dancer with a ballet company in London. We are… acquaintances, and I was surprised to meet him again here."

"Acquaintances," Niall repeated for Blake, mischief in his eyes.

"Is that the current word for it among young people these days?" Blake winked back at Niall.

Xavier pressed his lips shut and tried to look as though he didn't approve of the teasing. The problem was, whatever Blake and Niall were imagining, it probably wasn't that far off the mark. Xavier could only pray that they wouldn't force him to admit to it.

"Very well, then," Blake said with a chuckle, striding forward to clap a hand on Xavier's shoulder. "I'm glad you've made a friend. You should enjoy yourself on this voyage. Even though its purpose is a solemn one and the challenges that await us in New York are great, you're young, and you have the right to an experience you'll never forget as we make the crossing."

"And do go out there and make it one you'll never forget," Niall added with a cheeky wink. "That's what youth is for, after all."

"Yes, sir," Xavier said with a stiff nod. He couldn't imagine what else would have been a proper response to his employer's lover telling him, more or less, to go out and canoodle with a man he barely knew but yearned for, on a ship where every nook and cranny carried with it the possibility of being caught.

"Now," Niall went on, clapping his hands together. "Let's go out there and see if John and Gleason have killed or fucked each other yet."

Blake laughed as they headed for the cabin door. "My money is still on them killing each other first and fucking once they're both dead."

"I'll just finish tidying up here," Xavier called after them, face hot over their teasing and how easily the two of them could joke about the love lives of their friends.

"Carry on," Blake said with a smile and a nod as his parting salvo.

There really wasn't much to do in Blake and Niall's cabin. At home in Darlington Gardens, or before, at

Selby Manor, Xavier would have spent all day seeing to Blake's things, making certain everything he wore was in top condition, and repairing anything that needed sprucing up. On the ship, all he had to do was make sure everything was put away neatly and the cabin was in order. Once that was done, he wandered into the narrow hallways of the deck, then hesitated once he reached the lobby-like area separating the cabins from the public rooms.

If he was any sort of a friend at all, any sort of a man, he would go off and find Zander at once to apologize for his behavior the day before. Heaven only knew what Zander thought of him for dashing off the way he did. It was the second time he'd run off to leave the man to his fate. Zander must have thought he was a coward and a bounder.

But when Xavier marched out to the promenade and made his way from the first-class section of the ship to second class, he kept walking right past the door that would have taken him into the second-class public areas, where he would have expected to find Zander. He kept moving, making a full circuit around the back of the ship, heart racing as though it were more than a casual stroll.

What did he expect to have happen where Zander was concerned? He liked the man, genuinely and aside from kisses and the promise of more. Zander was full of life and had a wicked sense of humor. He seemed like the kind of man who wouldn't let a few setbacks stop him from living out his dreams. And then there were those kisses. Xavier didn't have all that much experience with love and pleasure, but he wasn't a complete rube. He could say beyond a shadow of a doubt that Zander was the most sensual and tempting man he'd ever known, and he wanted to know more.

So what was he waiting for? He scolded himself as he turned the corner at the end of the ship and started back up the other side. As Blake and Niall had told him, the voyage should be his chance to break a few rules and enjoy a few experiences. Why was he even thinking of hesitating?

With his mind made up, he marched boldly through the door into the second-class public space and made his way to the dining room. Breakfast was still being served, and if there were any place he'd be able to find Zander that morning, it would be among the crowd of his fellow second-class passengers.

Except that with one quick glance across the room, Xavier could see that Zander wasn't there. He dropped his shoulders in disappointment, but continued to scan the room, hoping he had somehow just missed Zander in his first glance. But as crowded as the room was, Xavier was certain he would have noticed Zander in an instant, even if he were in disguise or hiding under a blanket.

He turned to go, an odd, hollow feeling of disappointment in his chest, but paused as a few details of the room snagged his attention. The second-class dining room wasn't any noisier than the first-class one had been the evening before, but the conversations that echoed through the crowded space were being held in more languages and seemed to be far more animated and amusing. The tables were just as packed with people as first class, but the diners looked as though they were enjoying each other's company more. Everyone in first class had been deeply concerned with manners and propriety, and the ladies had deferred to the gentlemen as often as not. Second class was more of a free-for all. In addition to that, the crew attending the second-class dining room seemed less concerned with catering to the passengers, but more at ease as they moved about, making certain the buffet at one end of the hall was well-stocked.

Xavier left the room, contemplating the small but noticeable differences as he headed up the stairs to the highest deck and stepped out into the sunshine. He knew full well the differences between the upper and lower classes. He'd lived the last several years of his life as an interloper in the aristocracy, moving in their circles, but not really a part of them. He'd grown so accustomed to the odd, in between world he occupied, but seeing it played out in a tangible way as he walked from the second-class part of the ship to the first drove the distinction home. As soon as he reached the first-class deck area, the air seemed to vibrate at a different speed, and even the sea birds that circled above, following the ship, seemed to hold themselves with a more refined air.

"Xavier!"

The shout from an even higher deck near the very front of the ship had Xavier nearly jumping out of his skin and going hot and cold at the same time. He couldn't even begin to contain his smile of relief and joy and expectation as Zander called out to him, waving to him from the high deck.

"Don't shout like some carnival barker," the voice of Mrs. Pennypacker grumbled behind him, though Xavier couldn't see the woman fully until he scrambled up onto the high deck to join Zander.

Mrs. Pennypacker looked like a queen ensconced on a recumbent throne of some sort as she lounged in the morning sun. She wasn't even wearing a hat, like most respectable women would do, but the smile of contentment she wore made up for it.

"Oh, it's you," she said at the sight of Xavier. "You're just in time to fix my tea."

"I—oh," Xavier said, hopping into action as soon as he reached the deck.

Zander sent him a delighted grin as he returned to tucking the blanket covering Mrs. Pennypacker around her. "Do you need another pillow, ma'am?" he asked. "Anything I can get for you other than tea?"

Mrs. Pennypacker hummed, looking as mischievous as she did smug. "I wouldn't mind if you buttered one of those scones for me."

"Very good, ma'am," Zander said, bowing and playing the part of a servant perfectly as he circled around to the tray where Xavier was busy with the tea.

A huge tray laden with breakfast had been brought out and set on a portable table near Mrs. Pennypacker's chair. Xavier was impressed by the variety of breakfast foods it contained. He hadn't been aware that passengers could have their breakfast wherever they wanted. Then again, Mrs. Pennypacker was the sort of woman who got whatever she wanted, whether it was allowed or not.

That thought dropped straight out of Xavier's mind as Zander came to stand across the tray table from him and asked, "Did you sleep well last night?" with a mischievous glint in his eyes.

"No, I did not," Xavier murmured. He glanced around furtively. Mrs. Pennypacker wasn't the only passenger enjoying a little morning sunshine on the upper deck. An older gentleman was reading the previous day's *Times* in a chair several yards to one side, and a pair of young ladies stood at the railing, chatting quietly as they glanced out over the sea. "I slept abominably," Xavier went on in a soft voice. "Those with guilty consciences don't deserve to sleep well."

Zander's brow shot up as he cut a scone in half so that he could butter it. "Guilty conscience?"

Xavier tried not to be appalled at the mess Zander was making of the scone. "I'm sorry for—" He glanced to the gentlemen reading *The Times* and then to the young ladies, cleared his throat, then started over. "I'm sorry for dashing out on you yesterday. It was unforgivably rude."

Zander appeared to have a hard time not laughing at that. "I choose to believe that I overwhelmed you with my charm and magnetism," he said.

Xavier's face heated, and his skin prickled at the idea

of anyone overhearing what they were saying. Not so much because it would land them in trouble—they were being careful, after all—but because he wanted those words to be for him and him alone.

He turned back to Zander with a wicked grin. "Your charm and magnetism are impressive," he said.

Zander laughed. "I'm not the only charming one," he said, spreading a generous amount of butter over the butchered scone in a way that Xavier couldn't help but find erotic. Although, at that moment, Zander could have tripped and fallen down the stairs and he would have found it erotic.

Xavier cleared his throat and finished preparing Mrs. Pennypacker's tea, then stepped away from the table to present it to her. "Your tea, ma'am," he said in his most elegant voice. "I took the liberty of assuming you take it with cream and sugar."

"You are correct, young man," Mrs. Pennypacker said, accepting the tea with a smile. She held the saucer with one hand and crooked a finger to prompt Xavier to lean closer to her. When he did, she patted his cheek with a satisfied chuckle. "You are a handsome young lad. Both of you are," she said, speaking louder as Zander approached the other side of her chair with her scone on a plate. "I do so enjoy being surrounded by handsome young men."

"And I'm certain they enjoy surrounding you," Zander said, his whole face shining with good humor.

"Oh, they do," Mrs. Pennypacker said. "They always

have. You should have seen me in my heyday. That blackguard, Andrew Jackson, was president, Philadelphia was half the size it is now, and every young buck with a mind to line his pockets would practically beg to take me out walking along the river. My father had to beat them away with a stick, they were so eager. But no one other than Samuel Pennypacker would do for me. I knew that boy had smarts as well as looks, and that he would make something of himself one day. My parents were dead against the marriage, of course. They were Philadelphia high society of the day, and my father fought alongside George Washington himself as a young man, but it was Samuel or nothing for me."

Xavier grinned at Zander as they stood on either side of Mrs. Pennypacker's chair, letting her reminisce. Xavier wondered what it would have been like to go out walking along a river with Zander. He wondered if it would be possible to pry Zander away from Mrs. Pennypacker so that he could take a stroll around the ship. He wasn't finished apologizing yet, and he hadn't even begun following Blake's orders to enjoy himself with his new friend. And there was still so much he wanted to know about Zander.

Zander seemed equally as interested in Mrs. Pennypacker's stories, which was to say not much. The way he stared at Xavier with a secret little smile, as if reliving their adventures the day before and wondering when they could repeat them, had Xavier growing hot, in spite of the nip in the air as the ship sliced through the sea.

Zander had seen so much more of the world—and of life—than he had, and Xavier could see it in his eyes. If ever there was a man who could take him on an adventure he wouldn't ever forget, it was Zander.

Mrs. Pennypacker huffed suddenly, dragging Xavier's attention back to her. "Well, if the two of you aren't going to listen to my interesting and educational stories, why don't you do something else to make yourselves useful?"

"Ma'am?" Zander asked, peeling his eyes away from Xavier to smile benignly at her.

Mrs. Pennypacker fished through the folds of her blanket and came out with the key to her cabin. "Go fetch the book I've been meaning to read," she said, waggling the key at Zander with one hand as she held her cup and saucer in the other and balanced her scone on her lap. "It should be right there, on the table beside the bed, where I left it last night."

"You want us to go to your cabin to fetch a book?" Zander asked, staring at the key, then at Mrs. Pennypacker.

"Well, it'd be rather difficult for you to fly back to Dublin to fetch me a pint of good beer, now wouldn't it?" Mrs. Pennypacker snapped.

Xavier had to draw on all his powers of concentration not to snort. "Very well, ma'am," he said instead, then stepped around the back of her chair to join Zander. "We will return shortly."

"Yes, do," Mrs. Pennypacker said. "I'll probably need another cup of tea in a moment."

Xavier glanced to Zander with wide eyes, as though he couldn't believe the sort of errand they were being sent on, or that they'd been sent on an errand to begin with.

"Who would have thought this voyage would turn out to be so diverting?" Zander whispered as they hurried down the steps and strode across the deck.

"I certainly didn't," Xavier confessed. And the voyage had only just begun.

CHAPTER 7

Mrs. Pennypacker's key burned hot in Zander's hand, like a talisman that could lead him and Xavier to a magic portal. Whether that portal would lead to somewhere brilliant or exciting or whether it would take them to another level of trouble had yet to be determined.

"I sincerely hope no one is watching us right now," he murmured to Xavier, still managing to smile and think the whole thing was a lot of fun, as he ducked through the entrance to first class.

"What? Why?" Xavier blinked and followed him through the somewhat crowded entry hall. Xavier nodded to the short man with all-knowing eyes whom he'd pointed out as being a detective the day before. "We're only running an errand."

"Two young men letting themselves into the cabin of

a wealthy old widow traveling on her own?" Zander asked, one eyebrow raised.

Understanding dawned in Xavier's eyes. "I see your point. But if anyone asks, we'll simply tell them the truth, we're here to fetch her book, not to rob her blind." He paused, then said, "For a moment, I thought you were referring to other reasons two young men entering a cabin together might look suspicious."

Zander glanced over his shoulder at him as they turned the corner to head down the small corridor to Mrs. Pennypacker's room. He feigned a shocked gasp. "Mr. Lawrence, you have a wicked mind." He reached the door and fitted the key in the lock, then went on to add, "I like it."

Xavier snorted a laugh that he tried in vain to hide, his cheeks going a delicious shade of pink. The two of them slipped into Mrs. Pennypacker's room as quickly as they could. Zander felt a thrill of danger and mischief as the door clicked shut. He suddenly found himself in exactly the sort of position he'd hoped to be in with Xavier—alone in a place where they wouldn't be seen or disturbed. The possibilities that raced through his mind were endless.

"There's no book on the bedside table," Xavier pointed out as he crossed the room to the old woman's bed.

Zander's mouth twitched into a devilish grin as he walked up behind Xavier—far too close for it to be an accident. "Perhaps she put it in the drawer," he said, resting one hand on Xavier's hip and bending around him to pull open the draw.

The result of their positions had Zander's front flush against Xavier's back and his arms nearly enfolding him in an embrace. It was overt without being obvious, and it got the job done. Xavier sucked in a breath so suddenly that Zander wondered if it made him dizzy, and a small shudder passed through him. That only served to drive Zander even closer to madness and carelessness. His cock was definitely invested in his little charade now, and there was no possible way Xavier didn't feel it pressing against his backside, begging for more.

"No book," Zander observed once the drawer was open. He turned his face to Xavier, which placed his lips tantalizingly close to Xavier's neck. He could practically taste the salt of Xavier's skin, and he could most definitely smell desire rippling from him, but he held off. There was no point in simply biting into an apple when one could savor it for a bit first.

"No book," Xavier repeated in a shaky voice. His body started to sag into Zanders, but suddenly snapped straight again. "Good Lord."

The quick change in mood threw Zander off, although he didn't mind at all when Xavier leaned forward a bit, reaching into the drawer, and causing his ass to rub up against Zander's erection. For a moment, Zander reconsidered the timeline of his seduction, until Xavier straightened again as he took a diamond-studded, gold pocket watch out of the drawer. Then, even

Zander's blossoming arousal stopped abruptly as he gaped at the piece.

"What is *that*?" he asked, taking a step back as Xavier pivoted to show him the gaudy timepiece.

"I think it's supposed to be a watch," Xavier said, dangling the watch between them and trying hard not to snort with laughter again.

"That has to be the ugliest watch I've ever seen," Zander said, cupping his hand under the watch and examining it.

"It might be ugly, but it's probably worth both of us combined," Xavier said.

Zander glanced up at him, horrified by the thought. He took the watch from Xavier entirely and stepped closer to the shuttered porthole—which still let in quite a bit of light—to get a better look. "What would possess someone to have something this ridiculous made?"

Xavier shrugged as he continued to search the room, presumably for Mrs. Pennypacker's book. "Ostentatiousness?" he suggested. "Mrs. Pennypacker certainly seems to be that sort."

"True," Zander said. He opened the watch and found a small inscription, "*For my Millie. I will love you for all time, Samuel.*" He smiled as a burst of sentimentality hit him. It would have been wonderful to have a love that lasted through all time like that.

He closed the watch and glanced across the room to Xavier, who was opening drawers in the bureau. It was silly to think that Xavier was the sort of man he could love for all time—in essence, they'd just met—but it was equally silly to deny that there was a spark between them, and had been from the start, that he'd never felt with another man before. Like finding exactly the right pair of gloves that fit like a second skin, even though he'd just discovered the shop that sold them. When something fit, it fit.

"Do you know what I find odd," Xavier said without looking at Zander as he moved on to look in the wardrobe.

"Probably a great many things," Zander laughed, taking the watch back to the bedside table.

Xavier turned to him and laughed. The man was a work of art when he smiled. It made his beautiful eyes shine. "What I find odd," Xavier went on, "is that Mrs. Pennypacker doesn't have a single photograph with her."

Zander's brow inched up as he shut the drawer. "You know, you're right. Even I have an old photograph of my family with my things, and we never got along particularly."

"You didn't?" Xavier asked, turning to him.

Zander shook his head. "They had different ideas of who I should be than I had."

Xavier nodded, as though that were all the explanation he needed. "I have several photographs of my parents and sibling back home in London," he said, continuing his search. He continued with a sheepish grin over his shoulder for Zander. "I didn't bring them with me on the journey because I thought they might get wet and be ruined. But Lord Selby brought several photographs of his children."

"That's sweet," Zander said, shifting to lean against the bedside table. He knew he should join Xavier in his search, but at the moment, he was enjoying watching the man far too much.

"It's not entirely sweet," Xavier said. "We might need the photograph of Lord Stanley to help find the lad in New York, if Lady Selby continues to be difficult." From what little Zander knew of the situation from gossip, she probably would be. Xavier's tone shifted as he went on to say, "It strikes me that Mrs. Pennypacker must be a very lonely woman if she doesn't even have photographs of her loved ones to keep her company."

Zander thought he had a point. He also thought it was adorable that Xavier had such a compassionate heart. But what he found himself saying before he could think better of it was, "I certainly know what loneliness feels like."

He wanted to wince and take it back the moment Xavier turned to him with a sympathetic look. The last thing he wanted was for the object of his affections to think of him as weak or simpering somehow.

But Xavier said, "I think any man like us knows what loneliness is from time to time."

It was an astute observation, even if it raised all sorts of sentimental sensations in Zander that he wasn't in the mood to feel. Lust, yes. He was most definitely of a mind to feel lust at the moment. Excitement and daring too.

But instead, his fool heart had to go all mushy as Xavier gave up his search and came to lean against the edge of the bureau a few feet away from him.

"I'm glad I was accepted for membership into The Brotherhood," Xavier said. "I wasn't certain I would be at first, even though Lord Selby assured me that membership is not in any way restricted to the upper classes. Their club building is so luxurious, though, just like any other gentleman's club, and some of its members are quite lofty."

Zander blinked and shook his head. "The Brotherhood?"

Xavier seemed surprised that he didn't know what he was talking about. "It's an organization in London—well, all of England, really—that supports men like us. Sort of a mutual aide society, if one chooses to look at it that way."

"For men like us," Zander repeated in disbelief. When Xavier nodded, he went on with, "And you're a member?"

"I am. Since November."

"Ah, November," Zander said with a cheeky grin. "I've decided that I'm rather fond of that month."

Xavier blinked in confusion for a moment, then blushed up a storm when he remembered. "Yes, well, parts of it were lovely."

Zander pushed away from the bedside table and moved swiftly to trap Xavier against the bureau. "Yes, *parts* of it were," he said, slipping a hand down the front of Xavier's jacket to caress his cock through his trousers.

He didn't wait for Xavier to jump or wriggle away, or to find some excuse to bolt. He leaned in and slanted his mouth over Xavier's, kissing him into submission before he could even think of doing anything but kissing him back.

Blessedly, kissing him back was exactly what Xavier did. He let out a low whimper and molded his lips against Zander's for a moment before seeming to make a decision. He grabbed the sides of Zander's face and kissed him harder, teasing his tongue along the seam of Zander's mouth as if begging to be let in. Zander had no interest in denying Xavier anything, parting his lips and slipping his tongue against Xavier's.

It was beautiful and heady, and Zander could feel his control slipping with each second that ticked by. All the same, he leaned back with a teasing grin and asked, "You're not going to run out on me this time, are you?"

"No," Xavier gasped, shaking his head, his heavy-lidded gaze fixed on Zander's mouth.

"Good, because I've been aching for the chance to finish what we started for months now."

Xavier's only reply was a wordless sound of agreement as he surged into Zander, clasping his face again and kissing him with more aggression than Zander would have thought he had in him. Zander laughed deep in his chest as he gripped Xavier's sides and kissed him back, but only because the joy that filled him was too expansive to be kept inside. He returned Xavier's kisses, drawing his tongue into his mouth and sucking on it like he wanted to suck on other things. Xavier made a sound of approval that was far louder than Zander figured the discreet man had wanted to make, but he loved the pure, unfettered need in it.

There was more to be had than kisses, though. Zander worked through the buttons of Xavier's jacket, then waistcoat, then pushed the jacket off Xavier's shoulders. That simple movement seemed to drive the whole situation home to Xavier.

"Wait," he said, leaning back against the bureau and laying his hands flat on Zander's chest as if to stop him. "This is pure madness. We can't do this."

"You don't even know what I have in mind for us to do yet," Zander said with a mischievous flicker of one eyebrow, tugging Xavier's jacket farther down his shoulders.

"I think I have an idea," Xavier said with just a hint of sarcasm.

It was enough to fire Zander's blood and spur him on. "Then let's get on with it," he said, jerking Xavier toward him for another kiss.

He managed to disarm the man long enough to peel his jacket off his arms and to tug his shirt out of his trousers, but he had barely skated his hands across the hot skin of Xavier's stomach before Xavier stopped him again.

"We're in someone else's room," he panted, even more undone than his first protest. "We could be caught at any moment."

"Then I'll be quick," Zander said, leaning in to kiss Xavier's neck as he fumbled with the fastenings of his trousers.

"I'm not certain that's something you should brag about," Xavier laughed. That laughter turned into an overly-loud moan as Zander reached into his trousers to stroke his prick. Xavier jerked his hands back to grab the edge of the bureau, hopefully, Zander thought, because he was so aroused he might fall over.

Everything within Zander wanted to test that theory. He spent a moment thoroughly ravishing Xavier's mouth until the man was desperate and panting, then dropped to his knees. Xavier let out a strangled moan of disbelief and anticipation as Zander lifted his shirt enough to kiss his belly and swipe his tongue around Xavier's navel. He then made his way lower, bit by bit, grinning up at Xavier now and then as he did, all while Xavier's breath came in shorter and shorter pants.

Finally, everything was perfect. No one was lurking in the dark to arrest them or pounding on the door. Xavier was hot and breathless, and the tip of his cock was slick with pre-come. Zander stroked him gently for a moment before holding him steady and moving in not just to lick that slickness away—which caused another gorgeous, unfettered sound from Xavier—but to take his tip in his mouth.

Zander didn't consider himself an expert in the fine art of fellatio, but it was easy to give a lover an amazing experience when one cared so much about him. He started slowly, savoring Xavier's taste and texture and testing how much of him he could swallow as Xavier gasped and panted and gripped the edge of the bureau so hard his knuckles went white. Just knowing how much Xavier was enjoying their moment made Zander eager, and he added his hand to the teasing and pleasing he knew had Xavier near the edge.

Very near the edge, as it turned out. Zander was just starting to feel as though he were hitting his stride when Xavier let out a sudden, desperate expletive and came hard. Zander swallowed reflexively, trying not to either choke or laugh at how disorganized and unromantic the experience actually was. It didn't have to be romantic though, because it was undeniably sensual and arousing.

"Sorry," Xavier gasped, sagging to his elbows against the bureau as Zander let him go and wiped his mouth with the back of his sleeve. "God, that was rubbish. It just felt so—"

Zander rose to his feet, stifling his laugh by closing his mouth over Xavier's. Xavier made a sound of shock at the kiss that turned into another moan. His arms slid around Zander's sides as he took a breath and said, "You were not rubbish." He kissed Xavier again, then said, "You'll last much longer next time."

"Next time," Xavier repeated with stars in his eyes. He surprised Zander by slipping his hands around to the front of Zander's trousers to handle his erection. "I think you're ready for next time now."

Zander laughed deep in his throat and purred, "Honey, that's still this time."

Xavier laughed as well, sending Zander a mischievous grin that looked so good on him as he made quick work of unfastening Zander's trousers. They didn't have time for Xavier to go to his knees, and frankly, Zander was so far gone already that he didn't need it. He was just as vocal in his appreciation as Xavier had been as Xavier drew his cock out and fisted it. There were a thousand ways they could have done it better or been more refined, or even prepared, but Zander didn't need it. He could still taste Xavier on his lips and the warmth and scent of him was everywhere. The sound of their ragged breathing forming a perfect chorus was more than enough to send him soaring.

He came all over Xavier's hand within a minute. It felt so good to share that with Xavier that he wasn't even embarrassed about how quickly it was over or how messy he'd been. He intended to last far longer and be far messier with Xavier at their soonest possible convenience. He didn't even try to hide how much he'd enjoyed Xavier's touch by being quiet either, and once the burst of pleasure began to ebb, he grabbed the sides of Xavier's face and kissed him in thanks as though their lives depended on it.

The moment was sensual and sweet, and Zander was already calculating how long it would be until both of them were ready again and eyeing the bed sideways when the cabin door creaked open. Xavier went from sighing with pleasure to yelping as though he'd been branded with a hot iron. Zander gasped and clenched up as well, particularly when he twisted enough to see Det. Gleason in the doorway. Zander used his body as a shield to protect Xavier, but all Det. Gleason did was frown at the two of them.

"The two of you are making enough noise to wake the dead," the short, sharp man said. "Be a bit more discreet or you'll probably end up being thrown in the brig." He started to back out of the room, but turned to add, "And you're not going back out there looking like that. Clean yourselves up and look sharp."

With that, he stepped back into the corridor, shutting the door behind him with a snap.

Zander stood where he was for another moment, mouth hanging open, body wedged against Xavier's, pinning him to the bureau, hands still clasped on either side of Xavier's face. He and Xavier both were breathing so hard it was a wonder they didn't pass out.

"I think my entire life just passed before my eyes," Xavier said. His gasping turned into breathless laughter, and he rested his forehead on Zander's shoulder.

"He's not going to tell the captain or anything, is he?" Zander worried.

Xavier raised his head, shaking it. "Not unless he wants to find himself in trouble for the same sin." He wriggled under Zander, prompting Zander to back off slightly so he could tuck his prick back into his trousers and straighten himself. "I mentioned that Det. Gleason is one of us, didn't I?"

"You sort of did," Zander said, beginning the process of straightening himself up as well, "but sometimes our kind are the ones who end up turning us in to save themselves."

Xavier hummed and sent him a wary look, as though he had a good point.

They tucked, smoothed, buttoned, and brushed their way back into looking presentable. Gleason was right about them needing to fix their appearance before going out in public in more ways than one, though. They both had red, swollen mouths and disheveled hair, and it took more than a few splashes of water and the use of Mrs. Pennypacker's comb to get them back to looking anything less than debauched.

"Do I look presentable enough for the *Umbria*?" Zander asked at last, turning to face Xavier.

"Do I?" Xavier asked.

"Love, you look like the most beautiful creature to ever walk the earth," Zander said with a wink. When Xavier blushed deeply, Zander laughed and finished with, "If anyone asks, we'll say it's sunburn."

Xavier laughed with him, but as they reached the door to head out, he stopped Zander with a hand to his arm. "Thank you," he said, then came over all bashful. "And if we get a chance, I'd like to do it again."

"Honey," Zander said, leaning closer to him, "we're stuck on this ship for another five days or so with nothing to do but each other. Of course we're going to do it again."

He winked, and they left the cabin to head back to Mrs. Pennypacker on the upper deck. It was all Zander could do not to let everything he and Xavier had just done show on his face. As it was, he had to rack his brain for excuses of why he and Xavier had taken so long. And they never did find the book.

Not that they needed to worry about any of that. Once they returned to the upper deck, there was Mrs. Pennypacker, asleep in her lounge chair, an open book resting on her chest and a mischievous grin on her sleeping mouth, as if she'd planned the whole thing herself.

CHAPTER 8

The transatlantic voyage was supposed to feel like a death march to Zander. He was coming from a place of utter humiliation at the hands of English law and going to a place of uncertainty with a family he hadn't been part of for years, but from the moment he'd spotted Xavier gaping at him from across the *Umbria's* deck in Liverpool, his life had been nothing but happiness.

"No, no, *beta*, you are doing it wrong," Satish scolded him as he moved through a series of Satish's yoga poses off to one side in the second-class dining room the next morning. "Yoga is not just a series of athletic stretches. You need to train your mind and control your breathing as well."

"I thought that's what I was doing?" Zander said, unable to keep the joy and the teasing out of his voice, even though a part of him was exasperated.

How could he be anything but joyful when he and Xavier had spent such a lovely day together the day before? It had started with those few, precious moments of carnal bliss, then had gone on to the two of them roaming the ship together while Mrs. Pennypacker napped, talking about everything and nothing, and then making a splash by attending a concert held in the music room in first class with Mrs. Pennypacker, as her particular guests. All eyes had been on Mrs. Pennypacker and her "two handsome beaux", which, Zander figured, was exactly what the old woman was after.

Zander had hoped to spend the rest of the evening and the night with Xavier, but Xavier's duty toward Lord Selby—who seemed like a decent fellow, though somewhat agitated, in spite of the fact that he had a gorgeous and considerate lover in Niall Cristofori—had taken him away for the night, leaving Zander to toss and turn and conjure up images of everything he wanted to do to Xavier once they actually were able to spend more time alone. If not for the fact that Zander was sharing his second-class cabin with a stuffy, middle-aged clerk returning to New York after a business trip—because, of course, his father wouldn't have splurged for him to have a cabin of his own—he would have taken matters into his own hands in order to fall asleep, as it were.

"No! Gah! You are hopeless," Satish sighed, shaking his head at Zander as he executed a pose that had him standing on one foot, balanced in what felt like a perfect arabesque. "All wrong."

Zander laughed and dropped out of the pose—which, he noticed, had several young ladies and one powdered gentleman idling away their time at nearby tables sighing for a different reason than Satish—and planted his hands on his hips. "I think you're just being overly critical, Satish-ji," he said with a teasing smirk. "Seeing as I am the only one who took you up on your offer to learn this yoga thing you are so devoted to."

He was ribbing Satish on purpose, and his words had exactly the right effect. Satish looked as though Zander had insulted his mother and all of his ancestors. The man scrubbed a hand over his face. "You westerners think you know everything, simply because you invaded my country with your guns and your administration and your British ways. You know nothing about discipline of the mind and the attainment of higher states of consciousness. You are too busy being silly and concerned with the distractions of the flesh."

Zander grinned. Satish spoke the truth in more ways than he realized. Although, if Zander hoped to attain any sort of higher state of consciousness, as Satish called it, he would rather do it with Xavier, in a horizontal position. But what he said was, "You forget, I'm not British. I'm American."

"You are a fool," Satish said, rolling his eyes. Underneath it all, Zander was certain that the old man liked him. Otherwise, he wouldn't have taken the time to teach him anything—or complain about it.

"Now, again," Satish said, assuming a neutral stance and breathing in deeply. "Begin by centering yourself."

Zander started to mirror Satish's movements and breathing, but the distractions of the flesh that Satish had scolded him about came striding into the room at that moment. Xavier looked dashing and perfectly put together, as always, in spite of the fact that his shoulders and hat were damp from the dreary rain that beat down on the *Umbria's* decks and had since the night before. Xavier removed his hat, brushed off his shoulders, and glanced around the noisy, crowded room. The moment he spotted Zander, he broke into a smile that Zander felt all the way down to his core. Zander smiled back like the fool Satish had told him he was and waved as Xavier started toward him, dodging a group of restless children and Doña Ana as she tried to grab his sleeve for whatever mischief she and her friends were up to that day.

Satish made a sound of exasperation and threw up his hands. "Our lesson for today is over, I see."

"It doesn't have to be," Zander said, taking a half step toward Xavier as he came nearer. "You could make Xavier here your pupil as well."

"Me?" Xavier balked once he was near enough to reply. "Learn how to bend and pose like a dancer? I think not."

"And why not?" Zander asked, turning to him with a mischievous grin that was likely too flirtatious for a room crowded with people. "Are you too dignified for a little physical activity?" He arched one eyebrow salaciously.

Xavier turned pink, just as Zander hoped he would. "More like I am too awkward and clumsy for such an elegant and graceful discipline," he said, nodding respectfully to Satish.

Satish glanced between Xavier and Zander with a flat look, as though he weren't fooled at all. Zander didn't know what was considered normal or abominable in Satish's country, but whatever it was, the old man seemed inclined to accept what was right in front of his face without comment.

"Give yourself credit," Zander said, unable to keep his grin in check as he tugged on Xavier's sleeve to move them along toward some free seats at one of the nearby tables. "I'm certain I could have you bent into any number of exotic shapes in no time at all, and you'd be perfectly graceful in the process."

Xavier made a strangled sound of disapproval and peeked around furtively, though at the same time, he was no more capable of hiding his grin than Zander was. "In case you hadn't noticed," he whispered as he took a seat at the table while Zander perched on the edge of the table beside him, "we're not exactly alone in the room."

Zander chuckled and glanced around himself. "I think you'll find that the only place more private than an empty room in the middle of nowhere is a crowded room where everyone is busy talking to everybody else, and where a passel of wild children is running around vexing everyone they can."

No sooner had he said that than the pack of children

in question ran square into a stout, older gentleman, who proceeded to shout at them in what sounded like Portuguese while gesticulating rudely. The children merely laughed and ran on to where one of the ship's crew had just brought out a tray of snacks of some sort.

"See?" Zander said. He grinned and nudged Xavier's arm with his leg. "We could get away with all sorts of things in a room like this."

Xavier looked utterly unconvinced, though he didn't seem to mind the physical contact with Zander at all. "Not everyone is minding their own business," he said in a quiet voice, barely moving his mouth as he spoke. His eyes darted to the powdered man sitting at the other end of the table, reading a book.

"Don't mind me," the man said in a lilting, American accent, dragging his eyes up from the page to grin at Xavier and Zander. "I'm hardly in a position to go telling daddy that the two of you are playing hide the sausage."

Xavier coughed and looked like he might wriggle right out of his skin in an effort to escape. Zander merely laughed. He'd known from the moment the powdered man had started watching him exercise with Satish whom he was dealing with.

"Alexander Plushenko," he said, scooting along the table so that he was close enough to offer the man his hand. "My friends call me Zander." It just so happened that his movement made it necessary to drag one of his legs across Xavier's lap so that he was sitting directly in front of him, one foot propped on either arm of Xavier's chair. When the powdered man closed his book and switched seats to sit nearer to them, shaking Zander's hand with a wry grin, Zander went on to say, "And this is my friend, Xavier Lawrence, valet to the Duke of Selby."

Xavier's face was as bright as a beacon as he stared straight at Zander's open crotch for a moment before clearing his throat. He stood, leaning toward the table so that he could reach around Zander to shake the powdered man's hand. Of course, doing so brought his chest flush against Zander's in a position that really would get both of them arrested, if anyone was looking too closely. "How do you do?" Xavier greeted the man in a hoarse voice, then, as he shifted to resume his seat, whispered to Zander, "I am going to murder you in your sleep for this."

"That implies you'll be in my bed in order to do it," Zander murmured in return.

The powdered man laughed. "Jasper Werther," he introduced himself. "And I'd most certainly be willing to commit murder if it meant I was in either of your beds."

Xavier started coughing all over again, this time sounding as though he might have swallowed his tongue in the process. Zander just laughed and finished climbing over Xavier so that he could slip into the chair by his side.

"See? I told you," he said, nudging Xavier's arm.

"What gave it away?" Jasper asked with an amused grin. "Was it the green carnation? Perhaps the red tie?"

Zander blinked and took a closer look at the man. He was exceptionally well dressed, which Xavier would approve of, in a stylish suit that was cut to flatter his slim figure. But the red necktie he wore was a startling oddity, though one Zander had heard of before. So was the green carnation he wore in his lapel. Green carnations had been all the rage in London for the last few years among men who wished to identify themselves as inverts. Zander assumed red ties meant the same thing, perhaps in circles in New York.

"Actually," Zander said, leaning close enough to Xavier so that their arms touched, which was all the signal he needed to send to Jasper, "it was the powder and rouge." He couldn't help but laugh as he said as much.

"I'm testing a theory," Jasper said, then gestured for them to lean in closer. When they did, he went on with, "I'm attempting to see just how obvious I can be before anyone will make a comment."

Xavier's eyes went wide with shock. "Has anyone commented?"

Jasper grinned. "I've received snide looks and turned up noses from the better part of the fine, middle-class British families making the voyage, a few leering comments from that pack of Italian gentlemen in the corner, and no less than three offers from sailors manning the ship for a bit of a cuddle—" he tapped the side of his nose, "—when they are off-duty."

"And what did you do about that?" Zander asked, already laughing in anticipation of the answer.

Jasper sent him a falsely innocent look. "Darling, I'm not made of stone. One never says no to a sailor."

Zander burst fully into laughter. Xavier gaped at Jasper. "Aren't you afraid of being arrested?" he asked.

"By whom?" Jasper asked, blinking. "The sailors certainly aren't going to tell anyone. Not when they have a fairy flittering about their ship."

Xavier blinked. "A fairy?"

"I don't believe in hiding from what one is," Jasper said with a casual shrug.

"'Fairies' are what men like our friend Jasper here are called in New York," Zander explained. "Men who dress up as women, or who just behave in a certain way."

"Plucking eyebrows has become fashionable recently too," Jasper informed them, smoothing a finger along one unplucked brow, "but I'm not certain I'm ready to commit to that yet. It makes it much harder to hide when one needs to."

"I had no idea," Xavier said, looking dumbfounded.

"Neither do most people," Jasper said sympathetically. "By design," he added. "Our laws in New York aren't quite as draconian as yours in England, but that doesn't spare us from the court of public opinion, or an occasional visit to jail."

"What brought you to England?" Zander asked, pleased to be able to fall into conversation with someone who wouldn't immediately judge him and Xavier unjustly.

"It was a sartorial visit," Jasper said. "You should see

the size of the trunk I'm bringing home with me. London was devilishly tempting, and I could talk all day about Paris. I might just have a delightful confection from the House of Worth in that trunk of mine that will make me the talk of the Bowery once I'm home. That's why I'm traveling second class instead of first, you see," he added with a wink. "I spent my money on what is truly important."

"I would pay good money to see you in your purchase," Zander said with a wink.

"Keep your eyes peeled and you might just get the chance," Jasper replied. He shifted the conversation to ask, "And what of the two of you? Why New York?"

"I'm going home," Zander answered, not hiding how disappointed he was about it.

"My employer, Lord Selby, is in search of his son, who was abducted by his mother, an American," Xavier started.

Before he could go much further, an uproar sounded from halfway across the room. The obstreperous children had tried to steal the bag containing Doña Ana's tarot cards from her table, which resulted in Doña Ana and the rest of her friends shouting up a storm and attempting to chase after them. Much to Zander's surprise, the entire mad chase was headed straight in their direction, everyone screaming and shouting, arms flailing, and anyone in their path being knocked to the side.

"Looks like something needs to be done about this," Zander said, standing. As soon as he was on his feet, he stepped into the oncoming storm and hollered, "Stop!" with both arms raised, as though he were a policeman directing traffic at an intersection.

Surprisingly, both the group of wild children and Doña Ana and her friends froze in their places. The children glanced hopefully at Zander, as though wishing he would do something, or peeking over their shoulders at Doña Ana and her friends to see if they would keep up their pursuit.

"It's time for everyone to have a dance lesson," Zander announced, no idea what he was going to do or say until the words were out of his mouth. "Do we have any musicians in the room?"

Of course, there were always musicians whenever people were crowded together on a rainy day with nothing to do. A group of Irishmen was already playing fiddles, flutes, and a bohdran. They paused their song, had a quick word with each other, then got up and moved so that they could play closer to where Zander had the children's attention.

"A waltz, if you please," Zander asked him.

"But I don't know how to waltz," one of the young girls said.

"Yeah, and waltzes are for toffs," a boy added, crossing his arms.

"I'll teach you how," Zander said as the band started into a popular waltz tune, giving it a friendly feeling with their simple instruments. "And every man should know how to waltz," Zander went on. "That's how you catch yourself a sweetheart." He peeked over his shoulder at Xavier, who seemed utterly stunned by the turn of events.

"Now," Zander continued, pointing at the girl who said she didn't know how to waltz. "You. You're going to be my partner. Doña Ana, if you would pair up with our little tough."

Whether it was the rain and the monotony of the journey making everyone more willing to grab hold of whatever diversion was offered to them, or whether it was the eagerness of the adults in the room to give the children something to do, Zander's fellow passengers were quick to push chairs aside—although the tables were bolted to the floor—to clear space for the dance. Some of the children were eager to learn to dance, though a few of the others had to be forced into it by women who, Zander assumed, were their mothers or older sisters. Doña Ana and her friends seemed much more inclined to try to get the adult men to partner up with them, likely in more ways than one, but at least they joined in.

"The waltz is very simple," Zander announced. "Watch me. One-two-three, one-two-three, one-two-three."

It was simple. Most of the adults already knew the steps, even if they were more the sort to enjoy a livelier polka or some of the more recent dances to come out of Vauxhall or the resorts of the Lower East Side. It didn't truly matter if the children got the steps right either, as long as they were occupied.

Zander was pleased with his plan right up until the point when Jasper got up and came around the table to offer his hand to Xavier. A pinch of jealousy that came out of the blue squeezed his gut as he held his breath to see what Xavier would do.

He was far more pleased than he should have been when Xavier politely shook his head and held up a hand, refusing Jasper's invitation. Jasper accepted the rejection graciously, and moved on to find another partner.

His path took him past Zander, though, where he whispered a quick, "You're a lucky man. Loyalty like that is hard to find," before moving on to ask one of Doña Ana's friends to dance.

An impromptu ball was exactly what the entire second-class dining room needed. Before long, the dance spread until nearly everyone in the room was taking part. But once the strains of the waltz ended, the band reverted to Irish music, and the passengers shifted to whatever sort of dance they wanted to do, kicking up their heels and skirts and having a good time. Zander said goodbye to his little dance partner and slipped back over to sit on the edge of the table by Xavier's side, as he had earlier.

"You're not dancing?" he asked over the din that the party had raised.

"I need to conserve my strength for the first-class ball tonight," Xavier laughed.

Zander's brow shot up. "You're invited to a ball with the nobs tonight?"

Xavier looked embarrassed. "Lord Selby and his

friends are invited. Actually, everyone holding a first-class ticket is, and since that's technically the sort of ticket I have...." He let his sentence die off, but a flash of inspiration lit his eyes. "You...you wouldn't want to come with me, as my guest, would you?"

Zander's heart lifted so swiftly in his chest that it squeezed the air out of his lungs. "Xavier Lawrence, are you inviting me to a ball?"

Xavier blushed—as usual—and stood, nodding for Zander to step over to the side of the room with him. Not that it was any quieter over there. He leaned in and said, "I don't know how strict they plan to be about who they admit. You might not be able to get in. But if you do get in," he paused, lowering his head, then glancing up at Zander through his long, beautiful eyelashes, "I would love to see you there." He blinked, then said, "Not that we'd be able to dance together or anything. I doubt we would be able to be as free as Mr. Werther."

He nodded to Jasper, who was dancing merrily away with one of the young Italian gentlemen—who had one hand planted firmly on Jasper's backside as they cavorted through the cramped space of the dining room.

Zander laughed. "Italians always were much freer with their sexuality than Englishmen." He turned back to Xavier, longing to be able to be that free with him. "I would be happy to go to the ball with you, Cinderella," he said, warming inside and out. "And if there is any justice in the world at all, perhaps we'll be able to have our dance in the end, before the clock strikes midnight."

CHAPTER 9

Xavier was on pins and needles by the time he was called to help Blake dress for the ball. For the second day in a row, he'd spent most of his day with Zander, lounging about in second class, which was a complete departure from the life he usually led. He didn't have errands to run on Blake's behalf or hems to mend or boots to black. It truly felt like he was on holiday, as Blake had insisted he be when they'd spoken that morning. And while nothing half as exciting as the interlude he and Zander had had in Mrs. Pennypacker's cabin had happened since then, Xavier was still as happy as a clam.

Which was a direct contrast to Blake.

"Do we have to attend this ball?" he sighed, glancing to Niall with pleading eyes as Xavier helped the two of them dress in their cabin. "You remember what happened the last time I attended a ball," he added warily.

Xavier finished attaching Blake's cufflinks, then moved aside to brush his suit jacket one last time. Niall moved into the space Xavier had vacated so that he could tug Blake's tie loose, then retie it. Xavier would have been offended to have his handiwork ruined, except that he knew Niall's fussing had nothing to do with the tie's perfection, or lack thereof, and everything to do with making an excuse to stand close to Blake and touch him.

"Last time, the circumstances were different," Niall insisted. "Lady Norwich's ball was extraordinary in that the situation with Annamarie was fresh and everyone fancied themselves in the know."

"And the difference this time is?" Blake asked, one eyebrow raised.

"The difference is that we are aboard a ship in the middle of the Atlantic, and as far as I know, no one is fully aware of the situation. And if they are, they haven't made a single comment about it." Niall finished with the bowtie, then leaned in to kiss Blake's lips lightly.

Blake sighed, but rather then letting Niall step back, he kept his hands on his waist and pulled Niall in for another kiss. "What would I do without you?" he asked tenderly.

"You'd be miserable for ten years, marry a woman you could never love, and lead a hollow existence?" Niall suggested cheekily. That was precisely what Blake had done when the two of them had parted ways at university.

"I'm never making that mistake again," Blake said in a wry tone, stealing one more kiss before turning to Xavier.

Xavier had tried not to watch the whole, intimate scene directly. Of course, his position as Blake's valet had made him privy to more scenes than just that between Blake and Niall. He fancied himself as something between completely invisible and a trusted friend who would keep the details of Blake and Niall's intimacy like a secret he would take to the grave. Watching the two of them together now sent Xavier's thoughts straight across the ship to wherever Zander was, though. Everything between the two of them was fresh and new—though he would concede it was also intensified by the close conditions on the ship—but that didn't stop him from wondering what it would be like to love someone for a decade instead of just a day.

A knock sounded on the door, and Niall went to answer it as Xavier helped Blake on with his jacket.

"Are you lot ready?" John asked once the door was open. "Captain McKay will be beside himself if his ducal passenger isn't present to start the dancing." He sent Blake a teasing look, then winked at Niall, as if he were in on the joke.

"As I've told Niall, I don't want to go at all," Blake said with a frown, walking toward the door anyhow.

"Come now," John said. "You have to go. How else

will poor Xavier be granted admittance to a ball filled with the wealthy and titled?"

"Especially when he's gone through all this trouble to dress up," Niall teased along with John.

Xavier grinned over their teasing, peeking down at his ensemble. He hadn't thought he would have anything proper to wear to a captain's ball aboard a magnificent ship, but between what he had and the bits and pieces Blake and Niall had loaned him, he looked rather fine. His borrowed suit jacket was of the latest cut and style, and the waistcoat he wore under it had red embellishments. It was as far as he was willing to go to emulate Mr. Werther's style of a red tie as something to mark him out as who he was. Not that he was as brave as Mr. Werther in that regard. Things might have been laxer in New York—and he still wasn't convinced that was true, Mr. Werther was just bold—but he was an Englishman, no matter where he was, which meant he would look presentable and carry himself with dignity.

"Are you keeping your dance card open for Gleason tonight?" Niall teased John as they walked down the hall, Xavier a step behind the loftier men.

John laughed humorlessly at the jab. "I'd just as soon make the rest of the crossing in a dinghy tied behind the *Umbria*," he said.

"We'll toss Gleason in there with you," Niall said over his shoulder with a laugh. "That way, the two of you can resolve all of this tension between you."

John made a rude gesture, which he instantly had to

hide as they stepped out of the hallway from the cabins and into a more public area. Xavier caught the gesture, though, and had a hard time not snorting as they all made their way up the stairs to the higher deck and on to the music room.

Their little group broke up as soon as they entered the music room. Contrary to Xavier's worries, he didn't have any trouble at all being admitted to the ball. He gave credit to the suit and his proximity to Blake. Captain McKay was waiting near the door, along with a few other notable passengers, and as soon as Blake entered, he was whisked away to meet all of the ambitious passengers whom he hadn't already met. That left Xavier to exchange a wry look with John before wandering deeper into the room to search for Zander.

The music room was one of the more unique rooms on the ship, as far as Xander was concerned. It spanned the entire breadth of the ship, but for the deck on either side, and was as long as the dining room below, but the entire center of the floor was open to the dining room. A rail ran along the open section in the middle of the room to keep passengers from falling, but Xavier noticed quite a few people either still dining or enjoying the music and sights of the guests from below. The entire room was decorated as lavishly as every other part of first class, and the orchestra that had been hired to play was as competent as any that was hired for balls in the finest houses in London.

All of that was lovely, but it fell flat, since there was

still no sign of Zander. Xavier made a slow circuit of the room just to be sure Zander wasn't tucked away in any corners or busy conversing with any number of the first-class guests, who wouldn't have had the slightest clue who he was. After making an entire trip around the room without finding Zander, Xavier was worried something had happened and Zander hadn't been allowed in after all.

He had just about made up his mind to leave the ball in search of Zander when a gentle touch on his arm and the question, "Have you misplaced someone?" snagged Xavier's attention.

He turned to find himself addressed by a beautiful woman in an exquisite gown. Everything about her was loveliness and charm, from her elaborate hairstyle to her subtly painted face to the artful way she stood. And yet, there was something familiar about her.

"I was just looking for a friend," Xavier began before it hit him. He raised a hand to cover his mouth as he burst into laughter, then managed, "House of Worth indeed."

"Worth every franc I paid for it," Mr. Werther said, batting his eyelashes coyly.

"You will be strung up by your pretty little baubles if they discover you," Xavier whispered, inching closer to him.

"I had you fooled," Mr. Werther said, fanning himself coquettishly. "I dare say I have everyone else fooled as well."

"Xavier," John said, stepping away from his nearby

conversation and glancing between Xavier and Mr. Werther with a smile. "Have you made a new friend when the rest of us weren't looking?"

Xavier couldn't tell at a glance whether John knew what he was seeing or not. For Mr. Werther's sake, he decided to play along. "I have, in fact. John Dandie, I would like you to meet Miss—" he stopped, no idea what Mr. Werther wanted to be called.

"Rose," Mr. Werther went on in a convincingly feminine voice, offering John his hand. "Miss Blaise Rose."

"I had no idea Xavier had befriended such a beauty," John said, taking Mr. Werther's hand and kissing his knuckles. Judging by the slight quiver of John's lips, he must have had at least some idea of what he'd walked into. "Would you care to dance, Miss Rose?" he asked, offering his arm.

"I would be delighted," Mr. Werther smiled and simpered, then let John lead him to the portion of the room where couples were forming for the waltz. As they went, Mr. Werther turned to wink at Xavier over his shoulder.

As if that comedy of errors wasn't enough, almost by some sixth sense, Xavier turned toward the music room door just as Zander walked in, dressed to the nines, so handsome he made Xavier's heart speed up and his trousers suddenly seem too tight, escorting an overly-bejeweled Mrs. Pennypacker. The two of them made such an incongruent pair that Xavier found himself nearly dissolving into laughter all over again. Mrs. Pennypacker was dressed in a style that would have been divine a decade before, all silver silk and diamonds. Zander looked precisely like the sort of tantalizing young gentlemen that some older women hired to escort them around town, and then to take them home, if they were up for it. Which Zander most definitely was not, but that didn't make the image any less amusing.

"Ah, there's your friend," Mrs. Pennypacker said in a too-loud voice as both she and Zander spotted Xavier gaping at them. "The only thing better than being escorted through a room of people giving themselves airs and graces by one fine specimen of manhood is being escorted by two. Mr. Lawrence, come here at once."

Xavier jumped to do as he was told, dodging a few of the ball's guests to reach Mrs. Pennypacker's side. "Ma'am, you look lovely tonight," he said, falling back on manners as the only anchor holding him to reality.

"I look overdone and ridiculous," she corrected him, then swept him with a look. "But don't you look pretty. Doesn't he look pretty, Mr. Plushenko?" Mrs. Pennypacker turned to Zander with a wink.

"I wouldn't know, ma'am," Zander told her with a look that said the exact opposite. "I'm not much of a judge of male beauty."

Mrs. Pennypacker snorted. "Well, I'm telling you, the lad looks like a treat. Come now, let's take a turn about the room and make all the young ladies and fortune-hunters jealous."

Xavier had no idea he would enjoy a frivolous ball so

much. Perhaps it was the sea air going to his head, but he found it to be the easiest thing in the world to strut around the room, chin held high, Mrs. Pennypacker clinging to his arm, Zander sending him an occasional flirtatious look over the old woman's head. They drew far more attention than Xavier would have been comfortable with otherwise, but madly enough, Xavier found he didn't care.

"Mrs. Pennypacker, who are your delightful young companions?" Captain McKay asked, intercepting them before they finished a circuit of the room. He was still showing Blake off, which meant it was Blake's turn to try not to laugh at the ridiculous situation Xavier had gotten himself into.

"These are my boys," Mrs. Pennypacker explained. "I found them the moment I boarded the ship. Some careless souls somewhere completely misplaced two of the finest young bucks I've ever seen, so I've taken them on as a sort of charity case, you see. And as you can tell, they're quite taken with me." She sent flirtatious glances to both Xavier and Zander that tested Xavier's ability to keep a straight face. Especially when Blake and Niall were going red with the effort not to burst out laughing.

"I don't believe we've met." The Captain smiled benignly at Xavier, then Zander.

"Mr. Xavier Lawrence is a friend of mine," Blake stepped in, nodding to Xavier. "He is from the West Riding Lawrences."

"Oh, I see," Captain McKay said, his expression delighted.

Xavier cleared his throat and tried not to choke as he introduced Zander with, "Mr. Alexander Plushenko of New York."

"Yes, yes, the name sounds familiar." Captain McKay stroked his beard. "Something having to do with steel, perhaps?"

"In fact, my family does work with steel," Zander said, keeping a perfectly straight face.

Xavier's eyes began to water with the effort not to double over with laughter. He was willing to wager that Zander's family worked construction, though he'd never asked about it. To top everything off, the waltz ended, and John and Mr. Werther broke away from their dance to walk regally toward them.

"And here is another friend of mine," Xavier continued, stealing a peek at Zander as if to let him into the game. "Captain, I'd like you to meet the incomparable Miss Blaise Rose." He gestured as elegantly as he could to Mr. Werther as his hands shook with the effort not to break down into tears of hilarity.

"Madame," Captain McKay said, sweeping Mr. Werther with an appreciative look, evidently liking what he saw. "I am utterly charmed, and equally surprised that we have not yet been introduced."

"You must forgive me, Captain," Mr. Werther said, batting his eyelashes and looking perfectly demure. "I was not well for the first few days of the journey. One might say that this ball is my coming out."

Zander coughed suddenly, falling into a fit that seemed more like laughter than anything else.

"Oh, dear, Mr. Plushenko, can I fetch you a glass of water?" Xavier said, jumping on the chance to pull Zander away for a moment. "Please excuse us, ma'am," he said to Mrs. Pennypacker in his most apologetic voice. "We won't be but a moment."

Mrs. Pennypacker hummed suspiciously. "That's what you said last time."

Zander started coughing all over again, which gave Xavier exactly the excuse he needed to step away from the others, thump Zander's back, and walk him to the far corner of the room, where a small table of refreshments was set up.

"Dear God, that's Jasper, isn't it?" Zander choked once they were out of earshot of everyone else.

"It is," Xavier said, finally able to burst into laughter. "And his House of Worth gown."

They both glanced back toward their friends as they swallowed a few much-needed mouthfuls of punch from the crystal cups on the refreshment table. Xavier nearly spit his punch out as Captain McKay offered his arm to Mr. Werther to escort him toward the other dancing couples.

"She makes a lovely dance partner," Zander said in a dangerously fey voice, considering how many people were standing within earshot.

"I could never be so bold," Xavier said, finishing his punch.

"I don't think I could be either. She's either going to conquer the world or end up on the wrong end of the law someday," Zander said in an admiring voice. "And honestly, right now, I'm thinking the former."

Their conversation was interrupted as Mrs. Pennypacker turned to head in her direction. "Which one of you stallions is going to dance with me first?" she asked, as bold as Mr. Werther.

"I would be honored to do the job, ma'am," Zander said, setting his punch cup down and offering Mrs. Pennypacker his arm.

"Lovely," Mrs. Pennypacker said, then started to pull Zander toward the dancers. She turned to glance at Xavier over her shoulder and said, "Don't go too far. You're next."

Xavier couldn't wipe the smile off his face after that. He finished his punch and set his glass aside, then returned to where Blake, Niall, and John were standing off to one side, watching the dancers and whispering comments to one another.

As soon as Xavier joined them, Blake grinned at him and said, "When I told you to treat the voyage as a holiday, I didn't precisely mean to treat it as a holiday at the circus."

"I can assure you, sir, I didn't seek out any of this," Xavier told him with a laugh.

"But you are enjoying it," Blake said, seemingly pleased. "I'm glad."

"Your friend, Miss Rose," John said, arching an eyebrow at Xavier.

"Is extraordinarily talented, as I'm finding out," Xavier finished.

"Yes, he is," John said quietly, proving he knew the way of things.

Blake and Niall both snapped to look at him, then turned to Xavier with expressions of shock and amusement. Xavier was feeling cheeky enough that all he did was shrug in reply.

The dance continued, and everyone seemed to enjoy themselves without a care in the world. As diverting as it was to watch Mr. Werther with Captain McKay, Xavier only had eyes for Zander. He had excellent form as he led Mrs. Pennypacker around the dance floor. But of course, he would, as a professional dancer. Xavier found himself studying Zander's form in more way than one. He'd gotten a tantalizing glimpse of it the day before, but not nearly enough to satisfy him.

Zander seemed to know exactly what he was thinking every time their eyes met as he spun Mrs. Pennypacker across the room. Each new glance seemed more heated than the next, and Xavier was tempted to do something dangerous, like wink at Zander. Behavior like that might have gone unremarked on in the over-crowded second-class dining room, but he doubted he'd be able to get away with it where they were.

He was relieved beyond measure when the dance ended and Zander headed back toward him with Mrs. Pennypacker. That relief was short-lived, though, as it meant Xavier's turn was next. Dancing with an eccentric old woman draped with too many diamonds wasn't what he wanted to do just then. He would rather have found a way to dance with Zander. It would have been heaven itself to be held in Zander's strong, competent arms and whisked around a dance floor.

As if in some sort of answer to a prayer, just before Zander and Mrs. Pennypacker reached Xavier's corner of the room, one of the other first-class guests stepped in with a wide, lascivious smile…for Mrs. Pennypacker's diamonds.

"My lady, it would do me great honor to have this next dance," the man said in a round, gracious, American accent.

"It's not 'my lady', but you look like a strapping young fellow," Mrs. Pennypacker said, dropping Zander's arm and taking the other man's. She glanced to Xavier and said, "I trust you don't mind if this one takes a turn."

"Not at all, ma'am." Xavier bowed deeply.

The other man sent Xavier a smug grin, as though he'd stolen a prize right out from under him. As far as Xavier was concerned, the real prize had stayed with him.

"Have we gone through the looking glass?" Xavier murmured to Zander with a giggle, standing closer to him once they were alone.

"I think we might have," Zander said in return.

They both nodded to Mr. Werther as Captain McKay returned him to where Blake, Niall, and John were still standing, but another unsuspecting male passenger snatched him up for another dance before any sort of conversation could continue on.

Xavier sighed wistfully. "I wish we could dance," he said.

"Who says we can't?" Zander asked, his eyes suddenly full of mischief.

"Mr. Werther might be able to get away with it in his House of Worth finery," Xavier started, but abandoned the statement as Zander grabbed his hand. Instead, as Zander tugged him into motion and the two of them started across the music room, Xavier asked, "Where are we going?"

"You'll see," Zander said, sending him a saucy wink over his shoulder.

CHAPTER 10

Every time so far that Xavier had trusted himself to Zander's "You'll see," he'd ended up in a situation that turned his insides into knots. And not in a bad way. He followed Zander out of the music room with a frown, pretending that the two of them had some sort of urgent business that needed their attention. A few people paused in their conversations to glance at the two of them curiously, but no one bothered to stop them. Gleason had finally arrived at the ball, and he in particular noted Xavier and Zander's departure by raising one eyebrow, almost in warning.

Xavier wasn't certain where Zander would take him this time, but was somewhat surprised when he whisked him out onto the deck. The rain that had drummed the ship all day had mostly cleared up and the sky above was filled with stars instead of clouds, but the deck itself was still wet, and the humidity hanging in the air was noticeable. But that only meant that almost no one was wandering the deck, which gave Xavier and Zander privacy.

That didn't stop Zander from glancing up and down the length of the ship once they were a few yards away from the door, though. "There's got to be a good spot," he mumbled, mostly to himself.

At last, his eyes seemed to fix on something. He grabbed Xavier's hand and picked up his pace, drawing him toward the front of the ship. The portholes to the music room were all open to let a breeze in to cool off the dancers, but it also meant the melodic strains of the orchestra wafted out into the night. A lively polka was just ending, and after a brief pause that gave Xavier and Zander plenty of time to make it to the somewhat hidden upper deck where Mrs. Pennypacker had had her nap a few days before, they launched into the strains of a romantic waltz.

Zander turned to Xavier, extending his hand with a gallant bow, and asked, "Mr. Lawrence, may I have this dance?"

Xavier's heart fluttered, and the rest of his body heated in spite of the cold snap in the air. "What if someone sees us?" he asked, remembering the night in St. James's Park all too well. For more reason than one.

Zander glanced around, holding his arms out to his sides. "I don't think the fish will mind," he said, the teasing in his eyes illuminated by the light of a large, bright moon above.

Xavier grinned, feeling foolish for being so overly concerned, and took a slow step toward him. "I know how to waltz," he said, tilting his head down slightly and glancing up at Zander coyly, "but I've never danced the woman's part."

"It's a good thing I'll be the one leading, then," Zander said, his voice taking on a rich, deep tone of suggestion.

Xavier was certain he'd gone completely mad to take such a monumental risk, but the moon and the stars twinkled brightly above, the rain on the deck reflected the light like a thousand diamonds beneath their feet, and the orchestra seemed to be playing just for them. He held his breath, gazing into Zander's eyes with complete trust and adoration, then lifted his arms so that Zander could sweep him into dance position.

They stood frozen in each other's arms for a moment, as if waiting for the rest of the world to stand still for them, then Zander moved into the steps of the waltz. Xavier's fears that he would embarrass himself were proven immediately unfounded as Zander was such a good lead. Zander's body was firm and precise, and the slight variations in pressure and tension as he led Xavier through a series of simple steps, then added more variation, had Xavier feeling as though he were born to be right where he was, putty in Zander's hands.

"This is how our night in the park should have ended," Zander said, twirling Xavier around the empty space of the upper deck.

"On a ship in the night with nothing but the moon and the stars and the sea to keep us company?" Xavier answered, feeling like a sentimental fool and loving it.

"No," Zander laughed, swung Xavier through a more complicated turn, then held him closer. "In each other's arms, without a care in the world."

Part of Xavier wanted to argue that they likely had a great many cares in their world at the moment, but all of them seemed as distant as the sight of land. They truly were in limbo, not a part of any nation or custom, in the middle of a vast ocean. The night was theirs to create with whatever rules they wanted.

The orchestra finished the waltz, and Zander led Xavier through a final set of steps. But instead of letting him go, in the moment of silence that followed, he pulled Xavier closer. He splayed his hand across Xavier's back and held him flush against his body. Xavier could practically feel the wild pounding of his heart as the two of them gasped for breath, both from the dance and from the promise of everything that was to come, their open mouths mere inches apart. Another song began, one that was energetic and joyful, but rather than dancing, Xavier surged toward Zander, closing his mouth over his.

It was a moment so perfect that it was almost ridiculous. Zander dropped out of dance position entirely, sliding his arms around Xavier and letting out a sound of need as their bodies molded together. The tension of the dance was still in Zander's body, but it had taken on a far more erotic feeling. Xavier shamelessly slid his hand down to caress Zander's arse, which earned a smile from Zander that gave his mouth a whole new texture for Xavier to explore.

"Come to my room," Xavier whispered as Zander switched to kissing and nibbling his neck. He tipped his head to the side to give Zander more room to play, but as good as it felt, Xavier had far more things in mind for them. "I have a room to myself, in first class. No one will disturb us there."

"Yes," Zander said, taking a half step back, his eyes bright with arousal.

That was all Xavier needed to hear. He took Zander's hand this time, rushing to the stairs leading down to the main deck as fast as he could without slipping. There were more people stepping out onto the deck for a bit of fresh air as they made their way back to the first-class doorway, which made Xavier glad they'd ended their dance when they did. He hated letting go of Zander's hand as they ducked into the first-class common area, which was too crowded for any sort of display of affection, but when they made their way down to the stairs and on to the quiet halls of the first-class cabins, he took Zander's hand again, threading their fingers together.

When they reached the short corridor leading to his cabin and Blake's across from it, Xavier took one last look around to make certain no one was watching them, then tugged Zander on with a broad grin. He took his key from his pocket and fumbled with it, giddiness over what they were doing making him clumsy. When he finally managed to unlock the door and stumble through, pulling Zander with him, and shut the door behind him, Zander was on him in a flash.

"This is more like it," Zander hummed, pressing Xavier against the door and reaching to turn the lock. He then grabbed Xavier's hands and pinned them against the door over his head before diving in to kiss him with enough force to knock his soul right out of his body.

If the deck was romance personified, being trapped against a cabin door while the most gorgeous and wonderful man he'd ever known ravished his mouth to the point of bruising was the definition of lust. He couldn't decide which he liked better, but as Zander let go of his hands to make quick work of the buttons of his jacket and waistcoat, lust gained the upper hand.

"Don't worry about popping buttons," he panted as Zander struggled with the smaller buttons of his waistcoat. "I have a sewing kit."

"Exactly what every eager lover wants to hear his man say," Zander chuckled, unable to keep his mouth off of Xavier's for long, even as his hands worked. "But I'm not ruining the craftsmanship of this excellent vest."

Xavier laughed, surprised that craftsmanship was the last thing he cared about at that moment. He wriggled out of his jacket before Zander had made his way through his waistcoat, letting it drop to the floor. He started on the buttons of Zander's jacket, but the tangle of arms and hands was too much, so he left his arms hang at his sides while Zander hurriedly undressed him. It was deliciously erotic to have Zander do the exact opposite of what it was his job to do for Blake, and he wasn't sure how he would have the patience to just stand there as Zander peeled away his layers.

In the end, he gave up trying to be patient and shrugged out of his waistcoat and suspenders while pushing away from the wall and backing Zander toward the bed. He wanted the man naked and twisted up in his sheets as quickly as possible, and a few little items of clothing weren't going to stand in his way. He shed his waistcoat and shirt as they crossed the room, and Zander peeled out of his jacket and waistcoat, tugging at his tie as well, until the back of his legs bumped against the bed. All the while, they kept trying to kiss each other, lips and tongues brushing with increasing intensity, but less effectiveness.

At last, Zander broke into a laugh as he lost his balance and sat hard on the bed. "Shoes," he panted, shaking his head. "Shoes are going to get in the way of this particular dance."

Xavier solved that problem by lifting first one foot to rest on Zander's thigh, and, when Zander had plucked through the buttons on the side of his dress shoe, switched feet so Zander could unbutton that one as well. He kicked off his shoes just in time as Zander reached for the fastenings of his trousers and tugged him close so that he could undo them. He wasted no time in pushing Xavier's trousers and drawers down over his hips, skating his hands intoxicatingly down Xavier's thighs as he did, then drawing them back up again so that he could cup his balls with one hand and fist his cock with the other.

Xavier let out a wordless hiss that had started as an expletive in his mind and tilted his head back. He wanted to tell Zander that it felt good, that he wanted more, but also that he wouldn't last two seconds the way they were going. He was utterly incapable of speech, though. The moment was doubly erotic once he managed to clumsily step out of his trousers as that left him fully naked while Zander was still mostly dressed.

"I like you this way," Zander said with an impish grin, pulling Xavier closer, but also nudging his knees between Xavier's legs to that he was forced to stand awkwardly astride Zander's lap. "Not quite so properly British now, are we?" He circled his hands around to Xavier's backside, sliding his fingers along the cleft of his arse and fingering his hole.

Xavier sucked in a breath and grabbed handfuls of Zander's hair to keep from falling over if nothing else. "I'm going to come in your face if you're not careful," he managed to croak.

Zander laughed deep in his throat. "We wouldn't want that now, would we?" The teasing in his eyes said it might not be the worst thing that ever happened.

Xavier was on the verge of replying with what he hoped was witty banter when Zander leaned in to kiss Xavier's chest, right above his heart. That rendered Xavier incapable of speech, and moments later, as Zander flicked his tongue across one of Xavier's nipples, he was nearly rendered incapable of breathing. Every kiss and every touch was pure bliss, and even though he was sinking under a tidal wave of arousal, Xavier wanted more.

"You're rather fetching when you want it so badly you can't think," Zander said between glorious kisses, glancing up at him with a wink.

"I would come up with a clever reply to that," Xavier said with a gulp, "but as you've observed, I can't think at the moment."

"Good," Zander said, his expression turning wicked. "I don't want to think either."

He resumed kissing Xavier's chest, licking a trail lower to his navel, then lower still. Xavier thought he might lose his mind with pleasure, particularly when Zander caressed his throbbing cock again, moving his hand just enough to drive him to the edge without throwing him over. Although, when Zander licked the moisture beading on the head of his cock, then took the tip in his mouth like he was sucking on an ice lolly, the rush of energy and bliss that had been gathering deep within him flared out of control.

He could only give Zander a gasped, "Oh!" in warning before the lightning struck and he came with an all-encompassing rush. Zander moved just in time for Xavier to erupt over his hand instead of his face, as predicted. Xavier groaned in delight as Zander stroked every last drop out of him, then felt as though his limbs had turned to jelly as he sat unsteadily on Zander's knees.

"Sorry," he panted, leaning his head against Zander's shoulder for a moment, utterly spent.

"For what?" Zander laughed.

"For not lasting more than a minute," Xavier glanced up at him warily. "Again."

Zander laughed harder, rolling Xavier to his back on the bed. "Darling, the night is young and so are we. You'll be ready to go again in about five minutes."

"You probably have that right," Xavier agreed with a sly grin. With Zander, he felt like he could go again and again, all night, without worrying about recovery, he wanted the man that badly.

"And in the meantime," Zander said, rising to his knees between Xavier's spread legs, "I get to have my way with you while you don't have the energy to protest."

Xavier whimpered in excitement, adoring the idea of having Zander use him in every way possible. He didn't mind the show Zander put on as he undressed either. The man was every bit as beautiful as Xavier had imagined him to be. Zander's dancer's body was as perfect as any of the statues he'd ever ogled at the British Museum, and the color and texture of his skin was mesmerizing. Xavier was certain he could spend all day and night exploring the constellation of freckles and spots that made Zander's body a garden of delights.

And just as predicted, by the time Zander shed his clothes and shoes and crawled over top of Xavier, like some wild predator in the darkest jungles, Xavier was well on his way to being hard again.

"I don't suppose I need to ask which way you like it?" Zander said, grinning down at him with a wicked flash in his eyes.

"I like it any way you want me," Xavier purred, certain he sounded like a ninny, but not particularly caring at the moment.

He reached for Zander's thighs as he nudged his legs farther apart, tracing his hands up Zander's impossibly powerful muscles to caress his arse. Zander made a sound of approval, then leaned down to steal another searing kiss. As he did, Xavier surprised him by raking his nails hard across Zander's backside.

Zander tensed and let out a moan, then gazed down at Xavier with a bright-eyed look of surprise. "You little minx," he said. "You're going to pay for that."

Xavier's entire body trembled in expectation as Zander dipped down to bite his shoulder. The whole thing was wonderful and mad and easily the most erotic experience Xavier had ever had. He pressed his fingertips into Zander's sides and hooked one leg around Zander's thigh, arching into him to bring their pricks together. Once contact was made, all Xavier wanted to do was rut against Zander until they were both silly with pleasure. But he had one more surprise in store for Zander.

"Look on the table," he panted, tapping Zander's back to get his full attention.

Zander lifted his head from where he'd been biting

Xavier's neck and probably leaving a mark Xavier would have to spend days trying to cover up. When he saw it, Zander let out a sound of victory and gratitude.

"You absolute darling," Zander breathed, heavy with lust. He stretched to the side, grabbing the small jar of Vaseline Xavier had borrowed from Blake. "I'm not even going to pretend to be sweet and polite now that I have this," he went on, removing the lid, "I'm just going to fuck you into next Thursday."

Xavier laughed, even as he trembled in expectation. The moment was everything that he'd been waiting for, but now that it was there, a dozen different kinds of fear and worry mingled with his fondness for Zander and his need to give everything to him. He hid his nerves by flipping to his stomach so that he could hide the flash of uncertainty in his eyes and arch his hips up to signal for Zander to go forward boldly.

"Darling, there's no need to suddenly go shy on me," Zander said sweetly, positioning himself between Xavier's legs and nudging them farther apart. He set the open jar back on the table—and Xavier noticed quite a bit of its contents was gone—then leaned over to kiss Xavier's shoulder and neck. "We don't have to."

"Oh, I want to," Xavier said with more passion than he intended. He twisted a bit more so that he could meet Zander's eyes. "It's just...been a while, and it hasn't always gone well for me."

"That ends tonight." Zander kissed his cheek, then planted an awkward, sideways kiss on his mouth. "From here on out, it will go very well for you every single time."

Xavier grinned, his heart warming at the care and concern Zander showed for him. That grin turned into a gasp as Zander caressed his arse, fingering him with a bit of the Vaseline he apparently still had on his fingers. The contrast of cool and hot was heady, and Xavier let out a groan, burying his face against the pillow for a moment.

Zander didn't give him a moment to rest, although he gave plenty of time for Xavier to get used to things. He rained kisses all over Xavier's back, licking his way up Xavier's spine, while preparing and stretching him with one finger, then two, then three. It was all very precise and prescribed, but Xavier found he didn't mind the practicality of the whole thing at all. In fact, as he let go of his inhibitions, he began to move against Zander's hand, searching for more.

Even so, it came as more of a shock than he would have liked as Zander suddenly switched out his fingers for his cock. For a moment, everything tensed, and Xavier was desperately afraid he'd let Zander down. But as soon as the initial moment of resistance passed and Xavier relaxed into pleasure as Zander slid in deep, Xavier had no idea what he'd been so worried about.

"Yes," he sighed, adjusting his hips to accept Zander more fully. "Just like that. Yes."

"You are absolutely beautiful," Zander whispered, leaning in to nip Xavier's shoulder and kiss his neck for a moment, moving carefully. He started to say something else, but the words turned into a nebulous sound of pleasure as Zander moved more deliberately.

So quickly it made Xavier's head spin, every ounce of anxiety and fear of disappointment turned to undiluted pleasure as Zander hit his stride. He hit more than that, as the burst of white-hot pleasure that had Xavier moaning washed over him. How Zander managed to know exactly the right angle to thrust to leave Xavier liquid with arousal that shot through him like an electric current, was a sensual mystery, but everything about it was perfect. And just as Zander had predicted, it was only a matter of minutes before the swirl and pulse of energy that preceded orgasm had him in its grip. That would have been enough, but when Zander reached around and barely grazed Xavier's cock, he was gone.

He let out a desperate cry and jerked back against Zander as he spilled himself across the bedcovers. They'd been so eager for each other they hadn't bothered to slip between the sheets. Xavier's climax was so powerful that he was certain he would be spoiled for other men forever. And just as things turned overly-sensitive and borderline uncomfortable, Zander let out the most deliciously wild sound and tensed against him, filling him with warmth and a sense of completeness.

It was beautiful, perfect, and intimate, and as they collapsed to the bed, Zander pulling out so that he could roll Xavier into his arms and kiss him between gasps for breath, Xavier was certain he'd found the gates to Heaven themselves.

"You're wonderful," he panted, wrapping himself around Zander, even though they were both entirely too hot and sweaty for the contact.

"You're not too bad yourself," Zander said breathlessly.

Xavier hummed and nuzzled Zander's neck. "Let's take a nap, then do that again," he said in a hazy voice.

Zander laughed, "Yes, please."

CHAPTER 11

The only explanation was that the ship had sunk and Zander had gone on to his heavenly reward without knowing it. How else would he have been able to spend such a dazzling night in the arms of the most charming and alluring man he'd ever met? Dancing under the stars. Tumbling into bed in a first-class cabin. Barely getting any sleep because they couldn't get enough of each other. There was no possible explanation for such perfection, aside from suddenly finding himself in Paradise.

Zander woke to the subtle, far-off pulse of the ship's engine and the deep, steady breathing of Xavier asleep, tucked against his side. They'd made a complete mess of the bedclothes during the night, but there was something sweet about sleeping in a pile of untucked sheets and blankets that had gone askew. As sleep left him, Zander drew in a breath and shifted to his side, holding Xavier loosely against him. The man was utterly beautiful in slumber, all soft lines and carelessness. His English rose complexion matched the imperfect tones of his own skin perfectly as Xavier used his arm for a pillow. Xavier's lips were pink and swollen from passion, and Zander had every intention of keeping them that way.

He moved in to press a kiss to those lips, his heart stirring like the sunrise across the ocean as he did. Xavier stirred, humming in confusion. When his eyes fluttered open and he saw Zander right there with him, he broke into a lazy, self-satisfied smile and wriggled closer to Zander. His morning erection ground against Zander's hip causing his own prick to take notice.

"Good morning," Zander whispered, brushing a loose strand of hair from Xavier's face.

"Isn't it, though?" Xavier asked, sliding one arm around Zander's back to splay his hand across the muscles of Zander's back. He tilted his head, searching for another kiss, and arched his hips into Zander.

Zander laughed low in his throat, charmed beyond measure. "I thought I'd worn you out completely last night," he said, rolling Xavier to his back and settling between his legs.

Xavier shook his head, tracing his hands over Zander's sides and up his arms to thread his fingers through his hair. "Never. On the contrary, you give me stores of energy I never thought I had."

"That sounds divine," Zander murmured, kissing Xavier's lips, the tip of his nose, his chin, then his lips again. "Because having you here like this makes me feel like I have the strength of Hercules."

"Does that make me Iolaus?" Xavier asked with a cheeky grin, shifting to wrap his legs around Zander's.

"Yes," Zander said, kissing his lips again. He then pulled up and sent Xavier a reproachful look. "But I'm not helping you find a wife in the end, so you can get that out of your mind right now."

Xavier laughed. The sound and the vibrations it sent through Zander had him hard in no time. "Perish the thought," Xavier said with mock horror. "Though my mother would probably weep tears of joy if she knew her oldest son had turned out normal after all."

"You are normal, love," Zander insisted. "Don't let these silly notions of who should and shouldn't love each other distract you. You are a normal man with a normal heart."

"Truly?" Xavier arched one eyebrow. "Because I rather thought I was extraordinary."

Zander laughed, muffling the sound with a long, slow kiss. He moved against Xavier, treating them both to the delicious friction of two bodies that were still hungry for each other. But it was Zander's heart that wouldn't calm down. A handful of days was not long enough to know that you'd met the man you wanted to spend the rest of your life with, but his heart and his soul evidently didn't believe that practical notion. He didn't need time to know that he and Xavier could make each other blissfully happy.

Except time was the one thing they didn't have. New York was only a few days away, and once they reached there, his life would take a horrible turn into struggle and dreariness.

"I want to stay with you," he said, muscling himself above Xavier so that he could gaze down at him. It felt dangerous to say the words, like he was tempting fate while holding a losing hand.

"I want you to stay with me too," Xavier said with deadly seriousness in his eyes. He brushed his hands across Zander's sides to his hips, digging in his fingertips as if he could hold Zander where he was, against all the forces that threatened to keep them apart.

"I know we've only just met," Zander said, "but when something is as clear and obvious as this, you don't question it."

Xavier grinned up at him. "We haven't just met," he argued. "We've known each other for months."

Zander laughed, then lowered himself to kiss Xavier again. They'd shared a thousand kisses since their dance under the stars, but a thousand was only the beginning.

"There must be something Lord Selby can do," Xavier said breathlessly as Zander left his lips to kiss a trail down his neck to his shoulder. He knew the taste of Xavier's skin so well now. It would always remind him of the sea. "Perhaps Lord Selby could employ you as a footman," Xavier went on. "Not that we particularly need a footman in Darlington Gardens."

"I don't want to be a footman," Zander said, kissing

his way across Xavier's chest and circling his tongue around one of Xavier's nipples. "I'm a dancer."

"Perhaps you could be a dancing footman," Xavier teased, resting one arm behind his head and playing with Zander's hair as he made his way luxuriously down Xavier's stomach to his navel.

Zander laughed at Xavier's teasing, but the very real fact that he wouldn't truly fit into Xavier's life without making a sacrifice was like a burr under the saddle of the idea that the two of them could spend the rest of their lives together. "You could join whatever ballet company I find employment with," he said, following the line of hair that ran down Xavier's belly. "You would make a perfect supernumerary. Or a brilliant tree."

Xavier laughed, his brown eyes filled with heat and joy. "I certainly have that stiff as an oak part mastered." He wiggled his eyebrows as Zander reached his cock, which stood up proudly against his belly.

Zander hummed. "Yes, you do." He cupped Xavier's balls, then slid his hand up the length of his prick, lifting it so that he could kiss and suck the tip.

Xavier caught his breath, then let it out in a sound of blissful enjoyment. Zander was astounded with himself for ending up with Xavier's cock in his mouth yet again. It wasn't what he usually preferred, but with Xavier, everything was wonderful. As long as Xavier was happy, he would do anything. Perhaps even suck on his toes.

That thought made him laugh, and the joy of that made him bold enough to challenge himself to see how deeply he could take Xavier. What it did not do was to make him particularly observant. He should have heard the rattle of the lock or the hint of voices in the hall before the door to Xavier's cabin suddenly slammed open.

"Good God!" a gruff, male voice shouted at the site of Zander swallowing Xavier's cock.

Zander jerked in alarm so hard that he nearly choked. Xavier flinched dramatically too. Zander yanked himself away from Xavier, but there was no way whatsoever to make the scene between the two of them look even remotely innocent. There was no ambiguity whatsoever in what the two of them were doing.

All the same, the gruff man—who wore a ship's officer's uniform—demanded, "What the devil is going on here?"

Zander spotted two more uniformed men in the hall behind the officer, and, to his confoundment, Mrs. Pennypacker. He scrambled to cover himself and to throw a blanket over Xavier as well.

"Stand aside, stand aside." Mrs. Pennypacker shoved the officer and stepped into the cabin with a look of righteous indignation. She was still dressed in her ballgown and jewels from the night before, which made her look like some sort of merciless deity. "Those are the two," she told the gruff man with a scowl. "Alexander Plushenko and Xavier Lawrence."

Zander's mouth dropped open to defend himself, but he couldn't think of a thing to say. Mrs. Pennypacker looked livid, but she didn't seem at all surprised to find him and Xavier together in their current state.

"These are the men who stole your jewels?" the gruff man asked.

"What?" Xavier sat up straighter, clutching the blanket to his chest. "Stole your jewels?"

"Yes," Mrs. Pennypacker said. "It was them."

"I beg your pardon, Mrs. Pennypacker, but it was not," Zander said, his mind reeling over the surreal situation. He climbed off the bed, keeping a sheet wrapped around him. "We didn't even know your jewels were missing."

"A small chest containing Mrs. Pennypacker's jewels was stolen from her room last night during the ball," the officer reported. "The two of you were seen leaving the ball around the time the theft took place."

"They'd already seen the jewels," Mrs. Pennypacker said. "They knew they were there. And they were the only people who have been inside of my room since the voyage started. It must have been them. I was a fool to trust them."

"With all due respect, ma'am," Xavier climbed out of bed as well, draped in a blanket, "Zander and I have been otherwise occupied since we left the ball."

Zander wanted to wince, although even that would have been pointless. It wasn't as though there were any doubts about what he and Xavier had been guilty of.

But Mrs. Pennypacker laughed sharply. "There was plenty of time for the two of you to creep into my room, steal the jewels, and dash off for your sordid activities." She glared at Zander. "I expected better from you."

Those words stung far more than Zander anticipated they would. He'd thought Mrs. Pennypacker was a friend, or at least on his and Xavier's side. How many times had he been fooled by false friendships, only to have someone turn on him when it became convenient for them? That would teach him to trust strangers, even old women.

"Search the room," the officer ordered the two other men. "If they've taken the jewels, they'll be in here."

The two other men looked warily at the officer, seemingly reluctant to set foot in a cabin where so much sin had taken place. They did as they were told anyhow, but seemed reluctant to touch anything.

"You can search all you'd like, but you won't find a thing," Xavier said, attempting to gather clothes to dress in and hand Zander's to him while holding the blanket around his body. "Because we didn't take anything. You know we would never do that, ma'am. We are not thieves," Xavier appealed to Mrs. Pennypacker.

But Mrs. Pennypacker just laughed. "I trusted you, and look how untrustworthy the two of you turned out to be." She gestured to the two of them, as if their nature somehow meant they were criminals. "I should have known from the moment the two of you rushed to attend to me that it was all a scheme to rob me blind."

"Ma'am, *you* singled us out," Zander pointed out to her as he slipped his trousers on. Not that it would do any good. The woman's mind was made up, and even though they had nothing at all to do with each other, she must have felt that finding him and Xavier in bed together equated to the two of them being capable of larceny.

The two crewmen continued to open drawers and search through the wardrobe as Zander and Xavier dressed, their faces screwed into grimaces.

"Search the bed as well," the officer ordered them. "They could have the jewels hidden under the mattress."

"I ain't touching that filth," one of the men said, backing away from the bed.

Zander huffed with impatience, walking over to throw the rumpled sheets and pillows off the bed, then turning the mattress over with more muscle than was necessary. "Do you see?" he demanded. "No jewels."

"That's enough cheek out of you, Nancy," the officer snapped at Zander.

On top of all the other indignities they were being subjected to, that was enough to make Zander see red. "We have done nothing wrong," he insisted, taking a step toward the officer.

"Seize them!" the officer said, backing away.

The two crewmen seemed more than happy to leave off searching the room to grab Zander and Xavier and to wrench their arms behind their backs.

"Lay off us!" Xavier shouted, full of indignation.

That alone was enough to tell Zander that Xavier wasn't used to being mistreated. His heart ached for

Xavier as the crewmen shoved them to one side of the room and handled them roughly.

"We'll throw them in the brig until we find Mrs. Pennypacker's belongings," the officer said. "Once we reach New York, we'll turn them over to the local authorities."

"What is the meaning of this?" The door across the corridor opened, and Lord Selby stepped into the hall. Zander noted that he was careful not to let anyone get too much of a glimpse into his cabin, and likely his lover with it.

Xavier looked momentarily relieved, before the crewman holding him wrenched his arm hard enough to elicit a shout. "Your Grace," Xavier managed on the heels of his cry, "there's been a horrible misunderstanding."

Lord Selby stepped into the room, his eyes sharp with assessment. Zander was confident that he could see exactly what was happening. "Unhand my servant at once," he shouted at the man holding Xavier. "And his friend."

The crewman restraining Xavier let go, but the one holding Zander didn't. Xavier leapt away from his crewman, dashing to Lord Selby's side, but glancing to Zander with an anxious look, as though desperate to do something to help him.

"Lord Selby," the officer said, snapping to attention, but looking embarrassed at the same time. "I regret to inform you that your manservant has been caught committing an egregious crime. And he is suspected of stealing priceless jewels from Mrs. Pennypacker here."

"These two reprobates were the only ones other than me with access to my cabin," Mrs. Pennypacker said.

"In what way did they have access to your cabin?" Lord Selby demanded. "Did you entrust them with a key?"

"No, your grace," Mrs. Pennypacker said, deflating slightly. "But they had been to my room before and they knew what I was keeping there."

"Ma'am, I daresay that the entire complement of the ship, crew and passengers, knew what you were keeping there, as you have worn your jewels every day of the voyage so far," Lord Selby pointed out. "And if you did not give Mr. Lawrence and Mr. Plushenko your key, how could they possibly have entered your cabin?"

"They could have picked the lock," the crewman who had been holding Xavier said.

"As could anyone with those skills aboard the ship," Lord Selby pointed out. "That does not prove these two gentlemen are guilty."

"They're guilty enough of other things," the crewman holding Zander said, jerking him around and causing a flash of pain. Zander gritted his teeth to keep from crying out. "We saw 'em at it with our own eyes."

Lord Selby cleared his throat and glanced to Xavier. Xavier could only look guilty. Whatever Lord Selby thought about their carelessness, he kept it well hidden.

"What two men do in the privacy of their own cabin is no one else's business," he told the officer.

"Begging your pardon, sir," the officer said, "but it *is* our business. There've been reports that someone has been luring our good sailors into dirty deeds since we set out from Liverpool. The captain has gotten word of it, and he wants it stopped."

"Yeah, and we got lucky, killing two birds with one stone, didn't we?" the crewman holding Zander said, kicking his shin.

"Take these two criminals to the brig at once," the officer said.

The crewman holding Zander yanked him toward the door. The one who had been holding Xavier took a step forward, but Lord Selby stopped him.

"Do you know who I am?" Lord Selby bellowed.

"Um, yes, my lord, I do," the officer mumbled, looking at a loss.

"Then I demand you unhand that man and leave these two alone at once," Lord Selby said. "I will discipline them in my own way."

"My lord," the officer straightened and tugged on the hem of his uniform jacket, "I cannot do that. I have orders from the captain to find the thief and, as it happens, to find the wastrel leading our sailors astray. I've found them, and I must do my duty."

"And does your captain outrank a duke?" Lord Selby said with a ferocity Zander didn't think the man had.

"Er, during the voyage, yes," the officer mumbled.

"I won't have it," Lord Selby went on. "Release Mr. Plushenko at once."

The officer rubbed a hand over his face and groaned, as if he were dealing with a dispute over two dogs fighting rather than the lives and futures of men. "All right, your lordship," the man said, getting the form of address completely wrong, "I'll let you have your man back, but the other one goes to the brig."

"That is completely unfair," Lord Selby said. "They are both innocent, and they will both be allowed to go free."

"See, that's it, sir," the officer said. "They're not innocent. We caught them in the act. I'm willing to let your man go because he was just lying there—" he cleared his throat, "taking the male role, but that one's a cocksucker, and, well, you know how that goes."

Zander nearly laughed out loud at the preposterousness of the situation. Not just because of the nonsensical double standard some men had when it came to splitting hairs over the male or female role in sex, but because what they'd seen was a complete misrepresentation of everything the two of them had done the night before. Multiple times. That was beside the point even more because of the simple fact that, as far as Zander was concerned, neither of them had done a damn thing wrong. The difference was that Xavier had a duke on his side, whereas he was utterly alone.

"Come along," the officer said, gesturing for the crewman manhandling Zander to drag him out to the hall. "We can get this one down to the brig before too many of the passengers wake up. We wouldn't want anyone to be disturbed by this unfortunate mess."

"Wouldn't want them to be disturbed?" Lord Selby demanded. "You're suggesting holding an innocent man against his will."

"He's not innocent," Mrs. Pennypacker said from the other side of the room. She'd continued searching for her jewels while everyone else quibbled about sex. "And as soon as I find my jewels, I'll prove it."

"And when you do find them, we'll already have the culprit locked tight in the brig," the officer said.

"This is madness," Xavier said, following Zander and the crewmen and officer into the hall. "Your grace, can you do something?" he asked over his shoulder as Lord Selby stepped out of the room.

"I will certainly try," Lord Selby said.

But as Zander was dragged down the side corridor to the main hall, he doubted there was a damn thing the man could do, duke or not.

CHAPTER 12

Zander had suffered worse indignities in his life, but he couldn't think of many as he was dragged through the sleepy ship and down to the brig near the engine room. He hadn't been able to fully finish dressing before the officer had ordered him wrenched away from Xavier and the only hope of salvaging the situation he had. Early-bird passengers and crew alike stared at his unbuttoned shirt and bare feet as he was manhandled across the deck and down to the more functional parts of the ship.

"See how you like it in here, Nancy," the crewman who had taken great delight in yanking, shoving, and kicking him all the way to the brig said as he slammed the barred door shut.

The tiny room was hot, stuffy, and had no portholes or source of light other than the barred opening in the door. It contained a single, long bench built into the wall that Zander feared was supposed to be a seat, a table, and a bed. The only other furnishing, if it could be called that, was a dented, old chamber pot. There was no water —for washing or drinking—anywhere in sight.

"I demand to speak to Mrs. Pennypacker," he called through the window, gripping the bars like some clichéd illustration of a prisoner in a newspaper. "This is all a misunderstanding, and the sooner I can speak with her, the sooner it could all be sorted out."

In fact, as far as he could see, Mrs. Pennypacker was his one hope of getting out of the impossible situation. The woman had seemed so jolly, seemed like she liked him. She was likely upset about her missing jewels, and she probably hadn't slept the night before. Once she had a chance to rest and see the situation more clearly, she would come around to the truth that he and Xavier weren't thieves. And if he could charm his way back into her good graces, perhaps she would speak up for him the way the Duke of Selby had spoken up for Xavier.

Or she would continue to show her true colors and distance herself from him and Xavier as much as possible. The more Zander looked back on their interactions with the woman, the more he could see the old snob had simply been using the two of them for her own game.

"I demand to speak to someone," Zander called out all the same.

"Shut your yap," a different crewman—older and gruffer than the one who had dragged him out of Xavier's room—hollered back at him. "You're not going anywhere."

Zander blew out a frustrated breath and shoved a hand through his hair. "You cannot keep me in here indefinitely," he argued. "I have rights."

"Oh yeah?" the crewman guard marched over to the door, grimacing in at Zander. "You've got a right to keep quiet and be a good little fairy until the captain decides what to do with you."

"I'm not a fairy, I'm—" Zander started to defend himself, but gave it up as pointless. Evidently, word of what had happened had already reached the man. Who knew how quickly it would spread through the rest of the ship's crew, or its passengers? "Please, just let me speak with Mrs. Pennypacker," he said, trying a more reasonable tone.

"Haven't you done enough to hurt that poor old lady?" the guard snapped.

"She's hardly poor," Zander drawled.

It was the wrong thing to say. "So you did swipe her jewels after all, did you?" the guard asked, looking as though he had staged a coup in getting Zander to confess.

"I did not," Zander said through a clenched jaw. "And I could make her see as much if you'd just let me speak with her."

"No," the guard snapped, then turned to walk away.

Zander couldn't see if the man had only gone around the corner or if he'd gone to the far end of the ship. He could hardly see anything from the confines of the brig.

He paced back and forth for a few steps, brushing his hair with his fingers, then buttoning his shirt the rest of the way. Within a minute, he wondered if that were the best idea, since the brig was boiling hot, thanks to its proximity to the engines. It was loud too. The deep throbbing of the pistons that turned the screws that propelled the ship gave Zander a headache within minutes.

Those minutes felt like hours as they dragged on. No one came to speak with him about what happened. No one even brought him breakfast. His nerves began to fray, and the panicked thought that he'd been left entirely alone to die crept in on him.

"Hello?" he called out. "Is anyone there at all?"

The distant sound of shuffling came from around the corner, and the guard marched over to stand in front of the door once more. "I told you to shut your yap," the guard said.

Zander ignored the brute. "If I can't speak to Mrs. Pennypacker, at least let me speak to my friend, Mr. Lawrence."

The guard barked a cruel laugh. "I heard all about you and that lilywhite fairy friend of yours. You think I'm going to let that she-man anywhere near you?"

"Mr. Lawrence is not—" Again, Zander gave up and huffed instead of trying to defend Xavier or himself. He'd been down this path before—in London, in November. No one would listen, and no one would help. "Just let me speak to him," he said as calmly and carefully as he could.

"Not on your life."

The guard started to walk away, but Zander called after him, "At least let me have some water then. And some breakfast. I'm entitled to that, aren't I?"

The guard turned back to him with a dangerous look in his eyes. "You want to eat something?" he demanded.

Zander knew exactly what the man would say next and clenched his jaw, bracing for it.

Sure enough, the guard grabbed his crotch and said, "I've got a nice, thick sausage for you to swallow right here. Your sort likes that, don't you?"

"Never mind." Zander paced away from the door.

"Aaw, come on, pouf. You and I can work something out," the guard said. "You suck on what I have to give you and I'll make sure you have a nice, cool glass of water to tide you over until the captain decides whether or not to throw you overboard."

"I'll pass on that deal," Zander said in a wry tone.

"Your pretty, powdered friend took me up on it," the guard went on. "Nice, deep mouth that one has."

Zander whipped back to the door, his eyes going wide. It took him a half second to realize the guard meant Jasper and not Xavier. He couldn't help but feel just a bit of resentment toward Jasper. If he hadn't decided to make a sport of blowing sailors on the voyage—as Jasper had implied he had the day before—then perhaps he and Xavier wouldn't be in the mess they were in now.

Except Xavier wasn't in a mess. Xavier had a duke to clean up his messes. For all intents and purposes, Xavier was a toff himself, and the upper classes always got away with things that the working class had their heads lopped off for. It was a bitterly unfair pill to swallow.

"Just bring me a glass of water," he sighed, glaring at the guard.

"You've hurt my feelings by refusing to play nice, so I don't think I will," the guard said, walking away.

Zander boiled with frustration as he paced the tiny brig. He boiled with regular heat too, and before long, panic seeped in around his edges again. They couldn't keep him in the brig without food or water forever. Although, they had left him to dry out and starve for far longer than was right in the London prison. They were on a ship in the middle of the Atlantic, and for all anyone knew, the captain really could throw him overboard and pretend it was an accident. That might have been preferable to dying of dehydration, though.

Hours passed, and Zander grew desperate. He told himself it was his mind playing tricks on him and he was just a little thirsty, not on the verge of an emergency, but trapped as he was, no one there to listen to him or help him, those tricks of his mind started to gain the upper hand.

The only stroke of luck he had was when, apparently, the guards changed shifts.

"I don't want trouble from you," the new guard, a younger man who was tall and gangly and didn't seem to be the same, bullying sort as the first guard, said as he took over.

"Could I have some water?" Zander asked,

pretending to be meek and defeated in the hope he could play off of the young guard's sympathy. "And they haven't fed me yet either."

"They haven't?" The young guard looked shocked by that.

It was the first stroke of luck Zander had had since landing where he was. "No," he said, playing up his helplessness. "And...and, if you please, could you bring me a pen and paper so I could write a note to my friend to let him know what's become of me?"

"I'll see what I can do," the young guard said.

Zander resumed his pacing with a whole different feeling as he waited for the young guard to return. He nearly sang a hallelujah when the man came back not only with a large glass of water and some buttered bread, but with paper and a pencil too.

"Thank you," he said with a weary smile, accepting his bounty as the young guard handed it through the barred window. "A million times, thank you."

"I shouldn't be giving you the paper and pencil," the young guard said. "So write what you need to write fast, and I'll have one of the ship's boys deliver it."

Zander nodded and took everything straight to the bench. He thought for a moment about writing to Mrs. Pennypacker first to get her to see the truth of things, but that seemed pointless. There probably wasn't much that Xavier could do either that he wasn't already doing, but Zander poured his heart out to Xavier all the same. At the point things had come to, Xavier was his only hope.

. . .

"This is outrageous," Xavier nearly shouted as he paced beside the table in the first-class dining room that Blake and Niall, John and Det. Gleason had taken over for their meeting of the minds. "They cannot simply keep Zander locked away like a criminal when he's done nothing wrong."

The four other men glanced anxiously at him, and Blake tried to reach for him to get him to settle. Blake shot a look around the dining room. Quite a few of the other passengers were staring at him and whispering among themselves as Xavier paced. None of the tables immediately around Blake's table were occupied, possibly because the other first-class passengers saw Xavier as some sort of raving lunatic who might turn violent at any moment.

"The trouble is that the captain *does* seem to think Mr. Plushenko has done something wrong," Blake said in what Xavier thought was intended to be a soothing voice. "Both Britain and the United States have laws against sodomy."

"Who truly cares about any of that anyhow?" Xavier raged. In truth, his rage was fueled by guilt. For the second time, Xavier had landed Zander in prison while he himself had walked free. It was outrageous that the two of them could be held in such contempt for nothing more than expressing their love for each other. And yes, after everything he and Zander had shared and said, he was willing to call it love. He'd fight anyone who said it was anything else.

"Is your friend being held on charges of theft or sodomy?" Det. Gleason asked.

Xavier sucked in a breath, pausing his pacing to face the man. Oddly enough, being asked a blunt question by a man whose very profession was investigation felt as though they might have a chance of getting somewhere. "Both, if I understand correctly."

"But Mrs. Pennypacker and Captain McKay were willing to let you walk free, even though you are implicated in the same charges," Gleason went on with a frown.

"That's because of me, I fear," Blake said. "When I spoke to the captain earlier, he was willing to let me vouch for Xavier, but not Mr. Plushenko."

"Which is utterly and horribly unfair." Xavier resumed his pacing again. "Zander is no more or less guilty than I am."

Except that wasn't true. Xavier felt the weight of shame pressing down on him like a mountain. He should have been able to do something. He should have spoken up, come to Zander's defense with more strength. He should have been able to do something, anything, to keep Zander out of harm's way. It seemed as though right along with the love and passion he brought to Zander, he brought heaps of trouble as well. He wouldn't have been surprised if Zander hated him now and never wanted to see him again.

That thought sent Xavier into a spiral of panic. "We have to do something," he said, ragged and breathless. "We have to at least get Zander out of the brig."

"Captain McKay was adamant about keeping Mr. Plushenko locked up to keep his crew from being tempted into immorality," John said carefully.

"It wasn't Zander," Xavier huffed. "Or me either, if that's what you're thinking." He glared at John.

"I wasn't accusing either of you," John said, holding his hands up defensively. He lowered his voice to murmur, "We all know good and well that none of us can point that particular finger without pointing it at ourselves."

"I know who has been entertaining the *Umbria's* crew," Xavier muttered, resuming his pacing. He had too much restless energy not to pace. "But I'm not giving him away. It wasn't Zander."

"All of this is a moot point," Gleason argued. "A bit of diddling on a ship is to be expected. Believe me, I served in Her Majesty's Navy for nearly a decade, I know."

Xavier stopped his pacing, his brow shooting up as he stared at Gleason.

"We'd be better off proving that Mr. Plushenko—and Xavier—are not the ones who stole Mrs. Pennypacker's jewels," Gleason went on.

"And how do you propose to do that?" John asked with just a touch of his usual antagonism for the man.

Gleason shrugged. "By finding the real thief. And to

do that, I suggest we begin by interviewing Mrs. Pennypacker."

He nodded across the room to where the old woman had just walked in, a scowl on her face and dark circles under her eyes. Whether she had slept or not, she'd changed her clothes and now wore a gown that was as conspicuously simple and devoid of decoration as her ballgown the night before had been ostentatious. A twist of anger hit Xavier's gut at the sight of her, and he redirected his pacing to march toward her.

Gleason and Blake jumped up to chase after him.

"Easy, lad," Gleason cautioned him, catching up enough to rest a hand on his arm. "Let Lord Selby and I handle this."

Xavier was so consumed with bitterness over everything that had happened that he almost ignored Gleason so that he could shout at Mrs. Pennypacker and accuse her of turning her back on a young man who had been nothing but kind and helpful to her from the moment she boarded the ship. Good sense only barely won out. He hung back, letting Blake and Gleason step ahead of him.

"Mrs. Pennypacker, could we have a word?" Blake said, addressing the old woman with politeness Xavier wasn't sure she deserved.

"Good heavens," Mrs. Pennypacker said in a weak, tired voice, pressing a hand to her chest. "Is the Inquisition after me now as well?"

"Mrs. Pennypacker, my name is Detective Arthur Gleason." Gleason stepped forward, addressing the old woman with a softness Xavier hadn't thought he possessed. "Lord Selby has hired me to track down your missing jewels for you in the hope that we might exonerate Mr. Lawrence and Mr. Plushenko."

"I don't know why you're bothering," Mrs. Pennypacker said, eyeing Xavier as if he would steal the lace off her gown. "I know those two are guilty."

"That's what we'd like to determine, ma'am," Blake said, offering his arm to escort the woman to a nearby table. "We have been introduced, haven't we?" Blake asked cleverly. "Blake Williamson, Duke of Selby."

Mrs. Pennypacker rolled her eyes and sighed, "Oh, bother." She let Blake help her to a seat, though.

Blake and Gleason sat on either side of her, like friends, but Xavier was still too agitated to sit, though he hovered next to the table.

"Ma'am, can you think of anyone else who might have had access to your cabin? Anyone besides the maids and other crew, that is," Gleason asked. Xavier had the impression from his tone that Gleason was implying any member of the ship's crew could have been the thief. In fact, Xavier thought that was the most likely option.

"No," Mrs. Pennypacker said firmly, as if she knew the game Gleason were playing and wanted none of it. "It was those two, I know it. They left that ball last night right around the time my jewels were stolen."

"So the jewels were in your room when you left for the ball?" Blake asked.

"And missing when I returned, yes." Mrs. Pennypacker nodded.

"What time did you return to your room?" Gleason asked.

"Oh, well after midnight," Mrs. Pennypacker said with a smile. "You saw me last night. I danced until I couldn't stand, and then I sat and watched everyone else while being surrounded by the handsomest men on the ship."

Gleason exchanged a look with Blake, then Xavier. "Yes, I noticed you had quite a few dance partners and attendants last night. Do you happen to remember if any of them asked about your jewels?"

"Several of them," Mrs. Pennypacker said. "Mr. Walker asked where I'd obtained them. Mr. Cooper asked how valuable they were. Mr. Levins admired their shine, and Mr. Orton joked that they must weigh me down."

It took every ounce of strength Xavier had not to lean over and shake the woman. She'd just named four men who sounded far more suspicious than he and Zander were. The trouble was, she'd just named *four* men. Four that they'd have to investigate, along with who knew how many others.

He was about ready to peel away from the table, seek out the men in question, and interrogate them with thumb screws if he had to when one of the ship's boys came dashing into the room and, surprisingly, right over to him. The lad held a piece of paper that he waved at Xavier.

"Are you Mr. Lawrence?" the boy asked.

"I am," Xavier replied, blinking in surprise.

The boy thrust the paper at him. "This is for you, then, but no one is supposed to see me give it to you."

"Thank you?" Xavier took the paper.

The boy dashed off, leaving Xavier to puzzle over the note. As soon as he opened it, his heart dropped to his gut, and he sucked in a breath. He'd never seen Zander's handwriting before, but his love had signed it at the bottom.

"*Dearest Xavier,*" the note read. "*I am so sorry to have put you through all of this. If I could have figured out a way to be even more careful than we were, barring the door or something along those lines, I would have. You have to know that it was not my intention in any way to cause you trouble or harm. The brig is hot and miserable, and I can't say much for the hospitality I've been shown, but it's a relief to know you don't have to suffer through this with me.*

"*I would urge you to see if you can find some way to clear our names of these ridiculous charges, but I am certain you and your friends are already hard at work. Just know that I am sending you my love and my strength and praying that the whole thing is resolved as quickly as possible so that the two of us can be together again. And at this rate, I might take up a position as a footman after all just to be near you. Although I still think you would make an excellent tree. Yours, with love, Zander."*

Xavier made a strangled sound that was something between a laugh and a sob and pressed the letter to his throbbing heart. "We have to get him out of there," he told Blake in a broken voice. "He doesn't deserve any of this."

Blake sent him a sympathetic look, but one that was mingled with the sort of hopelessness that their sort always had to face when it was them against the law. "We'll try, lad. We'll definitely try."

CHAPTER 13

Within a day, Xavier went from feeling as though the transatlantic voyage would be far too short and wishing it would last forever out of a sense of joy and wonder, to praying that the *Umbria* would slow down or hit a storm so that they would have a few extra days to find the real jewel thief. Gleason was confident that they'd be able to ferret out the thief, provided they had enough time. But when they asked Captain McKay—pleading with him to let Zander out of the brig so that the whole mess could be resolved in the process—not only did the captain refuse to cooperate with them, he informed them they were ahead of schedule and would reach New York in a day and a half.

"Don't worry, lad. A day and a half is more than enough time for me to nab a thief," Gleason tried to reassure Xavier the next morning as they all sat at breakfast in the first-class dining room. "Searching the *Umbria* isn't like combing through London, looking for a missing heir." He shot a goading look at John, winking when John glanced back at him.

"Yes," John agreed, scowling at Gleason. "Even an arrogant idiot who thinks far too much of himself could find a jewel thief on a ship."

Xavier glanced up from the letter he was scribbling to Zander, jaw clenched. Most of the time he was amused by the heated interactions between John and Gleason, but not when his lover's freedom was at stake. "We have to find whoever it was and recover the jewels immediately, without faffing about," he grumbled, going back to his letter.

In the letter, he wrote about every detail of their search so far—about how they'd ruled out Mr. Orton and Mr. Levins, who had consented to have their cabins searched by the crewmen assigned by Captain McKay to the case. Surprisingly, they hadn't been able to find Mr. Walker or Mr. Cooper, which was odd enough on a ship *Umbria's* size and with just under four hundred passengers and crew. But it had been discovered that more than a few people had snuck into the ball the other night who shouldn't have been there—besides Miss Blaise Rose— and Gleason believed both Walker and Cooper had given Mrs. Pennypacker assumed names. Which meant their next course of action was searching the ship room by room, person by person.

"I have told you before, Mr. Gleason, I will not go traipsing about the ship with you, looking at people."

Xavier glanced up from his letter again to find that Gleason had left the table to approach Mrs. Pennypacker, who'd been the one to speak, as she entered the dining room. She was back to dressing in her usual, showy way instead of in some sort of pretend mourning, but she looked as put out as she had the day before.

"Ma'am, we need you to identify Mr. Walker and Mr. Cooper when we find them," Gleason tried to reason with her while also showing deference. He actually managed it too, which impressed Xavier to no end. "There are no men by those names aboard the ship, so we can only identify them on sight."

"No men by those names aboard the ship?" Mrs. Pennypacker made a scoffing noise and tried to walk past Gleason. "Nonsense. They told me their names right to my face. This whole voyage has been filled with deception and trickery. I never should have come to England."

Gleason hurried after Mrs. Pennypacker, going so far as to hold out a chair for her when she reached her favorite dining table. "I believe your dance partners at the ball were lying to you, ma'am," he said.

Mrs. Pennypacker's table wasn't far from where Xavier sat, so he felt the full impact of her scornful gaze when she glanced his way and said, "Like other young men were lying to me?"

Xavier's patience snapped. He stood abruptly from the table and, in spite of Blake's raised hand and appeal for calm, marched straight to Mrs. Pennypacker's table.

"I am very sorry to have caused you any distress,

ma'am," he said, barely able to keep his voice from shaking. "But for all your wealth and status, you have turned out to be a great disappointment to me."

"I beg your pardon?" Mrs. Pennypacker pressed a hand to her chest and gaped up at Xavier.

"Son, this isn't the time," Gleason murmured.

Xavier ignored them both. "Mr. Plushenko showed you nothing but kindness from the moment you set foot on the ship. He is not a member of the ship's crew and he did not need to help you in any way, and yet, he did."

"Helped himself to my jewels, you mean," Mrs. Pennypacker said, her eyes going wide.

"If you will recall, ma'am," Xavier went on, balling his fists at his sides in the hope it would help him to contain himself, "it was Mr. Plushenko and I who pointed out that, as your cabin did not have a safe, you should have asked the captain for a secure place to store your jewelry during the journey. We took great care to make certain they were hidden within your cabin."

"So that only you would know where they were," Mrs. Pennypacker said with a triumphant nod of her head, as though Xavier had proven his own guilt.

"Did you take the jewelry case out of its hiding place, ma'am?" Xavier asked.

"Well, yes." Mrs. Pennypacker deflated a bit. "I had to so that I could choose what to wear to the ball."

"And by any chance did you leave your jewels in sight of anyone who might have glanced through the porthole into your room?" Xavier asked on.

Mrs. Pennypacker's shoulders slumped further, and she didn't reply.

Xavier glanced to Gleason. "How is that for investigative questioning?"

He was too angry to wait for an answer from either Gleason or Mrs. Pennypacker. He turned sharply and marched back to the table, retrieving his writing things. His letter to Zander was more or less done, so he scrawled his name and a few words of love across the bottom, then folded it and marched out of the room to find the ship's boy who had been delivering letters for him and Zander since the morning before.

The boy wasn't that hard to find, but even after giving the lad the letter and a coin to ensure prompt delivery, Xavier was still restless and angry. He would have given anything to have the missing jewels drop out of the sky and into his lap, anything to convince Mrs. Pennypacker to go to the captain and tell him it was all a misunderstanding and Zander should go free.

That simply wasn't going to happen. Not only were the jewels unlikely to miraculously materialize, he doubted Mrs. Pennypacker would swallow her considerable pride long enough to admit she was wrong. He and Zander never should have trusted themselves to a stranger the way they had. There was nothing for Xavier to do with his restless energy but to pace the ship, wracking his brain for some way to resolve the whole, sordid mess so that he and Zander could be reunited. They'd only been apart for a day, but it felt like a lifetime.

His restlessness took him to the second-class dining room. It seemed like a distant hope, the idea that perhaps some of Zander's more colorful friends would know something that might help the situation. But the moment he stepped into the crowded, noisy room, he felt out of his depth. The only reason he was walking free while Zander was stuck in the brig was because of his connections to Blake. The way gossip traveled, everyone in the dining room probably knew it and likely hated him for it. He had an unfair advantage that none of the rest of them had—even though his class was no higher than theirs—and yet he couldn't help but feel like he needed their help.

"You look like a seagull flew off with your lucky rabbit's foot."

Xavier was startled by Mr. Werther's greeting as the man got up from a nearby table and came to meet him in the doorway. He rested a hand on Xavier's arm and gestured for him to join him for morning tea. Xavier took a few steps before stopping and pulling away from the man.

"I don't have time to socialize," he said, still glancing around the room, though he wasn't sure what he was looking for. He was overwhelmed with frustration and worry, and didn't know what he was doing anymore.

"You're concerned about your friend," Mr. Werther said, seeming to understand. He tried again, tugging on Xavier's sleeve this time to get him to come to the table. "Sit. Have some tea. It's the last of the good, British stuff I'll get for a while, and I'd like someone to share it with."

Xavier gave in and sat, but he did so with a tight sigh. "I'm sorry, Mr. Werther, I don't mean to be rude—"

"Jasper, please."

Xavier nodded, managing a small smile for the informality. "Forgive me if I find it impossible to rest easy while Zander is boiling away in the brig while a jewel thief is wandering free."

"Yes, I heard," Jasper said with a flat look. "And I'm terribly sorry."

"You're sorry?" Xavier's brow went up. "Are you the jewel thief, then?"

"No! Heavens, no," Jasper said with a laugh. "I don't have the constitution for theft. But as I understand it, your friend is being held for other reasons that I might have something to do with."

Xavier frowned. It was true. The captain was blaming Zander for seducing sailors when that had been Jasper's handiwork. But for some reason, Xavier couldn't bring himself to resent Jasper for that. Not when he looked so embarrassed and repentant about it. Jasper had only been trying to enjoy his voyage. Just like he had been by dressing in drag for the ball the other night.

That thought brought another with it that hit Xavier so quickly he felt like a fool for not thinking of it earlier. "Jasper, did you see anything at the ball?" he asked. "Anything suspicious from the men who danced with Mrs. Pennypacker?"

"Other than the fact that they were dancing with Mrs. Pennypacker and fawning all over that rumpled old turncoat?" Jasper asked with a sharp look.

"Two men in particular seem to have disappeared," Xavier went on. "A Mr. Walker and a Mr. Cooper."

Jasper shook his head. "Neither name sounds familiar."

"Those might not be their names," Xavier said. "None of us saw them, and Mrs. Pennypacker is not being cooperative. Perhaps you recall something? About anyone behaving suspiciously?"

Jasper leaned back in his chair, rubbing his chin. "This ship is teeming with suspicious behavior, as you well know."

Xavier slumped. "That doesn't help me at all. We need to find the real jewel thief before we reach New York tomorrow. Don't you have any idea how to narrow down our suspects at all?"

Jasper shrugged. "Well, there are the Dolan brothers. They were at the ball the other night, even though they weren't supposed to be."

Xavier blinked, irrationally angry all over again. "Are you telling me that you have known about interlopers at the ball all this time without telling me?"

"I was an interloper myself," Jasper pointed out. "And I had no reason to make the connection with your and Zander's troubles until just now. But yes, it is possible they're the thieves you're looking for."

"Then what are we sitting here for?" Xavier asked, standing. "We need to search their cabin."

Jasper grabbed his arm and forced him to sit. "We're on a ship in the middle of the ocean," he said calmly. "If they are the thieves, the Dolan brothers aren't going anywhere. And you'd be better off waiting until they come in here for lunch anyhow so that they don't have time to move or dispose of the jewels, if they stole them."

Xavier let out an impatient breath and sat, though he couldn't relax. Not even when Jasper poured him a cup of tea from the set on the table in front of him.

"Let's say you find the thieves and prove Zander is innocent," Jasper said, adding cream and sugar, then sliding the teacup across to Xavier. "How are you going to counter the good captain's complaint that Zander was the one diddling with his sailors, which he seems unusually upset about."

Xavier picked up the teacup and said, "The actual guilty party could always come forward to clear Zander's name." He took a sip of lukewarm tea.

Jasper laughed. "That would only land two of us in the soup. Especially since the rumor running around the ship is that the two of you were caught *in flagrante*." Jasper arched one eyebrow.

Xavier swallowed his tea, embarrassed to his core. "I don't know what's going to happen," Xavier confessed. "Which law governs aboard a ship, and what will Captain McKay do once we reach New York?"

"Do you have any friends or contacts in New York

that could help you, should Zander end up in a worse place than the *Umbria's* brig?" Jasper asked.

Xavier blew out a breath and put his teacup down. "No. Lord Selby is only making the journey to retrieve his son, who has been abducted by his mother. Her father is a Mr. Douglas Cannon."

Jasper had taken a sip of tea and nearly spit it all over the table. After he swallowed, he laughed humorlessly and said, "Good luck with that. Douglas Cannon is one of the most elite of New York's elite. And if your duke will be busy battling the Cannons to retrieve his son, he's not going to have any resources left to help spring a queer from jail."

"I hadn't even thought of that," Xavier said, sagging against the back of his chair. He rubbed his hands over his eyes, wishing he could go back two days and somehow figure out how to do things differently.

When he opened his eyes, Jasper had reached into the inside pocket of his jacket and pulled out a card. "Here," he said, handing the card to Xavier. "I might not be of any use to anyone on my own, but I could point you in the right direction, if you need pointing."

Xavier took the card and stared at the address it contained for some place called the Bowery. "Thank you, but I don't know how—"

He was cut off as Jasper suddenly sat straighter, his eyes going wide. He reached across to grab Xavier's arm. "Come on," he whispered, putting his teacup down and abandoning the table as he stood. "Now's our chance."

Xavier didn't have the slightest clue what the man was talking about until he twisted around as Jasper yanked him up from his chair. He spotted two men who bore a passing resemblance to each other walking into the room. They waved to another group of men in the far corner who were playing cards.

"Are those the Dolan brothers?" Xavier asked in a low, tight voice.

"They are," Jasper said, pushing him to the door. "And if they've come to play cards, we might have hours to convince the captain to search their room." They hurried out of the dining room, and Jasper added, "I was under the impression that they lost everything in a game a couple of nights ago, but if they're playing now, it means they've come into more money."

"So they have a motive, they knew Mrs. Pennypacker's jewels weren't well guarded, and they had the opportunity," Xavier said, picking up his pace to a near run as they headed out to the promenade.

"I'm sure your Det. Gleason would be proud of your powers of deduction," Jasper said, slapping Xavier on the back.

It all seemed so painfully simple and obvious to Xavier as they made their way back to the first-class dining room at the front of the ship. The Dolan brothers had to be Mr. Walker and Mr. Cooper. All they needed was to have Mrs. Pennypacker identify them—if they even needed that—then to alert Captain McKay so that their room could be searched. Xavier was certain they would find the jewels and the entire, terrifying interlude would be over. Zander could go free, they could laugh about how close they'd come to disaster, and then they could get on with their lives.

Gleason, Blake, and the others were equally as excited about the possibility once Xavier and Jasper found them, just finishing up their breakfast. They, too, knew in an instant that the Dolan brothers were the culprit. The six of them hurried off in search of the captain.

"Usually, I'm at the other end of the angry mob looking for justice," Jasper quipped as they headed to the wheelhouse.

Xavier laughed, but it felt far more like gallows humor than he wanted it to.

Captain McKay was actually willing to speak to them, which Xavier knew was entirely because of Blake's presence. In fact, Blake was the one who ended up speaking for them as they explained their theory of the Dolan brothers' guilt.

"And you believe that is who truly stole Mrs. Pennypacker's jewels?" Captain McKay asked, stroking his beard, after Blake finished explaining, with a few details added by Jasper. The good captain glanced right over Jasper, then did a double-take and narrowed his eyes. Xavier held his breath, but the captain shook his head and focused on the matter at hand.

"There is only one way to know for certain, sir," Blake said, "and that is to search their room."

"We'll search it, then," the captain said with a nod.

Their gang swelled from six members to seven as the captain joined them, then to ten as three crewmen were called on to perform the search.

"I can see the use of having a duke in one's pocket," Jasper commented to Xavier as they brought up the rear of the procession down the deck and into the hallway with the second-class cabins.

"I'm beginning to see the use of it myself," Xavier said with a sigh. See it and recognize how unfair it was.

In the end, the whole matter of the missing jewels was resolved with surprising speed and efficiency. The Dolans weren't in the cabin when the crewmen unlocked it and searched. Mrs. Pennypacker's jewelry case was sitting out in plain sight. Two of the crewmen marched into the second-class dining room to apprehend the brothers for the theft. They were so startled that they confessed to the crime, including picking the lock on Mrs. Pennypacker's cabin door. The whole thing was over like a storm at sea that blew itself out.

"And now, Captain McKay," Blake said with a smile once they were all out on the deck in the late-morning sunshine, "I trust that you will release Mr. Plushenko, as we have definitively proven that he is no thief."

Captain McKay balked at the suggestion. "Certainly not, my lord," he said.

All of Xavier's hope and trust in justice crashed around his feet. "But Mr. Plushenko is innocent," he argued. "We've just proven it. You have the real jewel thieves in custody now."

The captain stared down his nose at Xavier with a grimace. "Mr. Plushenko is most certainly not innocent, and neither are you. He is guilty of the grossest of crimes, and I fully intend to see that he is punished for his wicked ways."

"But Captain McKay," Blake appealed to the man, "surely a lack of judgement on the lad's part is no reason to destroy his life. I...I can't say I approve of the young men's behavior," Blake went on, face going red, unable to meet anyone's eyes as he lied through his teeth, "but Mr. Plushenko and Mr. Lawrence were in the privacy of their own cabin and the door was locked."

The captain drew himself to his full height. "It is not their filth that I object to, at least not in full," he said. "I will not have rumors of disgusting behavior aboard my ship travel any farther than the ship itself. I have a reputation as an upright Christian to maintain."

Xavier glanced desperately to Jasper, willing him to come clean with his part in the fiasco, even though he knew Jasper wouldn't. He wasn't sure he truly believed Jasper *should* confess either, not knowing how merciless Captain McKay would be.

"Then what can we do to change your mind?" Blake asked with a sigh. "What can we do to convince you to let Mr. Plushenko go free?"

"Nothing," the captain said with a shrug. "You cannot stand in the way of justice. When we reach port in New York tomorrow, I will turn Mr. Plushenko over to the authorities to do with as they see fit."

"But, sir—"

"This is the end of the discussion on the matter, my lord," Captain McKay said dismissively. "If you will excuse me, I have a ship to captain." Without another word, he turned and strode off, leaving the rest of them gaping after them.

"What are we going to do?" Xavier asked, panic welling within him. "We can't let Zander be handed over to the police in New York, we've no idea what they'll do to him."

"I have a fairly good idea," Jasper said with a sigh. When Xavier glanced desperately to him, Jasper went on with, "Whatever you can do to keep him out of a New York jail, I suggest you do it."

"We will," Blake said, as if to reassure Xavier.

Xavier had confidence in his master and friend, he just didn't have any idea whatsoever what they could do.

CHAPTER 14

Being locked in a dreary, London prison for more than a month was the worst experience of Zander's life. At least, it had been until he found himself trapped in the tiny, overheated, noisy brig of the *Umbria* for days. At least, he thought it was days. Time ceased to have any meaning within just a few, painful hours, and since he didn't have a window to the outside world, he had no sense of whether it was day or night except when the guards changed. The first night, the crewman who had been set to guard him kindly turned the lights out to allow Zander to sleep—not that he did that very well. The second night, the very first guard he'd had was back, and in addition to insulting Zander and withholding food and water unless he agreed to suck the man's cock, he left the light on all night.

The only indicators that any time had passed at all were the two letters that Xavier had managed to have delivered to him and the sudden appearance of two other men in the brig. Zander had cherished Xavier's letters, reading them over and over, and telling himself they were proof that not only Xavier, but a duke as well, was working hard to set him free. The letters lifted him up.

The two other prisoners were another story entirely.

"I'm not wasting away in here with this piece of shite," one of the two brothers that were shut in the tiny room with him complained as soon as the guard slammed the door on them. "There's no telling what this pouf will do to me."

"I wouldn't touch you if you were made of gold and rubbing your head brought seven years of good luck," Zander grumbled, hugging himself as he sat on the bench that doubled as a bed.

"Did you hear that?" the odious man shouted at the window. "He threatened to rub my head."

"And we all know what that means," the other brother said, backing into the farthest corner from Zander.

It was humiliating and disheartening. The Dolan brothers—Chaz and Burt, as he learned their names were when the guard hurled a series of insults at them—were *actual* criminals, but they sneered at him as though he were a plague-carrier. They kept to themselves in the far corner, even though the room wasn't big enough for all three of them to lie down on the floor at the same time, and when supper was handed through the barred window that evening, they wouldn't eat anything if

Zander had so much as touched the plate. They refused to take a piss in the chamber pot unless Zander faced fully in the other direction either. The whole thing was mortifying beyond reason.

He wouldn't cry. That was the one thing he told himself as he curled in the corner opposite the Dolan brothers, his face hidden against his knees. He wouldn't give any of them the satisfaction of seeing him cry. They could take away his dignity, treat him like vermin, and insult him all they wanted, but he would keep his pride. He thought of Xavier, of how wonderful it would be once the two of them were reunited. He didn't care what it took, he would find a way to be with Xavier, even if he had to take a job as a London street-sweeper to do it. He hadn't changed his clothes or bathed in nearly three days, he'd barely eaten enough to stop his stomach from gnawing, and the headache he had from the noise and heat of the brig, not to mention lack of water, hadn't let up for an instant, but he would never, ever let them see him cry.

Even that resolve came close to breaking as the minutes wore on to hours and more than a day passed. The first sign of hope of any kind he had was when the sound of the engine changed and the subtle roll that he'd gotten used to in the first few days of the voyage stopped.

"Make yourself ready," their current guard growled a good few hours after the change in the ship. "We've reached New York, and as soon as the authorities can come aboard to fetch you, you're not our problem anymore."

"What about my things?" Zander asked, pushing himself to his feet and lurching toward the door. His body felt horrible after so many days of disuse. He wanted to get out and move around, stretching his muscles and even dancing, just to feel normal again.

"What things?" the guard asked with a sneer.

"My belongings," Zander said. "My baggage, my clothes. Can I at least change clothes?"

The guard sniffed. "It's not within my authority to say."

That was all the answer he was going to get. It was as if he didn't have a right to anything at all anymore, not even his own possessions. He would have paced the cramped brig, but the Dolan brothers continued to glare at him, as if they would thrash him if he moved so much as an inch outside of the corner they'd boxed him in. His only saving grace was that neither man looked to have a single muscle on his body, whereas he had the physique of a dancer.

At last, the ship stilled completely and the engine died down. The silence of it rang in Zander's ears, even though he was certain there was as much noise as ever. His headache didn't let up, though. Not when the guards changed over, not when they were brought more drinking water, and not when a group of New York police officers marched up to the door to take them away.

Zander almost breathed a sigh of relief when the door swung open, though he stayed right where he was.

"Those two are the jewelry thieves," their current

guard told the police. "And that one's the pervert." It was clear from the man's tone which of them he thought was the worst offender.

Two of the officers grabbed the Dolan brothers by their arms and yanked them away into the hall. The third officer curled his lip and sneered at Zander. "What are we supposed to do with him?" he asked the guard.

"I don't know." The guard shrugged. "Isn't there some institution you can lock him up in? An asylum for his sort?"

The police officer snorted with laughter, then grabbed Zander's arm to yank him into the hall.

A strange sort of panic filled Zander. Men like him weren't actually thrown into asylums anymore, where they? He honestly didn't know, and after the madness of the last few days, he couldn't rule it out. Worse still, his legs felt rubbery and unsteady after being in the brig for what amounted to three days, and his head spun as the police officer dragged him up the stairs toward the deck.

"Ugh," the officer said with a grimace. "I thought you fairies were all pretty and powdered. You're downright rank."

"I haven't been allowed to bathe or change clothes," Zander told him.

That earned him a sharp slap. "No one said you could talk, pretty boy."

Zander clenched his jaw, praying for the strength not to lose his mind completely, attack the officer, and jump overboard into the harbor. A quick, ignominious death was almost preferable to the protracted humiliation he was being dragged through.

That thought sobered him up and, combined with the first breath of fresh air he'd had for days as he was marched out to the deck, then down the gangplank leading to a series of drab, clunky buildings adjacent to the city, gave him the strength to go on. The daylight hurt his eyes, but he forced himself to search down the ship to the other gangplank where passengers were disembarking. He didn't see any sign of Xavier, though. He thought about calling out for him, but that didn't seem as though it would do any good either.

All he could do was keep his wits about him as the policeman goosestepped him off of the ship and into the immigration office on shore. Barge Office was only a temporary facility for processing new arrivals to New York. The old building had been destroyed the year before, and the entirely new compound being built on Ellis Island wasn't even close to being finished yet. In a way, Zander felt like that gave him an advantage. The area he was marched to in order to be processed and while the police figured out what to do with him was unorganized and not as drastically separated from the queues that had formed to process the rest of the passengers coming off the *Umbria* as it could have been. There were more bars to contend with, though, but at least the cell where he was locked was separated from the one where the Dolan brothers now paced. His cell was closer to the arriving passengers as well.

More than a few of those passengers—people he recognized from the *Umbria*—stared and gaped at him. Zander was certain he looked a fright, but he didn't care as long as he could find Xavier in the crowd. And from what he could see, the first-class passengers had been allowed off the ship first.

What could have been a few seconds or a lifetime later, Zander spotted Xavier, his duke, and the others inching their way through the door into the immigration office as part of the queue.

"Xavier!" he called out, sounding both joyful and horribly desperate as he did.

Xavier snapped to face him, and his eyes went wide. "Zander!"

Zander moved along the wall of bars separating him from the other passengers to get closer to Xavier. Xavier pushed his way indiscriminately through ladies and gentlemen waiting to be processed at one of the desks at the far end of the room. They gasped and shrieked at his boldness, but Xavier didn't seem to care. At one point, he stumbled, but he kept moving on. Lord Selby and the others hurried after him, though they were more polite about it.

"What have they done to you?" Xavier demanded, his voice high and cracking when he finally reached the waist-high partition that separated Zander and the holding cells from the other passengers. Xavier's brown eyes were huge and glassy with distress.

"I didn't have the best accommodations for the last

part of the voyage," Zander said, fighting his own overflowing emotions to make light of things so that Xavier didn't cry.

"They didn't bring you your clothes or anything?" Xavier asked on his breath coming in shallow pants as he took in the full sight of Zander.

Zander shook his head. "I don't even know where my things are at this point."

"They can't just keep them from you." Xavier's tone switched to anger.

"Right now, I'm fairly certain they can do whatever they'd like," Zander said.

"No, they can't," Lord Selby said, catching up to Xavier. "This is a disgrace and a crime in and of itself. I'll see what I can do to get you out of this." He scooted along the partition, gesturing toward the police officers and harbor officials, who seemed to be lounging around chatting instead of doing their job. "Excuse me," he called to them. "Excuse me, your assistance is needed."

As Lord Selby flagged them down, Zander spotted Mrs. Pennypacker entering the immigration building. He had half a mind to signal to her, though he didn't know whether he would try to ask for her assistance or make a rude gesture at her and call her every name he could think of for landing him in his current mess. He hadn't decided what he felt when the old woman noticed him in his cell. For a moment, her eyes went wide, then she glanced away, as if pretending he wasn't there at all.

"That's the last time I trust someone without thoroughly vetting them first," Zander growled, his shoulders slumping.

"I'll never forgive her," Xavier agreed. He leaned over the partition, reaching for Zander. Zander stretched his arm through the bars, but the distance between him and Xavier was such that the best they could do was to brush fingertips. "Oh, bugger this," Xavier cursed, then lifted one leg to climb over the partition.

"Hey!" one of the harbor officials barked, pushing forward with a look so ferocious that Xavier changed his mind about climbing the partition. "Stay back!"

"Finally," Lord Selby nearly shouted. Xavier's attempt to reach Zander had done what all of Lord Selby's politeness couldn't do.

"What do you want?" the official asked in a growl.

"I would like this man released into my custody at once," Lord Selby said with a surprising amount of authority.

Authority that was completely lost on the harbor official. "Yeah? And who are you?" he asked.

"The Duke of Selby," Lord Selby replied, standing tall and proud.

"What do I care?" the harbor official sniffed. "You're in America now, mister. We got rid of your lot when we threw all that tea in Boston Harbor." He and the police officers laughed.

Xavier made a sound of indignation that would have warmed Zander's heart at any other time.

Lord Selby was livid. "This man is being held against his will on false charges," he insisted.

The police officer who had taken Zander off the ship ambled over to join the discussion. "They're not false charges." He nodded to Zander. "He's a sodomite."

The harbor official jerked toward Zander, his eyes going wide. "He doesn't look like a sodomite."

"He's not," Lord Selby lied. At least he did it convincingly. "He was falsely accused of theft, but the real thieves were caught." He gestured toward the Dolan brothers. "This man, Alexander Plushenko, is innocent."

"Plushenko, you say," the harbor official said, rubbing his chin. "There was a Dmitri Plushenko wandering around here earlier. Said he received a telegraph from the ship about his son."

"That's my father," Zander said, hope swirling through his stomach. If they'd telegraphed his father from the ship, he might have a chance of getting off without charges. The entire point of returning to New York was the hope he clung to that his family would be able to help him wipe the slate clean.

"The captain of the *Umbria* wants to press charges," the police officer said.

"What sort of charges?" the harbor official asked, as though the two men were discussing which music hall show they wanted to go see that night.

"Sodomy, I suppose," the police officer said with a shrug.

"And I tell you, the man is innocent," Lord Selby

said. "Can you not fetch someone in a position of authority to resolve this matter?"

The policeman and the harbor official grinned at Lord Selby as though he were a part of the music hall show. "I suppose we could do that," the harbor official said.

"Oh, sod this," Det. Gleason said, pushing his way past his friends and Lord Selby to reach the partition. He reached into his jacket and pulled out a wallet. "How much will it take."

The policeman and the harbor official exchanged grins. "Well, now, that's hard to say," the policeman said.

Zander's nerves felt as though they were shredding as the two men drew out the negotiation. He hated to admit it, but Det. Gleason's bribery might be the only thing to save his neck. Although, even if that worked, it might have been too late for his neck. Out of the corner of his eye, he spotted his father walking into the harbor office through the same side door he'd been dragged through, accompanied by another official-looking man. For better of for worse, his father already carried Zander's suitcase from the ship. An unexpected wave of sentimentality at seeing his father again after so many years swept through Zander. He stood taller, smiling with relief and waving to draw his father's attention. Everything would work out after all.

The moment his father saw him, the man's face clouded with bitter disappointment. The warm welcome Zander had hoped for was crushed by the disgusted curl of his father's lip and the hatred in his eyes. It was worse than prison in London and his time in the brig combined. That single look held nothing but coldness and alienation. It was a sure a sign that his father had changed, his family had changed, in the years Zander had been in England as if his father had turned orange. One look, and Zander suddenly knew that returning to New York had been as terrible an idea as cruising in St. James's Park, and that the outcome would be just as disastrous.

"Alexander," his father said, walking toward him with narrowed eyes.

"Father," Zander said, feeling as small as the child he'd been ages ago. One look, and it all came back to him —the feeling that he couldn't breathe, that he was in the wrong place with the wrong people, that he had been forced into someone else's life and was trapped there. It was a terrible time for his hopeful sentimentality to burn away, reminding him of all the reasons he'd left in the first place.

"I'll just take that." The policeman plucked the money Det. Gleason was offering out of his hands, then strode over to Zander's father. "You responsible for this one?" he asked.

"I was told my son was to be arrested," his father said in a thick, Russian accent.

"Yeah, well, if you get him out of here fast, we won't have to do the paperwork." The policeman tucked Det. Gleason's money into his jacket, then gestured for the harbor official to bring him the key. He glanced around as if he knew what he was doing was wrong, then unlocked the cell. "On your way, sonny, and we won't say another word about it."

Zander burst out of the cell, but instead of going to his father, he lunged toward the partition. Xavier shifted down and extended an arm toward him, but before they could get close enough to touch, Zander's father marched forward and grabbed him by the back of his collar, the same way he always had when Zander was a boy.

"You are coming home," his father growled, dragging him across the room.

"But my friends," Zander protested, disappointed to find that his father wouldn't be the savior he'd hoped he'd find, but rather just another oppressor.

"They are your friends no more," his father said, not letting up for a moment as he pushed Zander to the door. Nearly a decade had passed, and his father still had the iron grip and brute strength that he'd had when Zander was a boy, and now it was directed at him without mercy.

Zander twisted to meet Xavier's panic-stricken eyes. "Xavier, I—"

Before he could tell Xavier he loved him or that they would find a way to be together, his father yanked him out of the office and on to the bitter unknown.

CHAPTER 15

The Fairmount Hotel was one of the foremost luxury hotels in New York City. No expense had been spared in its construction, and the facilities it offered its guests boggled Xavier's mind. The suite that Blake had been given had an astounding view of Central Park from the fifth floor, and even though, once again, Niall had taken a lesser room in his own name that Xavier now occupied while he shared with Blake, that "lesser" room was on the fourth floor with an amazing view of the bustling traffic of Sixth Avenue. The hotel staff didn't know a valet from a viscount, so they treated him as though he were an equal to Blake and Niall, John and Det. Gleason.

But by the second morning after their arrival in the city, Xavier couldn't have cared less how comfortable and impressive the hotel was, how many works of art it contained or how sparkly the chandeliers in the dining room were. He would have stayed in a dirty backroom behind a slaughterhouse if it meant he could be with Zander, if he could even know where Zander was.

"The doorman at the Drake said Mr. Cannon no longer has an apartment there," Niall told John across the breakfast table as they discussed the findings of their search for Lady Selby and Lord Stanley from the day before. "But I believe the man is lying."

"Of course, he's lying," Det. Gleason said. "But that doesn't mean definitively that Lady Selby is there. He could have been lying when he said he didn't know where Mr. Cannon has taken up residence in the city now."

"If he even has," Blake sighed, pushing a hand through his hair. "Annamarie used to complain profusely about her father's dislike of the city and reliance on his house on Long Island. She preferred the society of Manhattan."

"And just because she's back doesn't mean she's getting her way," Niall added.

"It's far easier to hide in Manhattan than Long Island," Gleason said.

John turned to look at him with a brittle frown. "How would you know? Have you ever been to either before?"

"One doesn't need to have been to either place to know that a woman like Annamarie would be far more conspicuous in a rural area than in a city," Gleason snapped in return.

Xavier watched the entire argument begin to form, bobbing his leg restlessly under the table. He should be paying more attention. He should care so much more about Blake's son and heir and the underhanded way Lady Selby was behaving. His heart and his thoughts had only one aim, though.

He would never forget the desperation in Zander's eyes when he was dragged out of the immigration office. He would never forget the panic he felt either. He'd tried to shout after Zander, asking him where he was going, where he might find him, but Zander's father had yanked him away too fast. Xavier had tried to jump the partition again to chase after him and had nearly had his head bashed in by the policeman in the process.

In the end, he'd been forced to slog through the long line with Blake and the others to be registered as visitors to America or have his papers checked or to make certain he wasn't planning to stay, or whatever that blasted line had been for. He had barely paid attention to what was happening in his desperation to go after Zander. But by the time they'd made it through and been given leave to wander New York freely, Zander was gone without a trace.

"If only we'd been able to figure out which ship Ian Archibald sailed on to get to New York," Niall sighed, leaning back in his chair and tapping the fork he'd been eating breakfast with against the pristine tablecloth. "He could have told us so much."

"Are we absolutely certain that Archibald headed for New York at all?" Blake sighed.

"My sources said he took a ship departing from Lisbon," Gleason said. "Haven't we been certain all along that he is truly in love with Lady Selby and would do anything to win her?"

"Who knows?" Blake blew out a breath and rubbed a hand over his face. "All I want to do is find my son."

"And all I want to do is find Zander," Xavier blurted. As soon as the others froze and stared at him, he knew he'd spoken too loudly and with too much passion. He glanced sheepishly around at them, then decided there was no harm at all in being honest about his feelings. "I can't just let him slip away like this. He's somewhere in this city, likely being held against his will, and I have to find him."

The four other men exchanged looks and sipped their coffee or took small, awkward bites of their breakfast.

"Xavier, I don't doubt that you and Mr. Plushenko developed a fondness for each other on the voyage, but if he didn't tell you where in New York he lives at any point during your acquaintance...." John let his sentence fade off with a shrug.

"Are you certain that he even wants you to go after him, considering all the trouble you caused him?" Det. Gleason asked.

"Yes," Xavier said, drumming his fist on the table. "What we had was more than a dalliance. You lot might not believe it, but it's true."

"I don't doubt you," Blake said, sending Xavier a regretful smile. "But John is right when he points out that at no point did Mr. Plushenko tell you where he lives in New York."

"We didn't know we wouldn't have the entire journey to discuss those things," Xavier said through a clenched jaw. "And what we did speak of indicated to me that he was none too happy to be returning to New York to begin with." Blake started to say something else, but Xavier cut him off with, "I have to find him, and I would greatly appreciate your help in doing so." He glanced particularly to Det. Gleason. The man's entire profession was locating missing people.

But rather than having his statement returned with pledges of help and loyalty, the four men merely winced or looked sympathetic, or avoided looking at him at all.

"I'm sorry, Xavier, but finding Lord Stanley is our priority," John said.

Xavier clenched his jaw to keep himself from saying something he might regret. The tables of class had just been turned on him. His connection to a duke was enough to prevent him from being thrown in the *Umbria's* brig along with Zander, but now that Lord Stanley was involved, Xavier was back to being a servant and not worthy of attention.

"I understand," he said, seething, rising from his chair. "I'll find Zander on my own then." Though God only knew how he would do it.

He started to walk away, but Blake called after him, "Xavier, wait."

Xavier stopped and turned back to find Blake rising from his chair. A few of the other patrons of the hotel's restaurant stared at them as Blake crossed to Xavier's side. He cupped Xavier's elbow and walked him to the restaurant's door.

"I'm sorry that we don't have the spare resources to help you find your friend," Blake began.

"He is more than just a friend," Xavier said, fighting to hold onto his patience.

Blake nodded in understanding and reached into his jacket, taking out his wallet. "Here," he said, handing the entire thing to Xavier. "I cannot give you my time to help in your search, but I can give you other resources."

Xavier peeked inside of the wallet and nearly choked at the amount of money it contained. "Sir, this is...." He started to say it was too much, but the amount of money in his hands would go a long way in his search, from paying for transportation to bribing people for information, if it came down to it. He swallowed and said, "Thank you."

Blake thumped his arm. "I hope you do find him, and quickly."

It was the best Xavier was going to be able to do. He turned to leave the restaurant and the hotel in general, tucking the wallet into his jacket for safekeeping. The money lifted his spirits a fraction, but the moment he stepped out into the sunny but cold late-March morning and glanced around him—at busy streets, rushing people, and Central Park—his spirits sank all over again. New York City was home to millions of people, a number that staggered Xavier's mind. How was he supposed to find one man in the middle of it?

The only way he could think to start his search was to flag down a cab and ask the driver to take him to a place where Russian immigrants had settled. Zander had told him that his father had fled Russia after the failed attempt on Alexander II's life, so it would stand to reason that he'd seek out other Russians to live near. The driver seemed confident that he knew exactly the neighborhood Xavier was looking for, but when he let Xavier out and drove on, Xavier found himself abandoned in what appeared to be a Jewish neighborhood.

He sighed and pushed a hand through his hair, frustrated that he'd gone out without a hat and that he was now lost somewhere in Manhattan, no idea where Zander was and no idea where he was either.

"Excuse me," he asked an older woman walking by. "Do you happen to know anyone named Plushenko?"

The old woman shook her head and rushed on, seemingly terrified of speaking to him.

Xavier tried again a few more times, getting the same reaction. He was so frustrated he wanted to scream, but instead, he thrust his hands into his coat pockets and started to walk.

Within moments, he felt so far out of his depth that panic edged in to replace his frustration. He'd never seen anything like the southern part of Manhattan before. It was vast and teeming with people of all languages and complexions. The buildings around him were a mishmash of styles and states of repair. Some of them looked quite nice, but others gave Xavier the feeling that they could come crashing down at any moment. Lines holding laundry were strung between buildings down side streets, women laughed and shouted to each other in half a dozen languages as they went about their domestic chores, and there were as many children as there were dogs running about, making mischief.

It wasn't a thing like London, and under other circumstances, Xavier might have enjoyed watching the people and their ways. He stopped a few times to ask about Zander, but no one had heard of anyone named Plushenko, and even if they had, Xavier quickly saw it would be a fruitless search. There were just too many people, too many streets, and too much life surging around him to find one man just by asking about him on the street. He wracked his brain, trying to remember other details Zander might have told him—his father's full name, what the man did for a living—but he was so twisted around inside that he couldn't remember anything.

Finally, as lunchtime rolled around and his stomach began to growl, Xavier sought out one of the carts selling food and reached into his pocket to pull out Blake's wallet. His hand hit something else in the inner pocket as he did, though. A sudden jolt of inspiration hit him as he remembered Jasper's card. It was still in his pocket. He yanked it out and looked at the address. Jasper might not know any more than he did, but at least he wouldn't have to search alone.

He ran to the nearest street corner and waved for the first cab that would stop for him.

"One-fifty Bleeker Street, please," he told the driver.

Much to his surprise, before Xavier could hop into the cab, the driver gaped at him, eyes wide. "I beg your pardon?" he asked.

Xavier hesitated, looked at the card again, then repeated, "One-fifty Bleeker Street?"

The driver laughed. "You slumming it, then, m'lord?"

Xavier frowned. "I'm sorry, I don't understand."

"Usually when you fancy, foreign sorts go slumming, you do it in pairs or groups," the driver said. "So maybe you're going to The Slippery Slope for other reasons?"

Xavier still didn't understand. New York was probably full of words and phrases he didn't understand. "Yes, er, that's it. Can you take me there?"

"I'll drop you at the end of the street," the driver said. "Can't go ruining my reputation for respectability, now, can I?"

Xavier shook his head and leapt into the carriage. He had no idea what the fellow was on about, only that he needed to find Jasper—if he could—as soon as possible to get him to help with the search.

Less than half an hour later, he knew exactly what the driver was talking about. Bleeker Street in the area where he was let off didn't seem different from any other part of the city at first glance, but once Xavier took a closer look, he could see at once what he was up against. There was something just a little bit different in the air as he checked Jasper's card one more time and headed down the street toward one-fifty. A few of the women lounging about in front of some of the houses eyed him as though he were a piece of candy they wanted to unwrap —which would have been unnerving to the point of ridiculousness, except that a second look revealed they weren't women at all. The colors all around Xavier were just a little bit brighter, and the music pouring out of the buildings on either side of the street was raucous and inviting.

"And where are you off to in such a hurry, sweetheart?" a person who Xavier couldn't quite tell whether they were a man or a woman asked him, opening the doorway of what looked like some sort of music hall with a sign over the door that read "The Slide". "I've got everything you need right here." The person winked and sent Xavier a coquettish glance, then grabbed his, or her, crotch.

A thrill of excitement went through Xavier, not because of the salacious gesture, but because he knew instinctively he'd come to the right place. "Do you know Jasper Werther?" he asked the doorperson.

Their expression changed entirely, and they looked at Xavier as though he were a friend. "I take it the two of you became acquainted on her recent trip abroad?"

Xavier couldn't fight the hint of a smile that pulled at his mouth. He was most certainly in the right place. "Something like that," he answered cryptically. "I need to find him—er, her—in a hurry."

The doorperson grinned. "It's too early for him to be a her, so you'll probably find him at lunch at The Slippery Slope." They pointed across the street.

Xavier pivoted to find another club or music hall, or whatever it was, on the other side of the street with a sign proclaiming it "The Slippery Slope". A second surge of excitement shot through him. He was getting somewhere. "Thank you," he nodded to the doorperson before dashing across the street to the other club.

He was greeted at The Slippery Slope by a man in drag who wanted nothing more than to flirt and coo over the fact that he'd won Xavier away from his rival manning the door of The Slide—if that was even the appropriate word to use—but as soon as Xavier explained why he was there, all teasing stopped and the man directed him into the club and pointed him toward a long bar at one side of the vast hall.

Xavier was as astounded by The Slippery Slope as he had been with the rows and rows of shabby buildings he'd walked through in his search for Zander. He'd been to dance halls and concert halls before, and this one was no different. Tables were set up throughout the floor and a stage took up most of the space at the back of the room. A woman dressed as a man sat at a piano on the stage, playing for the few patrons who were there for lunch.

Xavier had the impression that lunch was not a particularly busy time for the club, but the people who were there—mostly men, but men of all descriptions and mannerisms—seemed to be having a good time. One slight, powdered man with his hair slicked back and rouge on his lips was sitting in the lap of a burly man who was clearly a sailor.

After spotting that, Xavier wasn't at all surprised to find Jasper sitting at the bar, gazing jealously at the couple. The moment Jasper spotted him, though, his wistful look turned into one of surprise and delight.

"My lord Xavier," he greeted Xavier with a particularly campy shout, slipping off his stool and rushing to wrap Xavier in a hug that knocked the sense right out of him. "I was worried I'd never see you again."

Xavier stumbled out of the embrace, brushing his jacket's sleeves and straightening the hem. He wasn't one for public displays of affection to begin with, but Jasper's exuberance seemed both reassuring and fitting for the environment they were in.

"I wasn't sure I would see you again either," he said, then cleared his throat, highly aware of most of the men in the room staring curiously at him as Jasper grabbed his hand and led him to the bar. "But I need your help."

"Troubles with your sweetheart?" Jasper asked, patting the seat of the stool next to the one he'd been sitting on, then hopping back onto his own stool and perching as though he were a parrot in a gilded cage.

Xavier took the offered seat, but stared at Jasper—and

the rest of the room—for a moment before replying. Jasper was clearly in his element, but his affected mannerisms had the feel of play to Xavier. Everything around him seemed to be playful and lighthearted, but with a sensual pulse underneath. It struck him suddenly that The Slippery Slope was what The Chameleon Club of the Brotherhood might have looked like on the other side of Alice's looking glass. It was a place where men like them could be themselves, just like The Chameleon Club, but in the maddest possible way. Everett Jewel would have adored the place.

He shook that thought out of his head and focused on business. "I didn't see you when we were leaving the ship," Xavier began, "so I don't know how much of what happened at Barge Office you are aware of."

"I had a little last-minute arrangement with one of the stokers from the engine room," Jasper said with a lascivious flash in his eyes, squirming a bit on his stool. "He was very good at stoking."

Xavier gaped at him for a moment before shaking his head once again and pushing on. "Zander was released to his father, but his father dragged him away before I could discover where they live or what was happening, or even before I could say a proper goodbye."

"And you wish to find your beau to say a proper goodbye?" Jasper asked.

"No, I need to find him so I can get him away from his father, so I can take him back home with me." Xavier hadn't intended to phrase it quite like that, like Zander was a puppy he wanted to take home, but it wasn't far off the mark.

"What do you know about your sweetheart's family and where they might be?" Jasper asked, turning serious.

Xavier shrugged, hating the helpless feeling that hung over him. "His father came from Russia in the late eighteen sixties after being involved in the failed assassination attempt of Alexander II."

"Didn't they blow that bastard up in the end?" Jasper asked.

"Yes, but not the first time," Xavier said, frustrated by the hint that Jasper would lose focus. "I assume Zander and his family are somewhere in the city where Russians live, but the cab driver took me to a Jewish neighborhood."

"Which makes perfect sense, since the majority of the Russians who have immigrated are Jews, but doesn't help you," Jasper said. He shifted to cross his legs and studied Xavier intently. "What else do you know? How much money does your Zander's family have? What does his father do?"

"I don't know," Xavier shrugged hopelessly. "All I know is that Zander's father was against him becoming a dancer. He wanted him to do something more practical."

"There you have it, then," Jasper said, slipping off his stool and taking Xavier's hand. "They're working class, which means they'll be somewhere on the Lower East Side. Russian but not Jewish could be a little more of a challenge, since there aren't as many of those. But I have a few ideas of where we can start looking."

"Truly?" Xavier's heart lifted for the first time in days. "You'll help me find him?"

"Darling, I'm simply mad for star-crossed love stories," Jasper cooed. "Of course, I'll help you."

CHAPTER 16

Xavier felt far more confident about roaming the southern part of Manhattan, now that he had a native New Yorker with him. He learned quickly from Jasper that different parts of the city had names, that they started in the Bowery and headed east into an area Jasper called "Little Germany", since it was predominantly occupied by German immigrants.

"They don't have the same monopoly on the area that they had two decades ago," Jasper explained as they walked. "A whole new crop of freshly-sprouted, soon-to-be Americans have been steadily moving in, so perhaps your sweetheart's family is here, since they don't fit anywhere else."

"Perhaps," Xavier said.

He kept his eye on Jasper as well as their surroundings as they walked briskly through a section of the city that could have been Hamburg or Berlin, for all he knew.

Jasper had transformed the moment they stepped out of The Slippery Slope. He'd dropped all of his playful, campy mannerisms and walked with a more sweeping stride, his back held straight. That attempt to appear as masculine as possible increased once they crossed into Little Germany, and as they headed south. Xavier was impressed with the way Jasper could alter his demeanor so completely to suit their surroundings. The one thing he couldn't do was remove the trace of powder and rouge from his face, which drew looks as they crossed over a street where the entire grid of the city shifted slightly.

Whatever the Germans going about their business around them thought of Jasper's appearance, it didn't stop them from pausing to answer Xavier's questions about Zander.

"No one named Plushenko at all?" he asked hopelessly once they'd had their tenth inquiry turn up nothing.

"Not around here," the woman they'd asked said in her thick, Bavarian accent. "But the two of you look too skinny. Come inside for some Knödel."

Xavier's stomach growled at the prospect, even though he had no idea what Knödel was. All he knew was that the scents wafting from the small restaurant behind the woman were enough to drive him mad.

Of course, another thing to drive him mad was when a second, middle-aged woman called out something to the first woman in German, then laughed. Xavier had no idea what she was saying, but when he caught the word "bratwurst" as the woman pointed to Jasper, he had enough of an impression to question how hungry he was.

"I'm assuming that was rude," Jasper said, one eyebrow raised, "but you look like you could eat a horse."

"Not here, though," Xavier sighed, pushing ahead. "It's not as though I didn't expect things to be as bad here as they are in London."

"They're bad everywhere," Jasper said with a shrug. "And they're good everywhere too. It depends on where you are and who you're speaking to." He gestured for Xavier to walk with him across the street to a small restaurant that was selling what looked like pretzels and bratwurst out a window in the front. "And as much as it might defeat the purpose of maintaining our dignity in the face of some people's chiding, I do like a good bratwurst now and then." He sent Xavier a flirtatious wink.

Xavier didn't know whether to laugh or curse or drag Jasper on so that they could make better time in their search for Zander. His resolve to keep searching without rest flagged a little as Jasper ordered sausages, pretzels, and sauerkraut from the restaurant. The sight and scents of the food were amazing, and for the moment, his stomach won out over his heart.

"Allow me," he said, reaching into his jacket to take out Blake's wallet when Jasper rummaged in his pocket for change.

As soon as Xavier opened the wallet and took out a bill, Jasper surged toward him, slapping his hands over the wallet, causing Xavier to both close it and their hands to conceal it. "Have you lost your mind?" Jasper whispered, glancing around quickly, eyes wide.

"I'm beginning to think I have," Xavier murmured in return.

"Look around you," Jasper hissed. "Do you think any of these people have seen that kind of money at any point in their lives?"

Xavier looked around with a different gaze than the one he'd used while taking in the colorful decorations and delicious sight of every kind of German food he could imagine. Even though things at street level looked clean and vibrant, there was something menacing about the rest of the area where they found themselves. Like the section of the city the cab driver had first dropped him off in, the streets were teeming with people dressed in worn clothes and shabby shoes. They seemed comfortable in their environment, but there was a certain degree of desperation about them. Clearly, he and Jasper didn't belong there, but that fact hadn't bothered Xavier until now.

"Is there a subtle way to pay for our lunch and leave?" he asked Jasper in a near whisper.

"Let me pay and you can pay me back," Jasper said.

Xavier nodded and slipped Blake's wallet back into his coat. He busied himself brushing off his sleeves and pretending nothing at all was out of the ordinary as Jasper paid for their German feast with a few coins from his pocket, then gathered up the paper containers and whisked Xavier along until they could cross over another major thoroughfare and take their food to a small park to eat.

"You have to be careful in the city," Jasper explained as they sat side by side on a bench, the paper containers of food between them. "It's not the way it was just a decade ago."

"You were in New York a decade ago?" Xavier asked, chewing on his pretzel and eyeing the sauerkraut suspiciously. He wasn't sure he liked the look of it.

"Let's see." Jasper tilted his head to one side. "I came to New York in seventy-nine, so yes, a little more than a decade. I would be willing to believe the city has doubled or tripled in size since then. At least, this part of it." He paused again, then made an off-hand gesture and said, "Perhaps not doubled or tripled, but it seems as though everyone from everywhere in Europe wants to come here these days. And I see no reason that will stop anytime soon. That's what all of this construction is about."

He nodded across from the park, where a huge team of working men were poring over a construction site. It looked as though several older buildings had been torn down and a massive, new one was being erected in its place. Xavier had never seen a modern building being constructed before and was surprised at how much metal was involved. He'd always thought of buildings as being made of bricks and stone and wood.

More interesting than the building materials were the workers themselves, though. They were all strong men with massive arms and broad backs and shoulders. Xavier couldn't help but stare at the way they moved, climbing the construction scaffolding and hauling loads of building materials as they did. They appeared to be from several nationalities, from swarthy to fair. One of the men working near the corner of the building reminded him of Zander. Or perhaps it was the way his trousers suddenly didn't seem to fit right that reminded him of Zander.

Jasper let out a happy sigh and bit off a piece of his bratwurst with a little too much relish. "I do so enjoy sight-seeing in New York," he said, tilting his head to the side as one of the bigger, swarthier workers bent forward over a steel beam to reach for something. "I like to come down here from time to time to see if I can't make a date."

Xavier nearly choked on his pretzel. "I'm sorry, a *date*?"

Jasper laughed and scooped up some of the sauerkraut from its container, adding it to his sausage. "I can see I am going to have to tutor you on all the new slang replacing every sort of poetic or decent language these days. The phrase 'to make a date' means to arrange to have dinner with someone."

Xavier blinked, then said, "No, I mean...with them?" He nodded to the construction site.

"Darling, they're hungry for it," Jasper explained. "Most of them are over here on their own, without their families and without their women. Who do you think they turn to in times of loneliness for a hug and a tickle?"

"I, er...." Xavier had no idea what to say about that. Particularly not when one of the construction workers happened to see them sitting there and waved at Jasper with a broad smile.

"Gianni is perfectly lovely," Jasper sighed, waving back. "If you weren't so in love with your dancer, I'd give you lessons on more than just the new phrases people use when talking these days. I'd teach you all about how to know which men like our sort and how to arrange to spend an evening with one." He dragged his gaze away from the construction site and glanced to Xavier with a teasing look. "Italian men are far and away the best."

Xavier could only gape for a moment before saying, "I can't even imagine."

"Perhaps that's your problem," Jasper said, finishing off his bratwurst. He pointed to Xavier for a few seconds as he chewed, then after he swallowed, he said, "You need to broaden your horizons and expand your acceptance of the way things are. Just because no one talks about it doesn't mean it isn't all around you."

"And is this what you learned when you came to the city all those years ago?" Xavier asked, taking another bite of his pretzel.

Jasper laughed with a sudden bit of bitterness. "No, what I learned is that when your family rejects you, you go and find another family." When Xavier merely stared at him, he took a breath and explained, "I don't know how much you are aware of over there on the other side of the pond, but the seventies were hard times for us here in America. For too many of us, life seemed to crumble as investments failed and speculation ran rampant. My family, like so many others, were forced to sell the land we had and to move to this glorious hell hole to take work in whatever factories would hire us."

"Oh, I'm sorry," Xavier said, not knowing what else would be right to say.

"I do not have the constitution for garment work myself," Jasper went on, "though I do love a well-made gown or suit. I suppose I was a bit obvious about that, because before too long, a rather charming man by the name of Gossling chatted me up on a walk home one day and whisked me off to one of the early clubs that had just opened on Bleeker Street. And that was the end of that."

Xavier blinked at the abrupt ending to the story. "Are you saying he...led you astray, and you just kept at it?"

"More or less." Jasper shrugged one shoulder.

Xavier gaped even harder, then swallowed the bite of pretzel he'd taken. "Are you a prostitute, then?" he whispered.

"No, love," Jasper laughed. "I don't ask for money for it." He winked. "I make my living as a bookkeeper for The Slippery Slope. Thus the address on my card."

Xavier supposed it made sense, in as much as anything about the world he seemed to have stepped into made sense. He supposed notorious clubs needed men to handle their financial matters as much as solicitor's offices did, and it stood to reason that they would want to hire one of their own.

He had opened his mouth to ask Jasper for more details when he noticed a pair of workers ambling toward them. The way the two men looked at him and Jasper instantly killed the last of Xavier's appetite.

"Oh, dear," Jasper said, shifting to sit straighter and to tidy up the remnants of their lunch. "I think, perhaps, we've stayed too long."

"Agreed," Xavier said, standing when Jasper did.

They were too late. No sooner had they gotten to their feet than the two men picked up their pace, moving in to corner Xavier and Jasper against the bench.

"What do we have here, Sal?" one of them, who had managed to sweat through his shirt, even though it was a cool day, asked.

"I think we have ourselves a couple of fairies, Mick," Sal answered with a toothy grin.

"What a nice thing to find just as we're off for lunch," Mick said.

Sal glanced around in a way that prompted Xavier to look as well, though he wasn't certain what Sal saw. A few of the other workers looked in their direction, but as many of them as not seemed to be deliberately avoiding acknowledging Sal and Mick.

Finally, Sal nodded. "Don't think anyone is in that alley over there." He glanced to Jasper. "If you're done with your lunch, how about a little dessert?" He grabbed his crotch.

Xavier's eyes went wide and he swallowed uneasily. The two men were much bigger than him and Jasper, which didn't bode well at all.

"Gentlemen, I think there's been some sort of misunderstanding," Jasper said with uncanny calm, sounding as masculine as Xavier had heard him sound. "You've mistaken us for a different sort of men."

"No, sweetheart, we haven't mistaken you for men at all," Mick said, reaching out suddenly and swiping his thumb across Jasper's lip. His thumb came away tinged red with rouge.

Jasper cleared his throat and peeked furtively at Xavier as if to apologize for getting them into a bind. Xavier's heart pounded, but as much as he wanted to run, he had to do something.

"I'm terribly sorry for the confusion," he said with his best manners. "We're searching for a friend. Perhaps you could help us find him. His name is—"

"I can be your friend," Sal said, inching closer to Xavier. "That is, if you're friendly to me."

Xavier attempted to jump back, but the bench was in the way. "No, thank you," he said, his throat squeezing closed. He darted a look around, praying there was a way out of the suddenly dangerous situation, or that one of the construction workers pretending not to watch the scene would intervene. He would even have settled for a policeman, though they had never done him a lick of good in the past.

"We're wasting time," Mick said. "You two are going to accompany us to that alley, and then you're going to suck our cocks, like two good little fairies."

"We are not," Xavier snapped in indignation.

Jasper wasn't so circumspect. He dropped the

rubbish left over from their lunch that he was still holding and smashed Mick across the face with a surprisingly effective punch. The violent gesture came as so much of a surprise to Xavier that for a split-second, all he could do was gape.

Mick raised a hand to his now bleeding lip, then scowled at Jasper, murderous intent in his eyes. "My cock won't be the only thing you're sucking on," he started.

Jasper didn't wait for him to finish the insult. "Kick him and run," he ordered Xavier.

Xavier felt utterly incapable of any sort of violence, but he did exactly what Jasper said and kicked Sal as hard as he could in the shin. Sal yelped and started to double over, and in the rush of horrified excitement that gripped Xavier, he somehow found the boldness to try to punch him the way Jasper had punched Mick. The result was a roaring pain in his hand as Sal staggered back.

"Run!" Jasper shouted, grabbing Xavier's free hand and pulling him away from the men.

They had only the thinnest hair of a head start as they peeled away from Sal and Mick and the bench. Somehow, Xavier found the strength and speed to shoot off across the park and toward the busy street running beside it. Sal and Mick chased after them, which sent terror through him unlike anything Xavier had ever experienced. There was no doubt in his mind what would happen if the two brutes caught them, and being punched in return was the very least of it.

"Across the street, across the street!" Jasper shouted, pointing to the rushing traffic ahead of him.

"Are you mad?" Xavier called back. Running into that sort of traffic would be close to suicide.

Then again, if Sal and Mick caught them, being flattened by a passing carriage would be the least of their worries.

Xavier followed Jasper's lead, dodging around pedestrians once they reached the sidewalk, then hurling himself out into the street full of speeding carriages and carts. He made a desperate sound that was something between a wail and an insane cry of victory as he leapt to one side, avoiding an ice truck, then sprinted ahead to stop from being trampled by a pair of horses pulling a carriage. Jasper was engaged in a similar dance for his life, flailing and shifting to the side before bolting on. Xavier leapt to avoid a pile of horse manure, and by some miracle, landed on the sidewalk on the other side of the street.

He and Jasper dashed on for another block before ducking around the corner of a shop entrance to see if they were still being chased. Thankfully, there was no sign of Sal or Mick. Xavier let out a groan of relief and leaned against the shop's doorframe. He trembled slightly, both from the sudden exertion and the fear of everything that could have happened.

"Welcome to America," Jasper panted, leaning against the opposite side of the doorframe.

"I think I prefer London, honestly," Xavier replied, gasping for breath.

"It's not so bad once you get used to it." Jasper pushed himself to stand straighter. "Remember how I said I would teach you how to meet the right sort of friend?" When Xavier widened his eyes slightly, Jasper finished his thought with, "Those were not the right sort."

Xavier swallowed, slowly becoming more aware of their surroundings. He leaned toward Jasper. "They were going to—" He couldn't bring himself to finish.

Jasper nodded. "It happens. You try to avoid it, but sometimes you can't."

"You mean, you've been—"

Jasper nodded, pressing a finger to his lips and moving on. "Let's not think about it. In fact, let's go home and have a few stiff drinks and not think about anything for the rest of the day."

That sounded like a brilliant idea, but as they walked on, Xavier turned to glance over his shoulder. "What about Zander?"

"Love," Jasper said with what Xavier now felt was a reckless amount of camp, considering where they were, "you're not going to find him today. We'll search again tomorrow, and next time, I'll think a little more carefully about my face before I leave home."

Xavier certainly hoped so. He couldn't exactly fault Jasper for being so willing to help him he hadn't stopped to clean up a bit, but from then on out, he would be sure to go to great lengths to disguise who he was.

CHAPTER 17

Three days after returning to New York, Zander felt as though he'd exchanged one form of prison for another.

"Zanya, come away from the window," his mother called to him from across the main room of the tiny, tenement apartment where the entire Plushenko family lived. "And shut the window when you come. The city air isn't healthy."

Zander couldn't disagree with her on that score, but after spending days in the *Umbria's* brig without any air or natural sunlight, he didn't care how much smoke and soot from the nearby factories he had to breathe in to get just a little taste of freedom. His mother, however, was washing laundry—the family's and other people's so that she could make a few extra nickels—and cloudy air didn't help her efforts.

All the same, Zander glanced wistfully out the

window again and told his mother over his shoulder, "Just one more minute."

His mother made a sound of disapproval and scowled at him, but she didn't order him to shut the window a second time. There was a time when she had tried to be supportive of him, but in the ten years since he'd last seen her, she'd become a faded shell of that woman, beaten down by poverty. His father's change had been worse. The man could hardly stand to look at him now. And his brothers had treated him like a filthy beggar dragged in off the streets from the moment he'd set foot in the tenement. His family as he'd known it, as he'd hoped to return to, had changed beyond recognition in the last ten years. He felt as though he'd stepped into a world of cruel strangers.

Zander let out a maudlin sigh and stared out into the city. He wanted to go home—home to London. He was a fool of the very worst sort to be listless and defeated by lost love and the predicament he found himself in now, but he couldn't help it. Three days had passed, and he could still feel the fleeting touch of Xavier's fingertips against his right before they were wrenched apart. He could still see the charming blush on his lover's cheeks every time Zander said something to startle or shock him. He could still hear Xavier's soft, plaintive moans of pleasure—and his louder, enthusiastic cries of ecstasy—as the two of them made love. Even though it had only been that one night. God help him, but he wanted so many more nights with Xavier. He wanted a lifetime.

But Xavier was somewhere out there in a city of over two million people, if Lord Selby had even wanted to stay in the city at all. Out there in the city, but certainly not the Lower East Side, where Zander was stuck under the watchful and suspicious eye of his family. Soon Xavier would return to London, and an ocean would separate them, possibly forever. God, he wanted to go home.

"Why are you sad?"

The question came from Anya, Zander's youngest sister, as she wandered over to stand next to him at the window.

"Anya," their mother snapped. "Don't talk to him. You have your chores." She pointed to the wringer that eight-year-old Anya was supposed to be turning to help their mother with the laundry. From the moment Zander had entered his family's apartments, Anya hadn't stopped working.

"Can't she have a few minutes to rest?" Zander asked. "She's been working that thing since sunrise." *When she should be in school*, Zander added for himself. He thought there were laws against child labor, but no one seemed to be checking up on Anya.

His mother continued to scowl and mutter something in Russian—a language he'd been raised with, but had grown surprisingly inept at after not using it for ten years. "You could offer to help," she said. "Since you refuse to go work with your father and brothers."

"I'm not refusing," Zander said, getting up, shutting the window, and moving over to the wringer so that he could turn the handle while Anya fed wet clothes into it. "I'm not a construction worker," he went on, speaking to Anya so that he didn't have to face the boiling resentment he felt for his mother. His own mother, whom he should love unconditionally and who should love him. It felt so wrong in so many ways that the family of his birth felt like complete strangers to him—hostile strangers at that.

"I'm a dancer," he told Anya with a sad smile. She'd been born after he'd moved to London. They'd met for the first time when his father had dragged him home three days ago, but it had been love at first sight. Just like him and Xavier. "If I'm going to find employment, it should be doing what I love to do best."

"I like your dancing," Anya said, her eyes huge and appreciative as she stared up at him. "It's pretty."

The day before, while out running an errand for their mother together, he and Anya had stumbled across a musician playing a street organ. He'd danced for Anya for a few bars—and nearly wept with relief at how good it felt to use his body for what it was intended to do—then danced with her. Those few, simple minutes had solidified their sibling bond in so many ways.

And now, here they were, both trapped in a stinking tenement, doing laundry.

Their mother huffed. "She calls you pretty. Even a child knows." She shook her head in disgust.

Zander swallowed the defensive comment he wanted to make. There was nothing wrong with who he was, and there was nothing wrong with loving who he did. That thought only made him long for Xavier a thousand times more and to feel the ache of painful emptiness in his heart without him. He rubbed a hand over the pocket in his trousers where Xavier's letters were nestled against his hip. He'd lost track of the number of times he'd read him. He'd taken them out at night more times than one and stared at them in the yellowish light from the streetlights outside, just to look at the shape of Xavier's handwriting. It was so elegant and proper, just like Xavier.

He was tempted to take the letters out again to show Anya, just to have someone to share his feelings with, but the sound of heavy footsteps on the stairs leading to their apartment not only stopped him from looking at the letters, it twisted his stomach into wary knots.

A moment later, his father and two brothers burst into the apartment, chattering excitedly to each other in Russian. They seemed to zero in on him the moment they entered the room, laughing and making comments to each other in a snide tone as they did. Zander kept working, even though Anya's expression had turned anxious and awe-filled as she stared up at him. Their mother made a curt comment to the men and waved them off. Zander could tell they were talking about something that had happened at the construction site where his father and brothers worked, but he couldn't piece things together well enough to know what was going on. He'd never felt so separate from his family in his life.

"Is something the matter?" he asked in English,

praying that, for a few minutes at least, they could speak the same language.

"There was a fight," his brother, Pavel, said. "Two of your sort were involved."

His mother left her work to rush into the corner that made up their kitchen so she could fetch lunch for the men. They lived close enough to the construction site where they currently had work to return home for lunch on days when Anya had too much work to be sent to the site with something, but only if their foreman didn't catch them.

"My sort?" The knot in Zander's gut grew tighter.

"Fairies," his brother Yuri said with a sneer.

"Are you a fairy?" Anya whispered, swaying closer to him, her blue eyes huge with wonder.

Zander swallowed hard and forced himself to smile for her. She only knew one meaning of the word, thank God. He crouched so he was at her level. "It's a secret, but yes, I am," he whispered back to her.

Anya gasped in wonder. "You're magic."

"I wouldn't say that." Zander touched her nose, then stood, facing his father and brothers with an entirely different demeanor. "What sort of fight?" he asked.

Yuri sent him a one-shoulder shrug and said, "Two painted and powdered fairies were sniffing around the site, looking for trade. Two of the men took them up on their offer, but they must have changed their minds. They attacked the men, like two cats in heat, then scampered off."

"They ran right off into traffic," Pavel finished the story. "Probably got themselves killed in the process. Mick and Sal were mad as bears and wanted to chase after them and beat them to death, but the foreman caught them and ordered them back to work or they'd be fired."

Zander frowned and opened his mouth to ask more questions, but his father cut him off with, "You remember work? That thing you should be doing instead of standing around here all day, pretending to be more of a woman than you already are?"

Zander took a deep breath to steady himself before getting into the same fight he'd had with his father every day for the past three days. "I will find work, Father, but there are other things I need to find first." Like Xavier. He'd gone out every day, hoping he'd be able to travel uptown to search for him, but something had always gotten in the way.

"You need to find nothing," his father bellowed so suddenly that Anya flinched and hid behind Zander. "You will come to work at the construction site with us, now, this very afternoon, or you will leave this house."

His father's words were like the door to the brig slamming on him all over again.

"I promise you, Father," he said, taking a step forward, "I am searching for work. Work that is more suitable to me." He had to find Xavier—or at least exhaust himself trying—before giving up and succumbing to the fate his father had in store for him.

"Work more suitable for you," his father said with a mocking sneer. "What sort of work is suitable for *you*?"

Inspiration hit Zander in a flash. "Work in a hotel," he said, brightening as the brilliance of the scheme struck him. "I've lived in London for the past ten years. I've gained the sort of refinement that the hotels uptown are looking for. And they pay well too."

The last statement was enough to soften the scowl on his father's face. He rubbed his beard, considering. Zander held his breath until, at last, his father said, "I will give you two days to find a job in one of these hotels. If you don't, you come work with us."

Two days was hardly any time at all, especially since Zander was certain his father was including the rest of that day as one of the two. Which meant he had to act fast. "I'll go right now," he said, crossing to the door and taking his coat and hat from the stand. "I'll head uptown and inquire at every fine hotel I can find." Although what he would be inquiring for had nothing to do with work. Surely, the employees at whatever hotel Lord Selby and his friends were staying at would know they had a duke under their roof.

His father didn't stop him as he headed out the door, which was a good sign. He hated to leave Anya to an afternoon of what was likely to be work that was too strenuous for her, but his new idea of how to look for Xavier had lit a fire under him. He didn't know why he hadn't thought to go to the fancy hotels uptown—hotels that would never let him through the door, looking as shabby and working-class as he did—ostensibly to inquire about work before. Coming up with the idea now made him feel as though he'd been an idiot and lost precious days in his search for Xavier.

His buoyed hopes began to sink at the very first hotel he went to, though. Not only were they not hiring, the manager he spoke to at the back entrance was utterly unwilling to divulge a single thing about any of the guests staying there. The second hotel was exactly the same, and the third. Zander understood the importance of maintaining discretion at hotels that catered to the upper-classes, but it had never been so damned inconvenient.

He tried lingering around the front of every luxury hotel on Broadway leading up to Central Park, looking in through the windows and hoping he might catch a glimpse of Xavier or Lord Selby or the others, but the hotel doormen caught on to what he was doing and chased him away, and by the time he neared Fifty-Ninth Street, he was certain a policeman was following him. And after the last few months of his life, he didn't think he would ever trust a police officer again.

He had no choice but to give up for the moment. At the same time, he was loath to head back to the crowded, noisy, dirty tenements of the Lower East Side. He crossed Fifty-Ninth Street and headed into the park, telling himself he had a chance of finding Xavier there. They'd met in a park, after all, so perhaps the fates would conspire for them to meet in a park once more.

Central Park was as crowded as the rest of the city in

the late afternoon, though. It didn't matter how deep into the park Zander walked or how desperately he searched the faces of the men idling away there or hurrying from one place to another, none them were Xavier. The terrifying thought that Xavier was gone forever, that they would never see each other again, began to tighten its grip around Zander's heart. His breath came in shorter and shorter gasps, and his hands started to tingle and go numb. He tried to force himself to breath, but the panic that had started to seep around him, like spilled ink spreading across parchment, wouldn't let him go.

He turned, intending to run back the way he came, and smashed headlong into a small boy who was tearing across the park in an odd reflection of the way Zander felt. The boy went crashing to his bottom after barreling into Zander.

"Are you all right, son?" Zander asked, crouching to check on the boy.

The boy was pale, with dark, curly hair that needed to be cut and soulful, hazel eyes. Something about him was familiar, though Zander couldn't put his finger on it. He was dressed in finely-tailored clothes, definitely a member of society's elite and not an urchin. The poor thing was stunned to find himself flat on his back.

"Let's get you back on your feet," Zander said, shifting to kneel and to lift the boy to a standing position. He set about brushing the dirt and grass off of the boy's fine coat. "Where's your nanny?" he asked, assuming any child dressed as well as the boy would have someone looking after him.

"She didn't come with us," the boy said in a British accent.

"No? That's a shame," Zander said, attempting to brush the boy's hair out of his eyes. "Who's looking after you, then?"

"No one," the boy said. "I'm running away. I want to go home."

"Running away?" Zander broke into a smile. He'd tried to run away on a regular basis when he was this boy's age.

"Don't listen to him," a well-dressed, exhausted-looking American woman said, charging toward him. "He's a filthy little liar."

"I am not," the boy said with a pout, moving to hide behind Zander.

The woman sighed impatiently. "Alan, enough of this. You're far too old for these kinds of tricks."

"No," the boy said firmly, stomping a foot. "I want to go home."

"You are home," the woman said. "And don't you like this big, pretty park? Don't you like the lovely apartment Granddad has bought for us all?"

"No," the boy stomped again.

"Alan!" the woman snapped in exasperation. "I won't have you behaving like this." She stormed forward, reaching for the boy.

The boy—Alan—tried to get away from her, but

tripped over Zander's legs, as he was still kneeling. That gave the woman—who Zander presumed was Alan's mother or perhaps aunt, since they had different accents and didn't seem to like each other much—the chance to rush in and catch him. She grabbed his hand and wrenched him to his feet. Poor Alan burst into tears. Again, Zander knew how he felt.

"Is there anything I can help you with?" Zander asked as he rose to his feet.

"No," the woman said without turning to look at him as she dragged Alan off across the park. She couldn't possibly be the boy's mother. She clearly didn't care for him at all, or so Zander assumed from the way she clamped her hand over his wrist to drag him instead of holding his hand. She might have been some sort of society nanny, although she was dressed too well for it.

He watched them with a frown, taking a few steps to follow them, as they headed toward Fifth Avenue. Something wasn't right, but he couldn't place what it was. His head was such a jumbled mess after everything that had happened to him in the last few days, the last few weeks, really. Even though the boy was younger, something about him made Zander think of Anya. Perhaps it was the way the woman had dragged the boy off. His heart went straight to worrying about how his little sister was treated by the rest of the family and what fate might befall her without a protector. That scrambled with the feeling of familiarity he had regarding the boy and the woman until all he could do was feel hopeless. He didn't want the world to be a cruel and loveless place, but he feared it was.

He turned and headed south, knowing he couldn't avoid returning home forever. His entire life felt as though it hung in the balance between hope and happiness if he could find Xavier and years of despairing misery if he couldn't.

CHAPTER 18

At some point, Xavier was going to have to start sleeping well again, otherwise he would fall apart completely, body and mind. But after the day he'd spent with Jasper, searching for Zander, and the evening he'd passed at The Slippery Slope, watching the cabaret act as Jasper plied him with alcohol in an attempt to get him to relax, that night wasn't it. He'd wanted to enjoy himself at The Slippery Slope, and he might have too, if not for the weight of Zander's absence pressing down on him.

In the morning, he was groggy, his head throbbed, and his mouth felt fuzzy, but he forced himself to get up, scrub himself vigorously, both to get clean and to start the blood moving through his veins again, and dragged himself down to the hotel dining room to join Blake and the others for breakfast.

"If it weren't for the fact that I know you've been

searching for your friend, I would say you had quite the night last night," Gleason teased him with a wry grin.

"If not for missing Zander, I would have," Xavier admitted. He should have been more circumspect. He should have shown deference to his betters and presented himself with decorum at all times. But his head was as thick as a whale omelet, his eyes stung, and there didn't seem to be enough coffee in all of Manhattan to make him feel human again.

"Any luck at all?" Niall asked sympathetically. Even though Xavier tried to refuse, he piled eggs, bacon, and toast on a plate in front of Xavier. In thanks, Xavier tried not to vomit at the sight. "It will make you feel better, believe me."

"If it stays down," Xavier mumbled. He took a few, ginger bites, then fought off the nausea by telling the others, "You remember Miss Blaise Rose, don't you?" When they nodded—and smirked—Xavier went on with, "She—that is, Jasper Werther—gave me his card. He's the only person I know in Manhattan. He lives and works at a club on Bleeker Street called The Slippery Slope."

To Xavier's surprise, a man seated at the table next to them, who was close enough to overhear, dropped his fork on his breakfast plate. He turned bright red, then immediately got up and moved to another table at the far end of the restaurant.

"It's that kind of a club, is it?" Gleason asked with a laugh.

Xavier nodded.

"That explains how wretched you are this morning," John said. He and Gleason shared a grin before John appeared to remember that he hated Gleason and frowned again.

"Jasper is a New Yorker," Xavier explained. "He thinks he can help find Zander. Last night, we asked nearly everyone who works at the club and the regulars to keep an eye out for Zander."

"That's the best way to find him," Gleason said with a definitive nod. He would know, so Xavier felt fractionally better.

"I wish we had the same sort of connections as you do in our search for Alan," Blake sighed, rubbing his eyes.

He looked as bad as Xavier did. Even though Blake had given him leave not to work as his valet until he found Zander, Xavier still felt responsible for the man. He assumed Niall was doing things like helping Blake dress and caring for his clothing, but as far as Xavier was concerned, Blake was wearing the wrong tie to go with his suit, the suit itself had wrinkles, Blake's collar wasn't pressed correctly, and if Xavier didn't find Zander soon so that the two of them could move forward together and he could resume his proper duties, more than one thing was going to drive him mad.

"We don't even know if Annamarie is in the city anymore," Blake went on with a sigh. "Nothing we've done so far has turned up so much as a whisper of her."

"Don't lose heart, darling," Niall said in a quiet voice, resting a hand over Blake's. "Just because Mr. Cannon's associates and friends have been unwilling to help us so far doesn't mean they won't help us today or tomorrow."

"I suppose that means we will all be continuing our searches today," John said, slapping his hands on the table so loudly that Xavier winced, then standing.

"It would appear so," Gleason said, rising with him and sending him a challenging stare over the table.

"I've told you, I don't need your help," John said. "Why don't you assist Xavier with his search?"

"Oh, so you've located Lady Selby, then, have you?" Gleason asked, flirting with John as much as he challenged him.

John muttered something that sounded very much like an off-color curse. Xavier's head pounded too much to bother following the course of their argument, or courtship, or whatever it was. He took a few more careful bites of his breakfast, a few more swigs of black coffee, and decided it actually was helping.

"You should stop at a chemist for some aspirin before continuing your search," Niall advised him as he and Blake stood to leave the table.

Xavier nodded his thanks, then watched his friends —if he could rightfully call them that when he felt so much below them—leave the restaurant. That left him alone. Alone in a world he didn't quite fit into. Alone with luxury and opulence all around him, but only emptiness in his heart. His employment was what it was, and he would always live right at the edges of a finer class of people than himself, but without Zander there to share it with him, that life would never seem like his own.

He ended up taking Niall's advice and stopping in at a chemist—which wasn't called that in New York and earned him a few strange looks before someone figured out what he was asking about—for aspirin. It hadn't fully taken effect as he rode in a cab back down to the Bowery, but by the time he stepped through the doors into the colorful, exciting world of The Slippery Slope, he felt at least half human.

"Darling, there you are," Jasper greeted him almost as soon as he stepped into the grand music hall, just before lunchtime. Jasper was dressed impeccably as usual, but unlike the day before, his face was completely clean of any sort of cosmetic. In fact, he hadn't shaved either, which gave his otherwise lean and beautiful face a touch of ruggedness.

"Jasper," Xavier nodded to him in greeting. He wished he hadn't moved his head quite so much after the gesture was done.

Jasper either didn't notice or didn't have time to make note of it. "I have news for you," he said, grabbing Xavier by the arm and tugging him across the room to a table near the empty stage at the front of the hall, where two decidedly masculine men sat having lunch with two elegantly-dressed fairies. "But you're not going to like it," Jasper added before they reached the table.

Xavier's already touchy stomach twisted. "I'm not

going to like it?" he asked, his sense of foreboding amplified by how horrible he felt.

"Well, you might like it, but there's a catch," Jasper said. Xavier wished he'd dispense with the theatrics and get to the point, but that wasn't particularly Jasper. Instead, he pulled Xavier over to the table and introduced him to its occupants. "Ladies and gentlemen, I would like to introduce you to Mr. Xavier Lawrence, valet to his grace, the Duke of Selby, and star-crossed lover in search of his missing heart."

Xavier's brow shot to his hairline, in spite of his headache. He'd never been introduced in quite such a grand manner before. "How do you do?" He bowed to the men at the table as though he'd just been introduced to the queen. And, in a manner of speaking, he was being introduced to the queen. Two of them, in fact.

"This is Lady Lollipop," Jasper gestured to a beautiful young thing dressed all in pink and white...who hadn't shaved yet either, "and her friend, Mr. Patterson." The man nodded. "And here we have Miss Terry and her beau, Mr. Fuller." The second couple nodded as well.

"It's always a pleasure to meet someone of obvious breeding and refinement," Miss Terry said in a bass that was at least an octave lower than Xavier's voice.

"Thank you." Xavier nodded elegantly, wondering if he were still tipsy from the night before. But no, The Slippery Slope was a haven for exactly the sort of people who lived life in more vibrant colors than everyone else. They had been kind to him the night before, and he had the feeling from the excitement in Jasper's eyes that they were about to help him again.

"Have a seat," Mr. Fuller said, pulling out the chair beside him.

Xavier sat, Jasper sitting next to him. "Tell them what you told me," Jasper said, a note of seriousness in his otherwise cheerful demeanor.

"You're looking for a man named Plushenko, right?" Mr. Fuller said.

"I am," Xavier nodded. "Alexander Plushenko, but he goes by Zander."

"Zander and Xavier?" Lady Lollipop asked, emphasizing the "Z" sound. "That sounds dazzling." She emphasized the "Z" again.

"Pure coincidence," Xavier said, smiling and trying to be patient. He glanced back to Mr. Fuller, urging him with a look to go on.

"There are a couple of Plushenkos working for Peterman Contracting right now on a new apartment building," Mr. Fuller said. "I handle payment of wages for Peterman. We've got three Plushenkos on a job down on Essex Street—Dmitri, Pavel, and Yuri. Do any of those names sound familiar?"

Xavier sucked in a breath as a faint memory from the middle of the chaos with Zander struck him. "Dmitri. Something about that sounds familiar, but I don't—"

"Wait," Jasper said, holding up a hand and grinning.

"Dmitri is the father of the other two," Mr. Patterson took up the story. "I work as a clerk for Mr. Peterman, and the day before yesterday, I overheard a conversation in which old Dmitri begged Mr. Peterman to hire his other son who'd just come home after being away."

Xavier jerked straighter, excitement pulsing through him so hard that it made his pounding head dizzy. "That's him," he said, so breathless he could hardly get a word out. "That has to be him."

"It could be," Mr. Patterson said, exchanging a look with Mr. Fuller as Lady Lollipop snuggled closer to him, hugging his arm. "Plushenko isn't the most common name around, but there are loads of them. So I wouldn't get your hopes up too high."

"But it's the best lead I've had since I started searching," Xavier said. He stood, turning to Jasper. "What are we waiting for? Where is this construction sight?"

"That's the catch," Jasper said gravely. "We've already been there."

Xavier sat with a thud. "It's where Sal and Mick work, isn't it?" he asked, already knowing the answer.

Jasper nodded. "Of all the places for your sweetheart's possible father and brother to work, they would work at a site that also employs two men who likely want to kill us, or worse."

Xavier blew out a heavy breath, blinking at the tabletop as he shoved a hand through his hair. It felt as though he were so close, but still miles and miles away.

He shook his head, deciding quickly. "We have to risk it," he said. "This is the best chance of finding Zander that we have so far. We have to figure out a way to ask around that construction site to see if those men are Zander's family without being seen by Sal and Mick."

"Good luck with that," Mr. Fuller said. "Those two you mentioned, Sal and Mick, they're what you might call big men on the job. The others look up to them."

Xavier rolled his shoulders and winced. "We still have to go," he said, knowing it was true, but dreading everything that might happen. He sent Jasper a look of appeal.

"Darling," Jasper said, sitting straighter. "Why do you think I have my manly look on today?"

Xavier smiled, grateful beyond measure that he had a friend who was willing to stick his neck out for him in an effort that could be far, far more dangerous than either of them needed. "It's still early," he said, rising again. "Perhaps if we're lucky, we can ask around before the workers are fully awake for the day."

"It's the best we can do," Jasper said, getting up to join them.

They said their goodbyes to Xavier's new friends, gathered their coats and hats, and headed out into the sunny morning. They were able to reach Essex Street and the construction site much faster than the day before, since they knew exactly where they were going and didn't bother to stop for food or to question locals along the way. Unlike the day before, however, Xavier's stomach twisted into knots at the sight of the place.

"How do we get close enough to ask questions without giving ourselves away to people we don't want to encounter?" Xavier asked as he and Jasper walked casually past the site, hats pulled low, collars turned up, as though they were two businessmen on their way to a meeting trying to fend off the chill.

"First, we should keep an eye out for our friends from yesterday," Jasper said in a near whisper, glancing over his shoulder as they passed the far end of the site.

They reached the street corner and paused, as if waiting for traffic to pass. Fortunately, there was a fair bit of traffic.

"Excuse me, sir, do you have the time?" Jasper asked a bored-looking gentleman waiting to cross the street as well. He gestured for Xavier to search the construction site for Sal and Mick as he waited for the gentleman to take out his pocket watch. Once the man did, Jasper knocked his arm, causing him to drop the watch. "Oh, I'm so sorry," he said, bending to help the man fetch it, but actually making it harder to pick up.

Xavier stepped to one side and squinted hard at the half-constructed building. He could see at once that it would be nearly impossible to tell if Sal and Mick were anywhere near. While a great many of the workers were within sight, just as many seemed to be working tucked away inside the unfinished structure. Xavier stepped to the side, craning his neck to see deeper into the building.

He had the oddest stroke of luck when one of the other men waiting to cross the street turned to see what he was staring at as well, and then another, and then two more. They all stared into the building as though there were something worth seeing in there. It was uncanny, but Xavier wasn't above using it.

"Dear Lord, what is that?" he asked in alarm, taking a few, bold steps toward the site.

The four men who thought there was something to see jumped with him. Their entire group moved in closer to the site, and as soon as they did, Xavier discreetly shifted to stand behind them, shielded from anyone who might be looking out at them.

"What do you lot think you're staring at?" a gruff man who seemed to be dressed just a tad better than the workers shouted at them from a spot near the front of the site. Xavier figured he might have been the foreman.

The men with him flinched and hurried back to the street corner. They'd done their job, though. Xavier spotted Sal and Mick working together with two other men to attach two beams together. Before they could so much as turn their heads or sense they were being spied on, Xavier rushed away, catching up with Jasper.

"They're there," he whispered. "Working near the front, slightly to the left side."

"Then we'll head around to the back on the right side," Jasper said, touching his arm, then leading him around the fully-constructed building next to the site.

To Xavier, it felt as though they were leaping through hoops and going to great lengths merely on the off chance that they might encounter someone who could possibly know where Zander could be located. There were far too man unknowns and a great deal too much fuss for his liking, but there was nothing else they could do. They circled back behind the buildings, heading through a dirty alley that left Xavier with the feeling that the walls would cave in on them if they breathed too hard.

Even there, they weren't able to continue with their mission alone. They encountered a small girl with blond hair, blue eyes, and a wary expression stepping away from the back corner of the construction site, carrying an empty bucket with a dirty cloth in it. She paused to stare at Xavier and Jasper as they scooted past her, but she didn't say a word.

"Now, how are we supposed to figure out which ones the Plushenkos are and ask about Zander?" Xavier said as they stepped out of the alley and into the noise of the construction site.

His question was immediately answered for him with a deep, furious cry of, "You!"

The shout was enough to freeze the blood in Xavier's veins, and he nearly tripped over a pile of construction refuse. That was only the beginning of his reaction. A moment later, he spotted an enraged man whom he remembered from the immigration office charging toward them—Zander's father. He was both elated to know the information they'd been given was good and Zander was now within his reach, and terrified at the look of murder in Zander's father's eyes.

"What do we do?" Jasper squeaked by Xavier's side, grabbing his arm.

Xavier didn't have time to think, only to act. "Where

is Zander?" he asked, backing up into the alley as the furious man marched up to him, his fists balled at his sides.

"You stay away from my son," Zander's father bellowed. "He wants nothing to do with you perversions of nature."

"I beg your pardon?" Jasper said, straightening in offense for a moment.

"Please," Xavier said, throwing caution to the wind. "I love him. I have to speak to him again. Just tell me where he is."

"No," the man shouted. He pointed a hard finger back down the alley. "You go! You will never see Alexander again. I will not have you fairies spoiling him more than he is already spoiled."

"Just tell him that Xavier is looking for him," Xavier pleaded with him. "Tell him he can find me at The Slippery Slope."

"You go now or I will kill you," Zander's father said, bending to pick up a long piece of lumber with a few, bent nails in one end. It wasn't much of a weapon, but Xavier was certain in the right hands, Zander's father's hands, it would be deadly.

"Please," Xavier called over his shoulder as Jasper tugged him along the alley, urging him to run. "Please just tell him Xavier is looking for him."

Zander's father roared at him, almost like a bear. It would have been comical if the man wasn't fully capable of ending their lives.

Xavier and Jasper tore back down the alley, heading for the street. They nearly bowled over the little girl—who had watched the entire confrontation with wide eyes—in their flight.

"What do we do now?" Xavier asked as they burst out onto the street, then immediately tried to appear casual, as though their lives weren't in danger.

The little girl wandered out to the street with them, staring at them silently.

Jasper shrugged. "We go back to The Slippery Slope," he said. "Perhaps someone else has heard something more specific about your sweetheart, like where he lives or if he's found a job other than working here."

Xavier nodded, wiping the sweat from his brow with the back of his sleeve as he did. "I suppose it's all we can do," he sighed. He just wished that fleeing the construction site and the first, real clue he'd found as to Zander's whereabouts didn't feel like giving up and letting Zander slip away.

CHAPTER 19

For the second day in a row, Zander met nothing but rejection and tight-lipped hotel staff as he searched for any sign of Xavier in Midtown and along Broadway. He'd been so certain when he started out that he would be able to catch a glimpse of Xavier or find some sort of clue that would lead him to Lord Selby. He feared that desperation was making him sloppy, but he couldn't help it. He was, indeed, desperate.

His father had gone back on his word to let Zander search for a job in a hotel the night before. He and Zander's brothers had returned from work in the evening with stories of how short-handed the construction project was and how Zander's father had promised the foreman he would bring another man with him to work the next day. It hadn't mattered how much Zander protested, his father was adamant that he give up his search for Xavier, give up his dreams, and do as he was told. For a man of Zander's age to be spoken to like he was a child was bad enough, but his father had spent several minutes railing at him to find a wife and start behaving like a real man too.

The only way Zander had been able to avoid being dragged off to work with his father was by waking up before the rest of the family, dressing in silence—which was difficult to do, considering he shared a room with both his older brothers and one younger brother who had employment as a newsboy—and to slip out of the apartment before anyone else awoke. He'd headed straight up to Midtown, watching the city wake up as he did.

He would have enjoyed the sleepy, predawn city and the relative calm that blanketed it before another workday began if not for his burning need to find at least some sign of Xavier. But by lunchtime, he was beginning to feel as though his plan to inquire in hotels was an abysmal failure. No one would speak to him, and once again, he ended up with a policeman on his tail. It all seemed so horribly hopeless, as if the world were against him after all.

Halfway through the afternoon, Zander gave up and headed south toward home. He walked rather than taking an omnibus, hands shoved in his pockets and collar turned up to hide his scowl from the throng of people walking along with him. He didn't know what to do, whether he should resign himself to the fate his father had mapped out for him, whether he should pack his things and leave his family to start a new life in the city on his own, whether he should try auditioning for ballet companies in New York, or perhaps Philadelphia or Boston, or whether he should try to somehow scrape together the fare to return to London and seek out Xavier there. His mind couldn't settle on just one thing, but the more he thought about abandoning his family, the more he worried about little Anya.

More than once, as Zander walked past a church, some of them with music and the scent of incense wafting out their doors, he thought of stopping and praying. Maybe God could help him if no one else could. Once he reached the Bowery, the raucous clubs and resorts beckoned to him with the same flashes of music and perfume. Unsurprisingly, the clubs held a far greater appeal for him. Zander found himself turning onto Bleeker Street and approaching one of the more notorious clubs that he'd heard of, The Slide. The club across the street, The Slippery Slope, looked to be doing a bit more business that day, but he wasn't sure he wanted that much company as he bought a drink to drown his misery.

"Are you certain I can't get you something else?" the pretty, painted fairy behind the bar asked him as he poured whatever drink Zander had ordered, he'd forgotten as soon as he ordered it. "You look like you could use some cheering up."

"I could," Zander said, sending the man a weak smile. "But not that way, not today."

"Trouble with your sweetheart?" the bartender asked.

Zander laughed humorlessly. "You could say that." He picked up the drink and downed half of it in one gulp. "I've lost him," he said, setting his glass down and staring at it with a sigh.

The bartender perked up as he raked Zander with a hungry gaze. "If you're looking for another sweetheart, I volunteer. You're just the sort I could eat for breakfast." He licked his lips to prove his point.

Zander sent the man an appreciative grin, but shook his head. "No, I mean, I've literally lost him. We met in London, enjoyed a beautiful ocean crossing—well, half of it was beautiful—but when we reached New York, we were split up, and now I can't find him."

"What a beautifully tragic story," the bartender said, resting his elbow on the bar and leaning with his cheek in his hand. "Still, I would never be so careless as to misplace someone as delicious as you." He sighed, drinking in the sight of Zander in a way that had Zander wriggling in discomfort. He'd forgotten what it felt like to be ogled in a place where no one cared who fancied whom. "You've got the physique of a dancer," the bartender went on.

"That's because I am a dancer," Zander said, lifting his glass to finish his drink.

The bartender stood straighter. "Are you? Because

we're hiring, if you're interested. Three shows a night and matinees on the weekend."

Zander nearly choked on his whiskey. It was the most bizarre solution to his problem that he could have thought of. No doubt working as a dancer at The Slide would involve more than dancing, but it would likely enable him to earn the money he needed to afford passage back to London.

Which was exactly the position he'd found himself in when he met Xavier in the first place.

"Did you say you just returned from England?" asked another man who had been sitting at the far end of the bar.

Zander wasn't keen on someone listening in to his conversation, but he nodded and said, "I did."

"And that you're looking for your sweetheart?" the man asked on.

An unexpected jolt of hope struck Zander. "I am."

"Any chance that sweetheart is an Englishman?" The man slipped off his stool as if he would move closer.

"He is," Zander said. "His name is—"

Before Zander could finish, the club's front door crashed open, and a gangling young lad of about fourteen scrambled in, out of breath and pink-faced.

"Ricky, Ricky," he gasped, rushing up to the bar and grabbing onto the edge. "The police are coming. There's going to be a raid."

As quickly as he'd dashed into the club, the boy turned and ran out again. Unfortunately, the man who seemed to have some sort of information about Xavier dashed out with him.

"No, wait!" Zander tried to chase after him, but before he could reach the door, a uniformed police officer stepped in with a menacing grin.

Zander heard the bartender—Ricky—mutter a curse as the policeman strode up to the bar. "Good afternoon, Officer Morton," Ricky greeted the man in a sweet voice. "And what brings you to our humble establishment today."

Zander took a few more steps toward the door, intending to leave before there was more trouble. The last thing he needed was to get caught up in a raid. But The Slide was the first place where he'd had even a little luck in tracking down Xavier, and if there was any chance he could learn more, he had to stay.

"Just checking in to see if you've paid your insurance money," Officer Morton said, leaning against the bar.

"Insurance money," Ricky said with a confused look, though he was still pretending to be friendly and biddable. "Let me see."

"Because your friends across the street didn't pay theirs," Officer Morton went on.

"Which friends?" Ricky played dumb. Zander was certain he knew exactly what was going on.

"The Slippery Slope," Officer Morton said. "They didn't pay, so it's likely they'll have a full house tonight for the show, if you know what I mean."

"Oh yes, I do," Ricky said, leaning across the bar to

flirt with the officer in what Zander thought was an outrageous move.

Zander knew what the officer was talking about too. The Slippery Slope was going to be raided that night. More than ever, he felt as though he needed to get out of the neighborhood and find another way to search for Xavier. But there was still the possibility that Ricky would know something, if Zander could just stick around long enough to find out.

"Why don't you join me in the back room, Officer Morton, and we'll just see about that insurance payment," Ricky said, batting his eyelashes and sashaying down the length of the bar toward a small door.

Officer Morton followed with a wide grin, though when he noticed Zander gaping at him, he snapped, "What do you think you're gawping at?"

"Nothing," Zander said, jumping into motion and rushing out of the club.

He didn't stop once he reached the street. He pulled his collar up, tipped his hat low over his eyes, and rushed on in the direction of home, hoping no one who shouldn't would see him on Bleeker Street and get any ideas about turning him in to the police. Twice was enough. There was no way he would go through that again. The only thing that might have stopped him was a hint of someone speaking in an English accent on the other side of the street, but when he turned to see if there was any possibility it could be Xavier, all he saw were the backs of two men attempting to conceal themselves the way he was as they stepped into The Slippery Slope.

He almost backtracked and crossed the street to warn the men, and perhaps the entire club, of the impending raid, but decided it wasn't worth the risk. He hoped that young lad who had warned Ricky would warn the owners of The Slippery Slope.

There was nothing else for him to do but to hurry on home. Whether he would pack up his belongings and leave his family for good or whether he would stay for Anya's sake and figure out a way to find Xavier and avoid his father's demands remained to be seen.

The choice seemed to be made for him the moment he entered the apartment to find that his father was already home.

"You," his father shouted, rounding on him the moment he stepped through the door. "You worthless, ungrateful son." His father marched over to him and slapped Zander's face before Zander could so much as ask what was going on.

Anya and their mother were the only other ones home. Anya gasped and burst into tears as Zander stumbled in the wake of his father's blow, but his mother meekly looked away.

"That was uncalled for," Zander protested, standing tall and touching a hand to the side of his face. "I'm not some child you can beat whenever you want."

"You are my son, and you will do as you're told," his father raged.

"I am a grown man with talents that would be wasted if I chose to do things your way," Zander protested.

His father didn't so much as blink at Zander's statement. "I found you a job. I gave my word that you would do it. How do you think it looks for me to turn up empty-handed when I promised another worker?"

"You shouldn't have promised anything on my behalf to begin with," Zander argued.

"You are my son, and you will do as I say," his father repeated. "You will not go around with your wicked, fairy friends and not send them looking after you."

Zander frowned, trying to deduce from his father's imperfect English what he meant. Did his father think the men who had caused the fight at the construction site the day before were somehow connected to him just because they shared a taste for men?

"Tomorrow, you will come work at the building," his father said with a firm nod.

"No, Father, I will not," Zander said. "I will go my own way and look for—"

Before he could finish, his father clamped a hand around his arm and marched him across the room. "You will do as I say or you will go," he insisted. "You will not get away from me again."

Zander thought those two points contradicted each other, but arguing would have done no good. His father marched him across the tiny apartment and threw him into the bedroom he'd shared with his brothers. Zander stumbled, and before he could regain his balance, his father slammed the door and locked it with a sharp click.

"This is outrageous," Zander shouted, throwing himself at the door, trying the handle, then banging on it when he found it was, indeed, locked tight. "You cannot lock me in my room like a prisoner."

"Are you willing to work for your keep?" his father asked through the door.

"Not doing construction," Zander called back.

"Then you stay where you are," his father said. His heavy footsteps marched away from the door.

"This is ridiculous," Zander growled, pivoting to lean his back against the door. He tore his hat off and threw it on one of the narrow beds—his father had grabbed him for the confrontation before he could get his coat and hat off—and slumped with his back against the door.

Once again, he was in prison. It seemed as though everything he did to save himself resulted in the walls closing around him more and more. He couldn't let things go on like this. There came a point when a man had to take drastic action, even if it burned bridges he wasn't certain he wanted to burn.

Not that he could burn anything when he was locked in his bedroom.

He sank to sit on the floor, burying his head in his hands and forcing himself to breathe steadily. He hadn't cried in the brig of the *Umbria*, and he wasn't about to cry now, but the temptation was hard to resist.

He wasn't sure how much time passed before a soft

knock sounded—not from the door, but from the window. Zander glanced up to find Anya staring in at him from outside. Considering how high up they were, the sight terrified him. He leapt up, rushing to the window and carefully opening it so he didn't knock Anya off the side of the building.

"What are you doing?" he asked, grabbing his sister around the waist and pulling her into the room.

She pointed over her shoulder out the window. "There's a fire escape."

Zander put her down and stuck his head out the window. There was a fire escape, but it ended three feet to the side of the window, outside of the window to the room his three sisters shared.

"Don't ever climb out like that again, Anya," he scolded her, staring down at a four-story drop. "You could have hurt yourself."

"I had to tell you something," Anya said.

Zander pulled his head back into the room and turned to her. "What do you have to tell me?"

"He said to say Xavier is looking for you," Anya said, staring up at him with her big, blue eyes.

Zander gasped, his heart slamming against his ribs. He dropped to his knees in front of Anya, grabbing her arms in a desperate grip. "Who said that? Where is he?"

"The fairies," Anya said. "Father said they were fairies too."

"Here?" Zander asked in disbelief.

Anya shook her head. "At the building. When I took

Father, Pavel, and Yuri their lunches. They were looking for you."

Zander couldn't help it. He burst into tears in spite of every effort he'd made to keep his emotions in check. Xavier was looking for him. He hadn't given up. Somewhere in the city, the love of his life was searching for him.

"Where is he?" he asked Anya. "Did he say where he was, where I could find him?"

Anya shrugged slightly and said, "They said they were going back to the slippery slope."

Zander's mouth fell open, and for a moment he thought he might be sick. If Anya had taken lunch to their father and brothers, she would have heard Xavier say he was looking for him just after noon. And if it was Xavier who had asked about him, and if he had gone straight back to Bleeker Street, there was a fair chance that Zander had been scant yards away from Xavier only a few hours before.

The joy he felt at that thought crashed quickly, though.

"There's going to be a raid," he said, dread pooling in his stomach as he wrenched himself to his feet. "The police are planning to raid The Slippery Slope tonight."

"How do you raid a slippery slope?" Anya asked.

Zander blinked down at her for a moment, no idea how to explain the sort of raid that would happen or the reasons why to an eight-year-old girl. He settled on, "The police think the fairies have done bad things, and they're going to try to capture them."

Anya clapped her hands to her mouth in shock.

Zander leapt into motion, lunging for the corner, where his suitcase from the ocean crossing sat. There wasn't room in any of the bureau drawers or the wardrobe for his things. He'd balked when his brothers insisted he keep everything he owned in his suitcase, but suddenly, he was glad for it. He had only a few things to throw into the case before closing it and buckling it shut.

"I have to go save the fairies," Zander said, heading for the window. He figured that was the only way to explain what he needed to do to a little girl. When he reached the window, he tossed his suitcase over to the fire escape, glad beyond measure when it landed safely. He stuck one leg out the window, calculating how he was going to climb over to the fire escape, then turned back to Anya. "Anya, I have to leave you," he said, heart full of regret. "But if I can find a way to come back, maybe even if I can find a way to take you with me somehow, would you want to go?"

"To fairyland?" Anya asked, her face lighting up.

"Possibly?" Zander answered with a laugh born out of his excitement.

"Yes, take me to fairyland," Anya said, rushing to the window.

"I'll come back for you if I can," Zander said, leaning toward her to kiss her forehead.

There wasn't time for more. He heard stirring in the

apartment, and whether that meant his father had figured out he was trying to get away, his brothers had come home, or someone was looking for Anya, he couldn't stay. Besides, Xavier was looking for him, and now Zander had a good idea where he might be. But he had to get to The Slippery Slope soon, before the raid started, or else the whole thing might be for naught.

CHAPTER 20

The sun had set and the yellow glow of lamplight that passed for darkness in New York City bathed Bleeker Street as Zander reached the corner of the Bowery and turned. He knew something was wrong from the moment he headed on toward the various clubs, resorts, and dance halls that were now glowing with life and sound after dark. He knew the area was popular with everyone from working class men looking for a bit of fun after their jobs were done to society's young people out "slumming" for a night, as they called it, but there seemed to be a few too many dour-faced men with anxious, suspicious looks, as if they were waiting to pounce. After what Zander had heard of the plans for a raid earlier, he could only believe that those men were police officers in disguise.

He gripped the handle of his suitcase and walked

faster, alternately praying he didn't draw anyone's notice and not caring who stared at him, as long as he could get to The Slippery Slope before whatever madness was in the offing started.

"Are you planning to stay a while?" a sweet-faced man in drag asked him from the upper window of a building beside one of the smaller clubs. "I've got room in my bed if you are."

Zander would have paused to banter with the young man on any other day. The entire area of the Bowery and Bleeker Street was famous for its wildness, and there were few other places a man could get away with exchanging a few, cheeky words with another man dressed as a woman.

"I'd be careful tonight if I were you," he called up to the young man. "It's going to be a busy night." He nodded back over his shoulder to the men he suspected were police at the end of the road.

The young man in drag gasped and pulled his head back through the window, closing it behind him. Zander could only hope he would warn others and that they would stay out of trouble.

Trouble was exactly what he felt like he was walking into as he reached The Slippery Slope. Whatever entertainments were on that night, they were already loud and exuberant, and men and women in various forms of dress and intoxication poured in and out of the door, gathering on the street in front of the club, laughing and fawning over each other. It was a recipe for disaster, but if there was any chance that Zander might find Xavier in the throbbing, swirling crowd, he would take the risk.

The main hall of the club was pulsing with noise, excitement, and an undeniable sexual tension as Zander pushed his way in through the crush around the door, using his suitcase to wedge people out of his way. A few took offense at his rough tactics, but just as many of the men with powdered faces and rouged cheeks gazed adoringly at him, as if they didn't mind being pushed around at all.

"Mine!" a rather large fairy with lovely brown eyes surrounded by kohl declared, grabbing Zander as soon as he stepped past the initial crush and into the sea of round tables packed with chairs, all of which were occupied, as far as Zander could see. "This one is definitely mine," the large fairy shouted.

"Actually, I'm already spoken for," Zander said.

He pushed to his toes and searched the crowded hall. There was enough smoke in the air from cigarettes and cigars to make it more difficult to see. The upbeat, almost jarring music being played by a small band on the stage combined with the chatter of hundreds of men and women made it next to impossible to hear anything either. Some sort of a cabaret show was taking place on the stage that involved a line of ladies that resembled French cancan dancers, but when they lifted their skirts to do their high kicks, it was blatantly obvious they weren't women. Zander would have found the ribald act hilarious, if he didn't know what was waiting for everyone on the street outside.

"I'm looking for Xavier Lawrence," he shouted to the large fairy, who still had his hand on Zander's arm.

"Oh! You must be the Russian dancer," the fairy said.

Even though Zander could barely hear him over the din, his heart dropped to his feet before leaping up to his throat. "You know Xavier? Is he here?"

The fairy turned Zander to the side and pointed toward the far end of the bar, just a few yards from the stage. There, seated next to Jasper Werther, looking like one of the only people in the room who wasn't enjoying himself, was Xavier.

Zander shouted wordlessly, but his cry of joy was drowned by the rest of the noise in the room. The large fairy let go of him, and he stumbled forward, shoving people out of the way as politely as he could when his whole being was overcome with pure happiness and relief for finding Xavier at last.

"Xavier!" he shouted at the top of his lungs, dodging a couple that were kissing as though they could swallow each other whole, right there in the middle of the public hall. "Xavier!"

At last, when Zander was about a third of the way into the hall, Xavier glanced up, and whatever he was saying to Jasper died on his lips. At first, Xavier's jaw dropped in surprise. Then his entire face lit with joy, and the blessed man burst into tears.

Zander thought he heard the distant sound of his

name as Xavier's mouth formed the word. "I'm coming!" Zander shouted in return. "I'm on my way!"

Xavier jumped off his stool and started toward Zander, but the crush of people blocked his way. Instead, as Zander ducked and dodged his way around far too many men having much too of a good a time, Xavier leapt toward the stage, climbing onto it and calling to Zander above everyone's heads. "You found me!"

Slowly, the noise in the hall began to die down as more and more people turned to see what Xavier was so ecstatic about on the stage and why Zander was pushing and shoving his way through the floor. As people caught on, they moved out of Zander's way, allowing him to make faster progress toward the stage.

To top things off, Jasper leapt onto the stage himself, and in a surprisingly booming stage voice declared, "Ladies and gentlemen, our star-crossed lovers are finally reunited!"

Whether the swirling mass of people around them had the first clue what Jasper was talking about or not, they all burst into loud applause and shouts of encouragement. It was like something out of a particularly wild dream as the crowd parted to allow Zander to run straight up to the stage. Xavier's face was bright red with excitement, and his eyes shone with relief and love. After more than a week of being kept apart, months of wondering who and where Xavier was before that, after imprisonment and betrayal, prejudice and frustration, Zander was only inches away from—

A booming gunshot rang out over the cheering, applauding hall. A split-second later, the sea of revelers burst into shouts and screams as dozens of uniformed and plain-clothes policemen flooded through the club's front door. The fairies and their patrons, everyone who had gone slumming for the night, and those who had simply come to see the show, scattered in every direction. What was more, the gap that had opened between Zander and the stage, between him and Xavier, quickly closed as the men who had made way for him moments before dashed and scattered to avoid the police.

"Zander!" Xavier shouted from the stage, rushing right to the edge and holding out his arms, as if he could pull Zander up onto the stage with him. "Hurry!"

Zander tried to do what he was told, but the surge of terrified patrons seemed to be pushing him farther away from Xavier instead of letting him get close. His suitcase was impeding his progress as well, but he'd be damned if he let that go. It felt like he was carrying his life with him, and if he could reach Xavier with all of his worldly possessions in tow, then the two of them could fly off together and he could leave this wretched world behind.

If he could reach Xavier to begin with.

"Stay right where you are!" a booming voice shouted over the scattering crowd, accompanied by the shrill sound of multiple police whistles. "Nobody move and nobody will get hurt!"

"Bully to that," Jasper shouted, leaping off the stage beside where Xavier stood. "This story is going to have a happy ending, dash it, and I am going to make sure that happens."

Jasper's determination spurred Zander forward once more. That, helped along by how fast the center of the hall cleared out as performers and patrons alike fled to the sides of the room, propelled Zander toward the stage. Jasper reached him halfway and grabbed his arm, pulling him along as if he could single-handedly force the outcome to the situation that he wanted.

Zander didn't care one way or another. He reached the stage, threw his suitcase onto it, then leapt up to Xavier's side with all the grace he could muster.

"Thank God," he gasped once he was able to drag Xavier into his arms. "I've been searching for you for days."

"I've been looking for you every moment since we arrived," Xavier groaned in return, then surged against him.

It was complete madness with the chaos of the raid happening all around them, but Zander clamped his arms around Xavier and kissed him for all he was worth. It was messy, bruising, and clumsy, but far and away the best kiss Zander had ever engaged in. It was so good that he didn't want to let Xavier go, even when Jasper shouted, "Time for that later. Run now!"

He had a point, particularly as the police whistles were growing louder and more men were being arrested and dragged out of the building. Zander let go of Xavier and lunged to grab his suitcase. Somewhere in the madness, he'd lost his hat, but that didn't seem to matter at the moment. Jasper had dashed to the back of the stage and was gesturing furiously for them to follow him, so Zander grabbed Xavier's hand and ran.

"The advantage of living in the building is that I know all of its secrets," Jasper panted, leading them down a backstage hallway, past a few dressing rooms, and on toward a door that appeared to be open to the night air.

Whatever had been going on in the side rooms and dressing rooms—and Zander had a good idea of what it was by the various states of undress of the men attempting to escape out the back door—news of the raid had reached everyone. Unfortunately, "everyone" included the police. Zander, Xavier, and Jasper were halfway down the hall when three uniformed officers appeared in the outside door, looking determined to arrest anyone they saw.

"No," Jasper shouted, changing directions abruptly and darting through a door that Zander almost didn't see.

Zander and Xavier followed Jasper into what turned out to be a stairwell. Jasper charged up the stairs—which instinct told Zander was a terrible idea, but they didn't appear to have much choice—and out through another small door three stories up. The hallway they ended up on was eerily quiet, compared to the rest of the building. Jasper fished in the pocket of his jacket, came up with a key, and had it ready to unlock one of the doors near the end of the hall.

"Welcome to my humble abode," he said in a hurry as

he threw open the door into a small but surprisingly neat apartment. "Please forgive me if I don't offer you tea and cake. We're in a bit of a hurry."

They darted through the apartment's main room and through to a bedroom. The bedroom was beautifully decorated as well, though just a bit fussy for Zander's tastes. Not that taste mattered as they shot toward the window and—Zander could now see the plan—the fire escape on the other side. Zander nearly laughed aloud at the sight of the House of Worth gown Jasper had worn to the ball aboard the *Umbria* handing from the wardrobe door.

"I hope you don't have a problem with heights," Jasper said, throwing open the window and stepping through. "Or questionably sturdy fire escapes."

"I'm amazed that the building has fire escapes at all," Xavier said, rushing out after Jasper.

"They're useful for more than just fires," Jasper said with a wink as Zander climbed out the window with his suitcase.

One look down once he was out on the fire escape and Zander wondered how anyone could risk their life on the brittle scaffolding that clung loosely to the side of the building. Jasper's fire escape was little more than a series of rusted, metal ladders connected by the narrowest of platforms. They weren't even as sturdy as the one at his family's tenement that he'd used to escape from home. Navigating that had been hard enough, but figuring out how to climb down the hair-raising ladders with a large suitcase was enough to take years off his life.

"Can't you just drop the suitcase and pick it up when we get down?" Xavier asked as Zander slowly made his way down the first ladder.

"I might have to," Zander confessed.

As soon as he made it down the ladder to the building's third floor, he fumbled his suitcase entirely, which sent it spilling to the street below, whether he wanted to drop it or not. He winced as the suitcase landed on its corner and split wide open, exposing everything he owned.

"At least we can climb down faster," he sighed, scurrying down the ladder after Xavier.

Not that speed did them any good. The shrill cry of a police whistle sounded at the end of the alley they were climbing down to, and before Zander and Xavier could reach the last ladder, just as Jasper jumped down to the street, two uniformed policemen saw them and broke into a run.

"Stop where you are!" one of them shouted.

"What do we do?" Xavier asked, pausing halfway down the last ladder.

"Keep going," Zander sighed. "We'll have a better chance if we're on the ground." A better chance of what, exactly, he wasn't sure.

"I've got this, lads," Jasper said, tugging at the ends of his sleeves, then marching forward to greet the policemen. "Gentlemen, there seems to have been some sort of a misunderstanding," he began.

As Xavier jumped the last few feet to the alley, Zander right behind him, and right as one of the policemen stepped forward as if to grab Jasper and subdue him, Jasper let fly a surprise right-hook that made contact with the policeman's face with a sickening crunch. Zander nearly stumbled and fell over at the surprising display of skilled violence from the otherwise refined fairy.

"You don't learn to survive in my line of work if you can't defend yourself," Jasper grunted, taking a swing at the other officer. "Go! Run!" he shouted over his shoulder at Zander and Xavier.

Zander lunged toward his ruined suitcase and the scattered pile of his clothes and belongings. He tried gathering them up, but it seemed like a fruitless endeavor.

"You're under arrest for perversion and assaulting a police officer," the first officer Jasper had punched growled.

"And my friends?" Jasper asked, ducking and dodging to avoid being grabbed by both policemen.

"They're under arrest too," the second officer said, starting after Zander and Xavier.

"You heard him," Jasper called out to them. He managed to stick his foot out and trip the second police officer, though that resulted in the first one clamping his arm around Jasper's chest and subduing him. "Run while you still can," Jasper shouted.

"You're going to have to leave it all," Xavier said, grabbing Zander's arms and tugging him away from his things.

With a growl, Zander rose and started after Xavier, toward the far end of the alley. He paused long enough to call out to Jasper, "What about you?"

Jasper was busy wrestling to get away from the first policeman. "Don't worry about me," he shouted. "Fairies have wings, remember?"

Zander started to laugh at the clever quip, but before he could, the policeman holding Jasper let go of him long enough to whip Jasper around so that he could punch him hard across the face.

Zander gasped and turned his full attention to Xavier and to outrunning the second policeman, who was still chasing them.

"Hurry," Xavier said, reaching for Zander's hand and pulling him along to the corner of the building. "I think we can cut through here and make it out to the street."

Zander nodded and picked up speed. He was more athletic than Xavier and leapt ahead of him in no time, but still held Xavier's hand and hurried him along. They made it out to the street before the second policeman was able to catch up to them. Their flight was helped by the fact that the street they burst into was a scene of absolute chaos as men in all forms and states of dress were being herded together by what seemed like a sea of policemen. Some of the unfortunate victims had their hands in cuffs, while others had given up fighting and stood sullenly in groups.

"There's a gap that way," Xavier whispered to Zander as they headed toward the edge of the group.

By some miracle, the policeman who was following them stopped his pursuit and turned instead to assisting the other officers who had already caught their victims. It was exactly the stroke of luck Zander and Xavier needed to rush past the edges of the crowd that had come to witness the raid and to walk on into the clear.

"My God, we actually got away," Xavier gasped as they slowed their flight to a walk, attempting not to look suspicious, then turned north as they reached the Bowery.

"We're not away until we're miles from here, safe and sound," Zander panted, his body aching and his emotions a wreck.

Xavier smiled at him, then reached out a hand to flag down a passing cab. It was another miracle, as far as Zander was concerned, that the carriage swung around to pick them up, although that miracle was less of a mystery when Xavier took a handful of bills out of his pocket and waved them at the driver.

"Fifty-Ninth and Fifth Avenue," he told the driver in as proper an accent as Zander had ever heard. "As fast as you can."

"Yes, sir," the driver said as Zander opened the carriage door.

"Never underestimate the power of a British accent and a handful of money," Xavier told Zander with a wink, jumping into the carriage behind him.

"After tonight," Zander said, sprawling across the carriage seat in exhaustion, "I never will."

CHAPTER 21

Xavier was out of breath, disheveled, and still slightly terrified for his life as he and Zander sank into the faded cab seat. His whole body ached from running and climbing, and from the general terror of nearly being arrested in a foreign country. But he'd never been happier in his life. Against all odds, he'd found Zander. And in a surprisingly short amount of time, all things considered.

He hadn't quite caught his breath yet, but he had to turn to Zander all the same to say, "You have no idea how—"

Zander stopped him flat as he grabbed Xavier's face, surged against him, and brought his mouth crashing down over Xavier's with blissful, punishing force. Xavier was helpless to do anything but moan and roll his eyes back and grab hold of Zander as if he might be torn away from him again at any moment. He couldn't get enough of Zander—his mouth, his tongue, the feel of his body, his entire presence. He kissed Zander back as if breathing didn't matter. All he needed was Zander.

He tried again with, "I didn't know if I would be able to—"

Zander cut him off again with a kiss and a possessive groan as he grabbed hold of Xavier and lifted him. Xavier wasn't entirely certain how it happened, and he hadn't known he was even capable of the position, but he found himself straddling Zander's lap, legs squashed madly against the seat, as Zander somehow tugged his shirt out of his trousers and slid his hands up the overheated, bare skin of Xavier's sides. His touch felt so good that Xavier went from panic to full arousal so fast he was afraid he'd come.

He wasn't sure he cared about that either, though. There would be plenty of time for proper seduction later, and as barmy as it was to slather desperate kisses all over his lover as they rode in a public carriage through some of the most crowded streets in one of the busiest cities in the world, that was all Xavier wanted to do. Zander was back in his arms at last.

The intensity of their burst of ardor couldn't last forever. Not when they were both so done in from their chase through The Slippery Slope. And as it turned out, breathing was important after all. He broke their kiss, and for a moment, he and Zander simply sat there, tangled in each other, foreheads resting together as they fought to catch their breaths. Gradually, Xavier became aware of how awkward the situation was. Zander still wore his coat over whatever other clothes he had on. Xavier had been surprised by the raid and had left his coat and hat at The Slippery Slope. He was now untucked and unbuttoned—though how Zander had managed to unbutton his jacket and waistcoat without him noticing was a mystery—and must have appeared thoroughly debauched.

All Xavier could manage to say as he gasped for air was, "What happened?"

"Do you mean just now? When we narrowly avoided me landing in jail for the third time in six months?" Zander said, somehow managing a clever smile. "Or when my father dragged me back to the festering tenement where my family of ten lives in three rooms? Or do you mean what happened when my entire life was turned upside down in the best way possible when I dragged a dapper valet aside for a little fumble in the dark in St. James's Park?"

Xavier couldn't help but laugh, then lean in to kiss Zander again—slowly this time, and with a smoldering passion instead of desperate lust, though he still felt that too. "Maybe all of it," he said, leaning back to look at Zander again.

"I don't know," Zander said with a shrug. "I stopped trying to make sense of my life a long time ago.

"That's probably wise," Xavier said, stealing another kiss.

Zander already had his arms around him, but he seemed to take that kiss as an invitation to let his hands roam free across Xavier's back and sides. It felt so good that Xavier seriously contemplated engaging in creative sexual acts with Zander right then and there. He only changed his mind about that when the carriage stopped at a crowded intersection. Even though it was dark, they hadn't closed the shades on the windows, and the pedestrians mere feet away outside of the carriage were frighteningly close.

It was enough to propel Xavier off of Zander's lap and onto the opposite carriage seat. "There's no sense in being arrested for gross indecency now when we've just gotten away from those charges," he said, tucking his shirt back into his considerably tighter trousers and attempting to do up his buttons with shaky hands.

"It's not called 'gross indecency' in New York," Zander said, adjusting the way he sat as well. "Although I can't remember what it is called here. Probably something that utterly misses the point, like public nuisance."

"Well, in my experience, you are rather a public nuisance," Xavier said, sending Zander a cheeky look.

Zander laughed, then reached across the gap between the seats, pulling Xavier back to his seat and kissing him again, in spite of the danger.

They managed to keep their clothes on and their heads about them all the way to Fifty-ninth Street and up to the doorway of The Fairmount.

"My God, is this where you're staying?" Zander asked, his brow shooting up, as they disembarked from the carriage and stepped up onto the curb.

"Mr. Cristofori insisted on a hotel overlooking Central Park," Xavier said.

"No, I mean I was here just yesterday," Zander said.

Xavier nearly missed a step as they crossed through the hotel door, which was held open for them. "You were here?"

"I told you, I've been searching for you," Zander said as they crossed the lobby. Several people eyed his and Xavier's disheveled state but did nothing to stop them as they started up the stairs. "I told my father I was looking for work in hotels."

"You were here?" Xavier repeated, blinking in disbelief. "Yesterday?"

"Yes."

"While Jasper and I were nearly being thrashed by some tough workman at the construction site on the Lower East Side where your father and brothers work?" The story Xavier had pieced together in his mind was laughable.

Zander stopped on the landing, gaping at him. "That was you and Jasper?" he asked. "My father and brothers couldn't stop talking about that fight yesterday."

"It wasn't much of a fight," Xavier admitted as they continued up the stairs. "Jasper punched the one fellow, then we ran for our lives."

"But still." Zander shoved a hand through his already messy hair. "You were within inches of me and I was within inches of you, so to speak, and neither of us knew it."

"I suppose that represents the fates trying to bring us back together," Xavier said.

Before Zander could comment, they rounded the corner of the landing and nearly ran headlong into Blake and Niall coming down the other way. Blake's look of frustration immediately lifted to delight.

"You found him," he said, beaming.

"Barely," Xavier admitted. "And nearly got arrested in the process."

"Arrested?" Niall asked.

"There was a raid on a club called The Slippery Slope," Zander explained.

Blake and Niall glanced between the two of them before Blake shook his head and said, "You'd better come up to the room and explain."

Xavier nodded—though he would rather have gone straight to his own room for a variety of reasons—and the four of them headed back up the stairs. When they reached the fourth floor, they came across John and Gleason.

"We were on our way to investigate the theater," John said.

"There's a premier tonight that my sources tell me Lady Selby is planning to attend," Gleason interrupted.

John narrowed his eyes at Gleason for interrupting, then went on with, "It looks like whatever this is might be more important than a show."

"Not in the hall," Niall said, stepping ahead to

unlock the door to his and Blake's room. "Just in case we say something that shouldn't be overheard."

Xavier felt a bit ridiculous as the six of them piled into Blake and Niall's hotel room. "I don't know what there is to say," he said. "I enlisted the help of Mr. Werther to search for Zander. Through his network of contacts, he was able to uncover a bit of information about his family."

"So that's how you ended up at the construction site," Zander said. Xavier nodded, and Zander went on with, "I've been searching hotels up here for the last two days, where I figured you all were probably staying. Before that, my father kept me a virtual prisoner in our family's tenement. He was insisting I take up employment doing construction with him and my older brothers." He turned to Xavier. "I wasn't having it. That's why I had my suitcase with me. I'd just left my father's house for good."

"What suitcase?" Gleason asked.

Zander sighed and shoved a hand through his hair. "It's gone, lost in the raid, and everything I own with it." He turned to Xavier. "I have nothing now, nothing at all."

"You have me," Xavier insisted, taking Zander's hand and squeezing it. It was a silly, maudlin gesture, but it felt right.

"I don't want to be a burden," Zander said, then glanced past Xavier to Blake. "Xavier once joked that I could go to work for you as a footman."

"You're a dancer, right?" Niall asked, a thoughtful look on his face.

Zander glanced to him, hope in his eyes. "I am. I was with the Markova Ballet Company until late last year."

Niall's mouth twitched into a grin. "I thought so. Which means you have theatrical experience." He paused, then said, "If you wouldn't mind returning to London, I might have a job for you at the Concord Theater."

Zander gaped at him as though Niall had just offered him a golden fleece. "I would love nothing more than to return to London," he said with feeling, clutching Xavier's hand. "It's where my heart is."

Xavier thought his heart might overflow with joy, but Zander lost his smile.

"There is one other thing," he said. "I have a sister, Anya. She's eight years old. I've only just gotten to know her, but I don't think I can leave her here to fend for herself. She's being treated like a servant by my parents, and I fear what might happen to her if she's left to their machinations."

Xavier's gut pinched with sympathy and uncertainty. He wanted Zander more than anything, but he wasn't sure he knew what to do with an eight-year-old girl, if they could even convince Zander's parents to let her go.

"We live next door to an orphanage for girls," Blake pointed out with a grin. "I'm certain Stephen and Max would make an exception and bring her into their fold, given the references your sister would have." When Zander and Xavier glanced to him, he winked.

Once again, having the power of a duke behind him

was proving useful to Xavier. "It's all a matter of convincing your parents to part with her, then," he said.

"It pains me to say it, but I'm sure money would—" He stopped midsentence, staring past Blake to the small table beside the bed. More specifically, he stared at the photograph of Alan resting there.

"Is something wrong?" John asked, glancing between Zander and the photograph.

"I saw that boy yesterday," Zander said, breaking away from Xavier to cross the room and take up the photograph. "Yes, this was definitely him."

"Where did you see him?" Blake asked, his voice suddenly hoarse and his eyes wide.

Zander put the photograph down and turned to Blake. "Just outside, in Central Park. He was trying to run away from his nanny or his mother, or someone who—" Again, he stopped cold, mouth dropping open. "I should have remembered," he said. "I should have put two and two together and realized that was Lady Selby and Lord Stanley." He glanced to Blake. "My lord, I'm so sorry. I was distressed because of my search for Xavier, and I didn't think."

"You say you saw them yesterday?" John asked, stepping forward and taking charge. "What else can you tell us?"

Zander's despair switched to hope. "The boy, Lord Stanley, was crying. He insisted he wanted to go home. The woman, Lady Selby, grabbed him and took him back to an apartment building across from the park. I watched them until they entered the building."

"Which building?" Blake asked with so much desperate energy that Xavier flinched.

"Maybe I can show you," Zander said, striding to the window.

Blake rushed to the window with him, as did Niall. Zander threw open the window and leaned out. It was already night, but there were so many streetlights and lanterns around that corner of Central Park that it was still possible to see the buildings on Fifth Avenue.

"There," Zander said, extending an arm to point. "That one. Five buildings up from the corner. That's the one they entered."

"It's the Drake," Blake said, jerking back into the room, his eyes wild with hope. "I *knew* that doorman was lying the other day. Come on," he said. "We might be able to catch them before they know we're here."

Blake and Niall dashed to the door, throwing it open and running into the hall. John and Gleason hurried after them. Xavier and Zander brought up the rear.

"Sir," Xavier called after Blake as they reached the stairs. "Am I needed for this endeavor? Because it's been a rather trying day and—"

"You're not needed," Blake called over his shoulder. "Go enjoy the fruits of your search."

Xavier had never been so relieved to be dismissed so curtly. He and Zander continued down the stairs with the others, but when they reached the third floor, they parted ways, walking swiftly down the hallway to Xavier's room instead. Xavier couldn't fish the key out of his jacket pocket fast enough—and he was grateful he'd thought to keep his room key and Blake's wallet in his jacket and not in his now lost coat—and unlocked the room as quickly as he could once they reached it.

"That's it, then," he said once they were safely inside the room with the door shut and locked. "All that activity and drama, all that heartache and searching. That's all done, and it's just the two of us now."

"Just the two of us," Zander repeated, unbuttoning his coat while fixing Xavier with a ravenous look. "And I don't know about you, but right now, I need real, tangible proof that it is the two of us, that we're together and safe, and that no one and nothing is ever going to part us again."

"I think that proof is exactly what I need right now too," Xavier agreed, letting out a breath it felt like he'd been holding for ages.

He pushed Zander's coat off his shoulders, letting it drop to the floor and ignoring his instinct to pick it up, brush it off, and hang it neatly. He did the same with Zander's waistcoat, noting that he wasn't wearing a jacket.

"When you said you have nothing left in the world, you meant it," he said, excited by the prospect that Zander was stripped bare and beholden to him in a variety of different ways. "Not even a jacket."

"What you see before you is all that I am and all that

I have," Zander said, fumbling with Xavier's buttons as Xavier tried to undress him. The result was a tangle of arms that threatened to make Xavier giggle—actually giggle—with excitement.

"I'll have to make you a whole new wardrobe," Xavier said.

"By yourself?" Zander's brow inched up as he shrugged out of his suspenders.

Xavier pulled Zander's shirt up over his head, nearly moaning at the broad, beautiful expanse of Zander's chest and stomach that he exposed. "I was a tailor before I was a valet, you know."

"You can dress me however you'd like," Zander said, peeling away Xavier's clothes.

"I think I might prefer you undressed," Xavier said, losing his breath and the power to speak entirely as he unfastened Zander's trousers and pushed them down over his hips.

There were so many things he wanted from Zander, so many ways he wanted to kiss and touch him, that he didn't know where to start. It didn't help that they still had clothes and shoes to remove, which was an unnecessary impediment that slowed things down just when Xavier wanted them to speed up. They managed to pull and peel off everything that was still in the way of the two of them falling into bed together and rolled between the sheets of the massive hotel bed with complete abandon.

Zander attempted to pin Xavier to his back, but Xavier managed to flip their positions, spreading himself across Zander's perfect body. "I've been dreaming about this for days," he bent down to kiss Zander, "weeks," he kissed him again, nibbling his lower lip, "months," he stroked his hands along Zander's arms, drawing them up over his head, "and you are going to let me do it properly."

"Love, you can do it however you want," Zander sighed, smiling lazily. "I'm all yours, now and forever."

They were the sweetest words Xavier had ever heard, and they made him bold. He slanted his mouth over Zander's, claiming him as his own with a deep sigh. It felt so good to be with him again at last that Xavier felt like he was floating in a cloud of pure joy. He threaded his fingers through Zander's hair as he kissed him, drawing Zander's tongue into his mouth and reveling in his taste. He couldn't help but move his hips against Zander's as well, loving the friction of their cocks pressed together, hard and hot and needy. He didn't want to rush things—he wanted to feel the bliss of arousal and contact and love for as long as he could—but his body was so excited by having what it had longed for that he already felt as though he were in danger of finishing too soon.

He broke their kiss, sagging against Zander and resting his forehead against Zander's shoulder. "I'm going to embarrass myself," he sighed.

"How could you possibly embarrass yourself?" Zander laughed, shifting his arms to stroke his hands down Xavier's sides to his arse.

The shudder of pleasure that simple gesture caused

left Xavier fighting not to come then and there, groaning as he did. "Because I've been waiting for this for so long that I've nearly come about three times now."

Zander continued to laugh. He kept one hand on Xavier's arse and brushed the hair back from Xavier's face with the other when Xavier muscled himself up to gaze down at him. "There is no right or wrong time to come, darling," he said. "If you want to, then do."

Xavier arched one eyebrow. "And then fall asleep in a puddle while you're still bristling with need?"

Zander sent a wicked look up to him. "Oh, you won't fall asleep, believe me. I won't let you."

The hint of command in Zander's voice cause Xavier to let out a shaky breath. "When you put it like that," he sighed, then leaned in to kiss Zander again. It was delicious and encompassing, and Xavier was certain he could lose his mind completely in Zander's arms. He held off for as long as it took to push himself up again and say, "One last thing."

"Now you're just delaying the inevitable," Zander teased him, raking his fingernails across Xavier's back.

Xavier caught his breath, then let it out on a pleasured sigh. He shook his head. "No, you'll like this. Look in the drawer." He nodded to the table beside the bed.

Zander turned his head to glance at it, then slipped out from under Xavier, scooting to the side of the bed, then pulling open the drawer. "You blessed man," he gasped, taking the jar of Vaseline Xavier still had from the *Umbria* out. "You truly have thought of everything."

Xavier had to swallow the urge to laugh by biting his lip as Zander unscrewed the lid and put the ointment to immediate use. Instead of gliding up behind him, though, he grabbed the extra pillows and pushed them under the small of Xavier's back as he lay face up.

"Would you believe I've actually never done it this way before?" Xavier gasped, feeling out of his depth and exposed in the best way as Zander lifted his knees.

"Then when it comes to this way," Zander said, leaning over him and slipping a slick finger into Xavier's hole to make certain he was ready, "you're all mine."

"Darling, I've been all yours since the moment I first saw you," Xavier sighed, relaxing and opening himself wider for Zander. "And I always will be."

Zander was clearly moved by the expression of love. He stretched over Xavier, kissing him soundly, his fingers working magic and leaving Xavier wanting more. More was exactly what he got a moment later as Zander straightened and slid firmly into him. Xavier let out a long moan of triumph that turned into a series of more desperate sounds as Zander started to move. What should have been absurd, what with the way he was spread and helpless as Zander watched him with passion-hazed eyes, was the most erotic and beautiful thing Xavier had ever done. Seeing Zander's expression shift between love and desire, then pure ecstasy as he thrust hard and fast was everything.

True to his prediction, Xavier didn't last long, but the explosive joy of coming with Zander inside of him made the wild throb of pleasure that pulsed through him as he spilled across his belly worth whatever messy indignity it brought with it. In a flash, he was nothing but white-hot, liquid pleasure, crying out with joy as he gave himself over to Zander completely. Zander loved what he saw, as was attested by the unfettered sounds he made with increasing intensity before tensing with a groan, and then shuddering as he collapsed over Xavier.

It was everything Xavier had wished and waited for, and as the two of them sprawled across the bed and each other, overheated and out of breath, he was happier than he'd ever been. Whatever it took, he wouldn't let anything come between the two of them again for the rest of their lives.

EPILOGUE

*A*rthur Gleason was not a heartless bastard. Or so he continually tried to tell himself. Other men had come to different conclusions over the years, but they were wrong. His heart went out to Blake Williamson as their little band of vigilantes were turned away from the Drake Apartments on Fifth Avenue. They'd stormed in with so much hope and confidence after Alexander Plushenko had reported seeing Lady Selby and the boy enter the building the day before, and they'd had those hopes thwarted when the doorman and concierge had not only refused to give them any information about any of the building's residents once again, but had threatened to call the police on them as well.

"Don't you know who I am?" Blake had demanded in a show that had made Arthur wince.

"No," the doorman had said, shoving Blake out into the street and closing the door on him.

It was an ignominious way for a duke to be treated, and really, the doorman should have known better, but there wasn't much they could do. They weren't in England anymore.

"This isn't the end," John said, thumping Blake's back bracingly as they headed back toward The Fairmount. "This is the beginning. We have solid proof that Annamarie and Alan were here just yesterday. Even if they're not now, they can't have gone far."

"We're close, Blake, I can feel it," Niall said.

Arthur's mouth twitched at the double-entendre. Blake and Niall were glaringly obvious in their affection, and unless they started behaving with a little more discretion—or closed themselves off from so-called regular society for the rest of their lives, which was certainly an option for an eccentric duke and a playwright—they would land in more trouble than either of them likely wanted to deal with. And that was *after* they found Lord Stanley and brought him back into their aberrant little family.

"Tomorrow, we'll try again," John said as they crossed the street. "And by the end of the week, I'm sure we'll have Alan back."

Arthur wasn't so sure. He veered away from the others, crossing Fifth Avenue to head into Central Park rather than returning to the hotel. They would most certainly get Lord Stanley back. He'd already made contact with a few people in New York who could help them with that. His network extended far beyond

England, even if he'd never been to New York before. It might take longer than a week, though, and it might get a tad messier than Blake wanted it to be. But anything worth doing was worth doing thoroughly. Even if things were broken in the process.

He stepped off the path, striding away from the parts of the park that were lit by streetlamps and into the shadowy areas created by shrubs and clusters of trees. All the while, he kept his ears pricked, waiting for those footfalls that he knew would come after him. Already, he could hear things taking place in the park that would likely make the ladies and tourists who traipsed through during the day blanche. London wasn't the only place where public parks turned into dens of iniquity at night.

Just as he'd suspected, within minutes, he heard the swish of John Dandie's footsteps coming through the grass. As if they'd planned the whole thing, he sidestepped toward the nearest tree and pivoted to lean against it, thrusting his hands into his pockets.

"I find it interesting that you claim to hate me, and yet, the moment you spot me slipping off into some darkened trysting spot, you follow me," he said, not bothering to hide his presence from John.

"This is about business, Gleason," John insisted. "It's about Lord Stanley."

"Sure it is," Arthur said, his voice dripping with sarcasm. "Just like it's been about little Alan all along."

John blinked at him and shifted nervously. "It *has* been about Lord Stanley all along."

It was charming that John thought so, charming that he still denied the infatuation he felt. Although Arthur believed that infatuation had taken a different turn when John had broken into his London flat and seen a few of the souvenirs he'd brought back from Japan hanging on his walls. Arthur's time in Tokyo after leaving the navy had been educational as well as pleasurable, and he hadn't met a man he wanted to share the skills he'd learned with since then.

Until John.

Arthur took a breath, pushing away from the tree and stepping right up to John. He loved the way John flinched whenever he got near, but forced himself to stay close, as if challenging himself. "If Lady Selby didn't leave the city immediately for her father's house in Long Island yesterday, after her encounter with Mr. Plushenko, she will most definitely leave now."

"How do you figure?" John asked, his voice deep, tension rolling off of him as the two of them stood close.

Arthur shrugged, pretending to be casual when really, he wanted to tear into John like a ravenous beast and bring him to the point of begging for mercy. "If she is still in residence over there," he nodded to the building they'd just tried to raid, "then the concierge will tell her, she'll realize Blake has found her, and she'll be gone from the city before dawn. If she's already left, then she's already left."

"So you think we'll end up on Long Island, then?" John asked.

Arthur grinned slyly up at him, "Darling, we'll end up in so many places together. Long Island is just one of them."

John stiffened noticeably, in more ways than one. "I am not just some toy you can play with, like a cat with a ball of yarn."

"You like it when I play with you," Arthur contradicted him. "You'll like it even more when I play with your balls."

John made a sound of disgust that rang hollow to Arthur's ears and backed away. "You are a menace," he said. "I wish I'd never invited you to come along on this investigation."

"That's a lie," Arthur laughed. "And mark my words, before this investigation is done, you'll be saying exactly the opposite. Right along with telling me all the things you want me to do to you."

"You're out of your mind." John took another step back.

"And you'll be out of yours by the time I'm done," Arthur promised.

"I won't—" John stopped himself, hands balled into fists at his sides. "I'm not staying here and listening to this rubbish anymore. We have an investigation to plan."

"We do," Arthur agreed, following John at a slower pace so that he could enjoy the sight of the man walking away from him, bothered to the point of madness. He hadn't found any man so intriguing and desperate to be taken since Shinobu. If he had his way, which he would,

John would be his just as completely before they found their way home again.

I hope you have enjoyed Xavier and Zander's story! I have so many authors notes to share with you about this one that it's almost silly, because I did so, so much research in preparation for this book!

First off, there may be a few things in this book that you might be tempted to think are anachronisms, but actually, they aren't. Life and technology was surprisingly advanced by 1891, and so was culture. Fire escapes were already being installed on buildings throughout New York (and trust me, I had quite the time looking up illustrations and photographs of what they looked like back then—yeesh!), although they wouldn't be made a requirement until the 1920s.

Another thing readers might be tempted to think are 21st century attitudes and values being placed on 19th century people—BUT THAT ARE TOTALLY NOT—is the vast and eclectic scope of gay culture of the late 19th and early 20th century in New York. Much of the academic research that I based Jasper Werther and The Slippery Slope on comes from George Chauncey's seminal work *Gay New York*. It might surprise you to know that the visibility of "fairies" in the 1890s and the ease and frequency with which they mixed with men of the working classes particularly was well known and somewhat ignored. It wasn't until closer toward the mid-20th century that the hammer really came down on the activities of the clubs, resorts, and people of the Bowery. In fact, The Slide was a real and very well-known "resort" of the late 19th-century that was notorious for its vibrancy and entertainments. And yep, young people of the upper classes and tourists to New York would frequent the Bowery, its clubs, and The Slide whenever they went "slumming", which was a popular pastime in those days. People of all sorts and with all kinds of intents kicked up their heels together in those clubs, which were as colorful and popular as they are today.

Also, drag culture—including the terms "drag" and "drag queen"—was already well-established by the 1890s. Drag shows were a popular draw, and drag queens would name themselves after popular female actresses and entertainments of the day. Lady Lollipop might sound anachronistic, but that is exactly the sort of name 19th century drag queens had. In fact, Chauncey talks about a famous queen of the era named Loop-the-loop, after a roller-coaster on Coney Island. Beyond, that, Chauncey talks quite a bit about how drag culture, and the entire fairy culture of the Bowery in the late-19th and early-20th centuries not only allowed working-class gay men to earn a living (albeit a dubious one), it gave middle-class gay men the ability to lead a double life. The city was large enough and compartmentalized enough that they could engage in perfectly respectable lives uptown, then head downtown to live it up and be more themselves.

Even though The Slide was closed by police in 1892, the wild culture of the Bowery continued, and continues to this day. And I'm not gonna lie, as I wrote Jasper Werther, intending him to be a fun way to help Xavier and Zander get back together, Jasper kept insisting more and more that he needed his own book. Which, of course, would require a whole new series, set in New York. I fully intend to get started on that new series next year, if I can. So keep your eyes peeled!

One other technical note.... I chose the RMS *Umbria* as the ship Xavier, Zander, and the others sailed on not just because it was one of the most well-known cruise ships of the day, but because some brilliant and creative soul has actually recreated the entire ship in Minecraft! I was actually able to "walk through" the entire vessel. So a lot of the details I've written in this story come from the fact that I've sort of taken a tour of the ship!

And on a personal note, I would just like to give a shout-out to my dear friend Satish, who I included in this book as an Easter egg for my friends. And yes, Satish has lectured me so, so many times about how yoga is a discipline and a spiritual practice, not just a bunch of stretching. You're the best, Satish!

Now that Xavier and Zander are together and Alan and Annamarie have been spotted, is it finally time for Blake to get his son back? It will be if John and Arthur have anything to do with it. And if Arthur gets his way, he'll get John too. And John might not mind. Can they locate and rescue Alan before their burning desire for each other gets the better of them? Find out next in the final installment of The Brotherhood, *Just a Little Rivalry*!

IF YOU ENJOYED THIS BOOK AND WOULD LIKE TO HEAR more from me, please sign up for my newsletter! When you sign up, you'll get a free, full-length novella, *A Passionate Deception*. Victorian identity theft has never been so exciting in this story of hope, tricks, and starting over. Part of my West Meets East series, *A Passionate Deception* can be read as a stand-alone. Pick up your free copy today by signing up to receive my newsletter (which I only send out when I have a new release)!

Sign up here: http://eepurl.com/cbaVMH

ARE YOU ON SOCIAL MEDIA? I AM! COME AND JOIN the fun on Facebook: http://www.facebook.com/merryfarmerreaders

I'M ALSO A HUGE FAN OF INSTAGRAM AND POST LOTS of original content there: https://www.instagram.com/merryfarmer/

ABOUT THE AUTHOR

I hope you have enjoyed *Just a Little Mischief*. If you'd like to be the first to learn about when new books in the series come out and more, please sign up for my newsletter here: http://eepurl.com/cbaVMH And remember, Read it, Review it, Share it! For a complete list of works by Merry Farmer with links, please visit http://wp.me/P5ttjb-14F.

Merry Farmer is an award-winning novelist who lives in suburban Philadelphia with her cats, Peter and Justine, who tear around the place and knock stuff over while she's trying to work. She has been writing since she was ten years old and realized one day that she didn't have to wait for the teacher to assign a creative writing project to write something. It was the best day of her life. She then went on to earn not one but two degrees in History so that she would always have something to write about. Her books have reached the Top 100 at Amazon, iBooks, and Barnes & Noble, and have been named finalists in the prestigious RONE and Rom Com Reader's Crown awards.

ACKNOWLEDGMENTS

I owe a huge debt of gratitude to my awesome beta-readers, Caroline Lee and Jolene Stewart, for their suggestions and advice. And double thanks to Julie Tague, for being a truly excellent editor and to Cindy Jackson for being an awesome assistant!

Click here for a complete list of other works by Merry Farmer.

Printed in Great Britain
by Amazon